IS THIS REALLY THE END OF SPOCK?

IS THE ROMULAN "INVISIBILITY" SCREEN A MIN-IATURE BLACK HOLE, AN ANTI-GRAVITY FORCE FIELD, OR SOMETHING COMPLETELY DIFFERENT?

WHO WILL KIRK CHOOSE FOR HIS NEW FIRST OFFICER?

These are just a few of the puzzles explored in this latest *Trek* collection. You'll discover the true story about Kirk and his son, learn the past and future history of the Star Trek universe, and delve into the characters, the worlds, the movies, the TV episodes—everything that has made Star Trek so real for so many people.

THE BEST OF TREK® #6

More Science Fiction from SIGNET

THE BEST OF TREK #6

FROM THE MAGAZINE FOR STAR TREK FANS

EDITED BY WALTER IRWIN AND G. B. LOVE

A SIGNET BOOK

NEW AMERICAN LIBRARY

TIMES MIRROR

SIGNET TRADEMARK REG. U.S. PAT. OFF AND FOREIGN COUNTRIES
REGISTERED TRADEMARK—MARCA REGISTRADA
HECHO EN CHICAGO, U.S.A.

SIGNET, SIGNET CLASSIC, MENTOR, PLUME, MERIDIAN and
NAL BOOKS
are published by The New American Library, Inc.,
1633 Broadway, New York, New York 10019

First Printing, September, 1983

1 2 3 4 5 6 7 8 9

PRINTED IN THE UNITED STATES OF AMERICA

ACKNOWLEDGMENTS

Eagle-eyed readers noted the absence of our acknowledgments in *Best of Trek #5* and wondered why. Were we mad at everybody? Was there no one to thank? Or did we do something incredibly stupid and inept like forgetting to include them?

Ahem.

Thanks, as (almost) always, are due to the many, many people who have helped and supported us over the years and have helped to make this sixth collection possible: Sheila Gilbert of NAL, editor, friend, and Evelyn Wood valedictorian; Jim Houston; Pat and Bill Mooney; Elaine Hauptman; Leslie Thompson; Christine Myers; and especially to the writers who have contributed so very much! To all of the above, and our readers, this volume is dedicated. Thanks.

CONTENTS

INTRODUCTION

Thank you for purchasing this sixth edition of articles and features from our magazine, *Trek*. We are sure that you will enjoy this collection just as much as you did the previous five.

As always, the articles included in this volume reflect the continuing growth of Star Trek fandom. Not only did the success of *Star Trek II: The Wrath of Khan* bring many new fans into our hobby, it also revitalized the interest of many fans who had fallen by the wayside during the lean years when there were no new Star Trek productions. Happily, this situation will not occur again for some time, as production is scheduled to start on *Star Trek III* in April 1983, with more films to follow. The strength of Star Trek as a draw for audiences has been twice proved, and we fans may be forgiven if we feel a little bit like saying "I told you so!" Because *Wrath of Khan* was so stimulating to fans, you will find a major portion of this volume given over to discussion of that film. Other articles are included as well; we feel we again have a fine mix, with each article reflecting an important, interesting, or maybe even humorous aspect of Star Trek. We think you'll find all of them extremely readable, informative and educational, and downright fun!

If you enjoy the articles in this collection and would like to see more, we invite you to turn to the ad at the back of this book for more information on how you can order individual issues of *Trek*. (And please, if you have borrowed a copy of this volume from a library, copy the information in the ad, and leave the ad intact for others to use. Thanks!)

And if you have been stirred to write an article or two yourself, please send it along to us. We would be most happy to see it, as we are always on the lookout for fresh and exciting new contributions. (Please don't send us Star Trek stories, however. We do not and *cannot* publish Star Trek fiction.) As was the case in our previous volumes, all of the contributors in this volume sent us articles after buying and reading one of our earlier collections. They did it; perhaps you can too.

We want to hear from you in any event. Our lines of communication are always open. We welcome (and heed!) your suggestions, comments, and ideas; you readers are the bosses. Although we cannot give you the addresses of Star Trek actors, or forward mail to them, or help anyone get a professional or amateur Star Trek novel or story published, we *do* want your comments on *Trek* and Star Trek in general. It is only through your letters that we know if our efforts, and those of our contributors, have been successful.

Again, many thanks, and we hope you will enjoy *The Best of Trek #6!*

WALTER IRWIN

G.B. LOVE

NEW LIFE, NEW CREATION: STAR TREK AS MODERN MYTH

by Barbara Devereaux

We often hear that religion and theology have no place in the world today; that they are outmoded concepts unneedful of comment or concern. But it is not often we hear such pronouncements from a Star Trek fan. Fans seem to have an abiding interest in matters spiritual; this, coupled with the ever-present fan skepticism and a willingness to examine and accept all viewpoints, makes for some interesting opinions. Of course, philosophy and psychology are not forgotten; adding them into the mixture serves to spice up the result.

In the following article, Barbara Devereaux takes a few cues from earlier Trek *articles (especially those of Joyce Tullock), then adds a number of interesting thoughts of her own. Chances are you won't agree with her opinions or conclusions, but we guarantee you won't be able to ignore them.*

Once upon a time there was a very small planet, far, far away at the edge of the galaxy. The planet teemed with life of all kinds. One kind was intelligent, but the intelligent life form was sad, for the planet was dying. Its crystal-clear streams had grown dark and its atmosphere was filled with poisonous gases. Wars raged across the face of the planet; they were fought for power and land, religion and honor, freedom and peace. Thousands died and the intelligent life form was very sad indeed. Yes, great was the suffering on the planet. There were many who were very poor and many who were very hungry. They longed for bread and freedom, dignity and peace; above all, they hungered for hope. They watched in fear as the terrible weapons of war grew bigger and bigger and they wondered if there would be a tomorrow.

Then, one day, toward the close of a bloody, fearful century (as time was reckoned on the planet), an idea appeared. It took the form of a simple story that was a wondrous tale of courage, love, and a future filled with hope. The story went straight to the heart of the sad little life form, and it held the story tight and would not let it go. The story grew and grew until it penetrated every corner of the planet. The story revealed to the life form something of the truth of its own condition. In doing so, the story became a myth and the myth was called Star Trek.

There were many myths half-buried in the life form's consciousness. They were valiant attempts to bring order to a chaotic reality, to find logic and reason in an absurd and lonely existence, to transcend the limits of failure and death. Over and over again, the new myth explored the old, probing it gently, prodding it for signs of life. At a time when the life form feared for its dying planet, its eyes were turned to accounts of the planet's creation, to the beginnings called Genesis.

The life form had scorned the stories for many years, thinking them unscientific, tales for children or the very naive. Finally, the wisest of the life forms realized that truth has many faces and that a myth is not fantasy: It is truth in another guise.

"Eden," whispered the new myth, and proceeded to explore paradise. There were a few problems. . . .

To begin with, the mythic hero called Kirk didn't really like the idea of paradise. As Joyce Tullock explained in some detail in her article "Bridging the Gap: The Promethian Star Trek" *(Best of Trek #3)*, Kirk believed that to succumb to the temptations of paradise was to become stagnant. To accept Eden was to give up a fight—and Kirk believed life was a fight. Eden was for sissies. As he demonstrated in "The Way to Eden," Kirk had very little interest in pursuing mythological worlds and very little patience with people who were intent on doing so. Utopias should be made, not discovered.

But the mythic hero called Spock reacted to the idea of Eden in quite a different way (a fact that bothered Kirk not in the least). In "The Way to Eden," it was Spock who was sympathetic to the idea of finding paradise—so much so that he offered to assist in the search. Again, in "The Apple," it is Spock who suggests that the people of Vaal might have a viable society and that in tampering with it, Kirk gave them only pain, suffering, and death. Kirk's reply to Spock's concern ("Is there anyone on this ship who looks even remotely like Satan?") is a less than honest answer to Spock's question.

In "This Side of Paradise," it is Spock who discovers love (or thinks he does) on Omnicron Ceti III. It takes a great deal to tear him away from paradise, and eventually it is only his loyalty to Kirk that keeps him from returning. Joyce Tullock pointed out that a happy Spock is a boring Spock; however, as we shall see, *Star Trek II: The Wrath of Khan* demonstrated that this statement is not entirely true. Nor did the rest of the crew walk out of paradise as Kirk suggests—the captain, with Spock's help, quite literally dragged them away.

Finally, in *Wrath of Khan*, it is Spock who welcomes the Genesis Device. There are dangers, as the third mythic hero, McCoy, points out. The power to create is also the power to destroy. And (as McCoy neglected to point out, but as Spock was no doubt aware) creatures have a way of rebelling against their creators. To be alive, they must be free. The need to choose comes early, the ability to choose wisely comes much later. But still and all, Spock is willing to take the risk.

The idea of paradise is part and parcel of Kirk's heritage, but time after time, he rejects it. Maybe he's afraid of it. Spock, on the other hand, may be attracted to the idea for the simple reason that there never was a paradise in Vulcan mythology. It is truly an alien concept to Spock, and one that is enormously appealing to him. He is certainly not threatened by a myth that seems to contradict those of his own planet; rather, he is convinced that differences in themselves are good and eventually will combine to create something new and marvelous.

More intriguing than the question of paradise is the question of the Creator of paradises, God. His existence is rarely mentioned explicitly, yet the question of the Almighty hovers over the *Enterprise* like the biblical cloud by day and pillar of fire by night. Joyce Tullock has suggested that the heroes of Star Trek have outgrown the need for a god or supreme being. God was a handy theory to have around to fill in the gaps in our scientific knowledge, but once those gaps are filled, the need for him ceased. There are a number of points that argue against Joyce's position.

In "Who Mourns for Adonais?" a rather pathetic, lonely Greek "god" demands that his "subjects" (the crew of the *Enterprise*) worship him. Kirk calmly replies that they find one

God quite sufficient. Now that is a remarkable accomplishment. To be able to recognize a false god and refuse to worship him is an accomplishment indeed. The sad little life form must have blinked his eyes in astonishment as he watched this episode, for the road through his century was littered with rusty idols that included everything from half-mad dictators to designer jeans. And the life form had worshiped every one of them. Kirk is so adept at recognizing false gods that he can even spot them in his own life. It took him a few years to walk away from the shrine of his own ambition, but he finally managed to do it.

However, there is an even more remarkable lesson to be learned from the new myth. In "Bread and Circuses," Uhura corrects Spock's false assumption that people with an advanced ethic of total love and brotherhood would worship the "sun." Her face was radiant as she explained that they worshiped the Son of God; obviously she was very pleased with the idea. The others on the bridge were equally pleased. Joyce dismisses this reaction as naive, saying that if the crew would remember that the history of Christianity included crusades and inquisitions, they might be less than enthusiastic. They're not naive. Certainly Spock, who seems so well acquainted with Earth history, would not be foolish enough to blind himself to the crimes committed in the name of religion. Vulcans are not known in the galaxy for their foolishness. Did our heroes chicken out and decide that no one can knock religion? Star Trek is not known for cowardice in the face of tough issues. So what precisely is the crew's reaction to the possibility of a new Christianity?

Check this out:

There were 430 people on board the *Enterprise* on its first voyage. They were of different sexes (two, at least), different nationalities, different races, different species, and presumably different religions. They lived and worked together twenty-four hours a day (or however they measured time) on one ship for five years. Even a ship the size of the *Enterprise* can feel a little cramped after five years, but, miracle of miracles, they all got along. Better than that, they liked each other. Better than that, they learned to love each other. As Deanna Rafferty observed in her article "*Star Trek: The Motion Picture*—A Year Later" (*Best of Trek #4*), the crewpersons are comfortable with each other and their work (except in *STTMP*—an aberration from the norm). And because they are at peace with each other, they are at peace with their God.

Think about it.

Enterprise crewpersons are a feisty lot. They don't tolerate each other because a Starfleet regulation tells them to or because they are threatened with eternal damnation if they don't. They really believe in all that stuff about brotherhood, and when they find each other, they find God. They don't care if he is called Father or Christ or Allah or The One or The All any more than they care if a person is black or white or Vulcan or human. It's such a simple idea you'd think someone would have thought of it three hundred years earlier. Naive? Hardly.

There are 430 crewpersons, and on the *Enterprise*, God wears 430 faces. He is not a threat, he is not a weapon—maybe he is not even a "he." He is not the exclusive property of any one religion. He doesn't take sides in wars or football games. And the crew is neither frightened nor embarrassed by his presence in whatever form it takes.

Let us consider two of the 430 faces of God aboard the *Enterprise*: the God of the old myth, Genesis (because the new myth so often explores it), and the God of Vulcan (just because it's interesting).

Unlike other creation myths that were popular at the time (such as the Babylonian creation myth), the Genesis account is the story of an orderly creation. Step by step, the planet is filled with living beings; God approves of his creations, including those made in his own image, man and woman. What does the story tell us of the Hebrew God? He is reasonable, logical, gentle; he is a lover of all that is good; he is a God who can be trusted, perhaps even loved. *Star Trek: The Motion Picture* observed that we all make God after our own image. Not quite. The God of Genesis is not an image of what humans are, but of what they long to be.

Now, what of Vulcan? If you were God, how would you reveal yourself to Vulcans? Perhaps you would appeal to what is best in them, what is closest to your own heart. In a human, it is love; in a Vulcan, logic. The God of Vulcan is the eternal mind; the Cosmic Mind that flows through, with, and in the universe. Gene Roddenberry tells us in the novelization of *STTMP* (a point regrettably omitted from the film) that Vulcans are natural mystics. They are blessed with a *seventh* sense, which is like a window opening to the All. They are completely united with the All and yet they retain their individual sense of identity. For humans it takes years of prayer, fasting, discipline, and (in western traditions) the gift of grace to achieve mystic union with the One. A Vulcan does it by closing his eyes.

Let us return to the Genesis myth, for it is more than a description of God; it also describes the fall of man and raises the question of his subsequent redemption. In the second generation account in Genesis, Adam and Eve eat of the fruit of knowledge of good and evil, and suddenly become ashamed of who they are. Humanity loses sight of the fact that it is made in God's image, becomes afraid of God, and feels impelled to hide from God. In betraying their relationship with God, humans do not simply discover evil; rather, they forget their own intrinsic goodness—they no longer understand the meaning of their own humanity.

Joyce is correct that "The Empath" is Star Trek's story of redemption, its passion play, but she is off-target in thinking that the episode was a refutation of religion. It was certainly a refutation of bad theology and the false images of God that abound in religion. McCoy does become a Christ-figure in the episode; he offers his life for the others because he knows they are worth dying for. McCoy, more than anyone, knows their weaknesses, and knows that weaknesses don't matter. Kirk and Spock matter simply because they are Kirk and Spock.

There are any number of theories that attempt to explain the crucifixion—the area is even a specialty within the study of theology called soteriology (from the Greek *soter*, meaning "savior"). One theory (refuted by "The Empath") suggests that man was so evil that God surely would have destroyed him, except that Christ died to make up for that evil and to hold back the avenging hand of God. According to that theory, Christ died in order to change the Father's mind about destroying us—his death affected the Father, not us. Was it God who needed changing? Was God really intending to do us all in with some mighty cosmic blast? Doubtful. Look back at the creation myth. It was not that man became evil, but that he lost sight of his own goodness. To be freed from sin is to be freed from illusions, freed from our false selves and restored to our real selves who are made in the image of God. Christ died for us because we are worth dying for. He believed in our goodness, but most of the time, we don't. It is this second idea of salvation that "The Empath" affirms.

The fact that McCoy is an unlikely Christ-figure is not that surprising. Christ-figures are always the unexpected, least-likely persons . . . poor, uneducated carpenters or simple country doctors.

Although McCoy is often surprising and unpredictable, it is Kirk who is the most complex part of the triad. Joyce tells us he is "ambitious, lusty, bored with orthodoxy." At times he is all those things, but he is also a great deal more. Hedonism should not be equated with heroism, and we all know Kirk is an honest-to-goodness hero. There is a Promethean streak in him; he is a man who defies God and enjoys it. It is not a small coal he wishes to snatch away while God isn't looking, it's immortality. Courageous though he is, there are many things that frighten him: He is afraid of the peace of Eden (too much time to think?), enduring relationships, growing old, death. As he finally admits in *Wrath of Khan*, Kirk has never really faced death—he has tricked death, cheated it, but he has never faced it. Understandably, he takes a certain pride in his own unique solution to the *Kobayashi Maru* simulation; he did, after all, receive a commendation for original thinking. It is the same pride he takes in his other conquests.

Promethean theology assumes that God has created humans with the desire for divinity (or immortality), but if they dare draw close to God, they are punished. It's the kind of double bind that literally drives people crazy. Apollo might play that game if he's in the mood, but the sadistic God of Promethean theology hardly fits a description of the God of Genesis—or the God of Vulcan. The irony lies in the fact that Kirk wishes to steal what is already his.

The Trappist monk Thomas Merton wrote that one problem with the Promethean mentality is its basic assumption about ownership and conquest. Kirk has always had to own the things he most cares about—*my* command, *my* crew, *my* ship, *my* friends, *my* life. No wonder he can't face death; he is a man who has never learned to let go. The Promethean man assumes that God won't let go either.

Another aspect of the Promethean mentality is its obstacle-course theory of life. Life is not to be lived, it is to be conquered. Life is a fight, and Kirk was a scrapper from the word go. He fought his way into and through the Academy, fought to get and keep command. In "Friendship—in the Balance" (*Best of Trek #4*), Joyce Tullock comments that things happen *to* McCoy, but that they happen *for* Kirk. It is an excellent distinction; however, we can't overlook the fact that Kirk is very liable to *make* things happen. He is fiercely competitive, and his quiet comment "I don't like to lose" in *Wrath of Khan* is one of the great understatements in Star Trek annals.

The feeling extends to Kirk's explorations in deep space. Space is indeed the final frontier, and it is a frontier that Kirk

intends to conquer. The conquest won't be military, of course—
the Federation is beyond that—but very often the spirit of conquest is still there. It is Kirk who is first to ignore the Prime
Directive, and we all know the man's not afraid of a fight.

Then there are the women—during the three-year series they
seemed to average about one a week. Just watching the man was
exhausting. In fairness to Kirk, most of the women were first-
class featherbrains. (Despite Beth Carlson's defense of Rand in
Best of Trek #4, Rand's still a featherbrain. Even Starfleet can
make a mistake. Edith Keeler and Miramanee were notable
exceptions; but Edith was an extraordinary woman and Kirk's
involvement with Miramanee was equally extraordinary.)

It wasn't until *Wrath of Khan* that women were portrayed as
intelligent individuals, as exemplified by Carol Marcus. Apparently,
Kirk acceded to her wishes and stayed away: It was what she
wanted—or was it what she wanted Kirk to believe she wanted?
She never told him about David, but (as Vonda McIntyre says in
the novelization), Kirk never asked.

Did the Promethean spirit of conquest in Kirk also extend to
his friends? No one could doubt Kirk's affection for Spock and
McCoy. They are old and dear friends and he cares for them
deeply. No one would argue the point that the Triad works.
However, when *Wrath of Khan* begins, Spock and McCoy are
orbiting Kirk like two worried satellites. In the novelization of
Wrath of Khan, we are told that Spock considers himself a
caretaker for the *Enterprise* until Kirk is ready to assume command.
He holds the ship in trust for Kirk. We are never really told what
McCoy is doing with himself and why he just happens to be
available to tag along with Kirk on a training cruise; Kirk seems
to take his availability for granted. Both Spock and McCoy are
aware that Kirk is unhappy, and both believe that part of the
solution lies in his retaking command of the *Enterprise*.

It is easy to admire Kirk's fighting spirit, but the problem with
the obstacle-course theory of life is that it doesn't work with
those things that are most important. How does one win the love
of a son or keep score in friendship? How does one conquer
death? Fortunately, when Kirk must finally face up to those
problems, Spock is around to help.

And what of Spock and the Vulcan God? (Surely, there's a
Vulcan name for God, but like Spock's first name, we probably
couldn't pronounce it.)

As pointed out earlier, there never was a Vulcan Eden, nor
was there a fall from grace. Vulcans are inextricably linked with

the One; it is not a matter of faith, but fact—biological fact, and it is a bit of Vulcan biology that would not be discussed with a non-Vulcan. The strength of the link varies with individual Vulcans and depends both on innate talent and fidelity to Vulcan disciplines. Although half-human, Spock was no doubt recognized very early on as being exceptionally gifted, and, trying to compensate for his "bad blood," he pursued the disciplines with grim determination.

In "The Savage Curtain" we learn that there was a specific moment in Vulcan history when its leaders chose peace over war, nonviolence over violence. It was probably at the same time that they determined emotion was the source of violence and that the complete repression of emotion was the price of peace. Vulcans perceived logic as being the opposite of emotion, and thus logic became the highest Vulcan ideal.

From earliest childhood, Vulcan children are taught that any emotional display is in extremely bad taste. If they know any parental affection at all, it is not affection that can be demonstrated in emotional terms. If a human were raised in an atmosphere of such stringent emotional repression, he would wind up becoming a psychopath. When a Vulcan child is raised in that atmosphere, he winds up like Spock. The difference lies in the Vulcan link with the One.

Even before a Vulcan child can walk, talk, or calculate decimals, he is aware of his link with the cosmos. In the most profound sense, the child is never and can never be alone. Later, the link is extended to other Vulcans, and occasionally to members of other species, in the form of the mind meld.

When a Vulcan talks about logic, he is not talking about two plus two equaling four. He is talking about the order and reason that permeate the very substance of the universe. A Vulcan can feel the pulse of the universe and knows that when an argument or action is logical, it is in harmony with the universe itself.

Although on a superficial level there is some competition in nature (the survival of the fittest), on a deeper level, there is a strong degree of cooperation and interdependence. Even on a subatomic level no particle can exist by itself. Vulcans, who were several centuries ahead of humans in their understanding of physics, realized that they themselves were part of a larger ecosystem. The thought of doing violence either to each other or to the environment was appalling; Spock's well-known vegetarianism is typical of the Vulcan attitude toward nature. Vulcans understand that it is not necessary to harm or destroy nature in order to preserve their own lives; rather, their lives depend on the continued preservation of the environment. Vulcan logic makes the preservation of one's environment imperative.

Thus, logic is not "cold reason," as McCoy and other humans often label it. In fact, it is the source of gentleness and sensitivity that is so characteristic of Vulcans in general and Spock in particular.

In "Requiem for Methuselah," McCoy tells Spock that he will never really understand what Kirk is experiencing because the word "love" isn't written in Spock's book. As is often the case when humans are dealing with Vulcans, McCoy was half right. The word "love" does not exist in the Vulcan vocabulary, and there is nothing that carries an equivalent connotation of emotion, romance, and sentiment. There is, however, a corollary to the principle of logic to which Vulcans would never attach the human word "love," although a few stubborn humans might insist that the term is appropriate.

From a Vulcan perspective, to act for the good of another is to enable the other to achieve an attitude of peace and harmony in the universe. It would never occur to a Vulcan to ask for anything in return. "Requiem for Methuselah" is a good example of the Vulcan corollary:

In the episode Kirk has unknowingly fallen in love with the android Reena; he and Flint come to blows over who will possess her. Spock, suspecting that Reena is not human, warns them several times to desist, knowing that the fragile humanity awakened in her by Kirk's love may be shattered in the face of violence. Kirk angrily tells Spock he doesn't understand what it means to fight for a woman (implying that Spock doesn't understand what it means to love). Unable to choose between the men, Reena dies (it is, presumably, a kind of heart failure). Spock then explains to the stricken Flint and Kirk that "the joy of love made her human, its agony destroyed her." In his adaptation of the episode, James Blish had Spock add, "The hand of God was duplicated. A life was created. But then—you demanded ideal response—for which God still waits."

After their return to the *Enterprise* and McCoy's lecture, Spock (apparently wearied by the whole thing) does not answer McCoy. However, after McCoy leaves, Spock uses the mind meld to attempt to alleviate some of Kirk's pain and remorse.

The events of the episode speak for themselves. We add only that Spock's analysis of the situation and his subsequent actions are perfectly logical and are consistent with the Vulcan corollary.

It is this understanding of logic which explains why we could never really accept the Spock of *Kolinahr* in *Star Trek: The Motion Picture*. We were, of course, fascinated by Leonard Nimoy's performance, but like so much of that film, it was another aberration from the norm. Logic and cruelty are not complementary; rather, they are contradictory. We could understand that Spock had failed to achieve the full mastery of emotion that is the goal of *Kolinahr*, and that he was venting his pain and frustration on his human friends (although even that is not truly in character), but we cannot accept the idea that Spock could sustain that position for a very long period of time. When one subtracts warmth, compassion, and understanding from a Vulcan, the result is a character that is merely disagreeably human.

How does Vulcan theology compare with Kirk's Promethean theology? In every instance, Spock's theology is the exact opposite of Kirk's. Kirk, for instance, is busy trying to steal immortality from God. Moral problems of thievery aside, Spock has no reason to steal, for all that is the One already belongs to Spock. Vulcans have never known anything but union with the One; Spock does not need to own what God possesses, nor does he need to own the things that Kirk seems to need. Although Spock is intensely loyal to the *Enterprise* and its crew, he has no need to possess them; he enjoys command but is quite willing to return command to Kirk without a second thought; he has "no ego to bruise." Spock's sense of identity has never been sustained by possessions, but there is one notable exception to his freedom in this regard—Kirk. That's what comes of being half human. In any case, Spock even manages to turn the friendship around: "I am your friend. I have been and always shall be."

Kirk is also busy conquering space; Spock has no need to conquer what is already his. In early Star Trek episodes (especially in "Journey to Babel") we are given the impression that Spock is in Starfleet because he cannot find a home on either Earth or Vulcan. However, the Spock of *Wrath of Khan* has grown and changed. This is a Spock who is at home anywhere; the universe is his. Unlike Kirk, Spock has never had to conquer the stars, for in some sense, he was always part of them.

In *Wrath of Khan*, Spock reminds Kirk that there are always possibilities; he does not add (perhaps he doesn't need to) that not everything is possible. No one can be all things, do all things, accomplish all things. It is not possible for both the *Enterprise* and Spock to survive, therefore Spock does what is logical. In such a situation, Spock would no more attempt to hold on to his own life than we would try to hold on to command when logic insists that Kirk is the better choice. And by letting go of his life, he—paradoxically in human terms, logically in Vulcan terms—gains everything.

At the end of *Wrath of Khan*, Kirk is a different person. When he tells David he should be on the bridge (admittedly a half-hearted ploy to avoid talking to his son), it has a ring of truth. He *should* be there, but it is probably the first time in Kirk's life that he *doesn't* want to be on the bridge, *doesn't* want to be in command. He no longer needs it, no longer has that hungry abyss of ambition to fill. He no longer must prove himself to God, to himself, or to anyone else. Kirk is finally free to command the *Enterprise* simply because he is the best and—as Spock said—anything less is a waste of Kirk's gifts. If Kirk commands, fewer people will die.

Of course he feels younger. The weight of a lifetime of struggle has been lifted from his shoulders, and he discovers in laying it aside that there remains a sense of honest accomplishment. He is even forced to let go of his closest friend and discovers, again as Spock promised, that the friendship has not been lost.

Dying and rising, death and rebirth are the theme of *Wrath of Khan* (and we all await the resurrection in *Star Trek III*), and one might be tempted to say that the new myth has replaced the old and that humans, in creating life, have become gods. Has the Promethean Gap been bridged? Has man become divine?

Perhaps it is not that the old myth has been replaced, but that it has been restored. Humans have not become divine, but they are rediscovering their own humanity. Kirk is becoming almost as human as Spock was all along. As Joyce Tullock said, man is no longer "standing, hands in pockets, toes kicking the dirt." But neither is he a defiant teenager out to prove he's his own person, shaking his fist and yelling "I'll show you" at God. In the twenty-third century, man is, at last, evolving into an adult. He no longer needs to own the stars, nor is he hell-bent on destroying what he loves. The author of new life can look into the face of his own Creator and know that he belongs.

And what of our sad little life form who searches for truth in the ruins of a dying planet? He brushes the dust of centuries away from the old myth and takes a new look at it. It is an incomplete work, an unfinished creation. For the life form, the new myth is not an answer at all, but a question.

STAR TREK MYSTERIES SOLVED —ONE MORE TIME!

by Leslie Thompson

Once again by popular demand, Leslie Thompson presents another of her Star Trek Mysteries articles. We would like to thank Sam Popular of Peoria, Ill., for requesting . . .

Yes, we know it's an old joke, but we've just about run out of things to say about these articles. It probably wouldn't hurt to say that we got a lot of letters pillorying us for not having a Mysteries article in BOT #4. Save your brickbats—Leslie's promised another for BOT #7, conditional upon her getting enough questions from our readers. On the personal side, those of you who've become friends with Leslie will be happy to learn she's done got herself engaged and plans to become a happily married woman sometime between the time you read this and the next arrival of Halley's Comet.

The appearance of *Star Trek II: The Wrath of Khan* has done more than cause a major revitalization of Star Trek fandom . . . it has caused a flood of mail to be dumped into my box by Walter and G.B. with the unsubtle instruction "Answer these, kid." Arrogant editors aside, I do love to offer solutions to mysteries in Star Trek, but I must admit *Wrath of Khan* has been giving me some headaches! That doggone movie is just so beautifully *complex* it boggles the imagination (and after five years of doing these articles, I don't have much imagination left to boggle, I'm afraid). But it's always interesting and always fun,

23

so like my sister-in-size, Pat Benetar, I'll hit ya with my best shots.

One of the first letters to come in was from Mark Bach of Chicago, who sent in five *Wrath of Khan* questions.

1. If (as I stated in an earlier mysteries article) the turbolift cars "follow people around," then why did Dr. McCoy have to wait for one in *Wrath*?

You'll remember that Saavik entered the car Kirk was already in; this was "his" car, and since there was no emergency to override its instructions, it would operate normally and stop for other passengers. But Saavik hit the "stop" button, halting the car so she could speak to Kirk, and while it was stopped, it blocked that particular tube and prevented McCoy's car from reaching him. As the doc, like all senior officers, is used to instant service, it was little wonder he was annoyed.

A smaller mystery is why McCoy referred to the lift car as an "elevator." Great pains were always taken in the series *not* to use the term; it apparently is not in Starfleet's lexicon and to call a turbolift car an "elevator" would be as great a crime as calling the deck the "floor." It could be that McCoy's sojourn on Earth has caused him to be a little rusty concerning Starfleet terminology (something he was never too big on to begin with), or else he's just getting more and more crotchety in his advancing years and goes out of his way *not* to use Starfleet terminology. (A bonus of this would be that it would irritate Spock.)

2. When Kirk realized that Khan was about to detonate the Genesis Device, why didn't he beam it onto the *Enterprise* and from there into deep space, as he did with Nomad?

I wondered about that too, Mark. They probably wouldn't have even had to bother bringing it onto the *Enterprise*; instead they could have just beamed it straight from the *Reliant* to deep space. Or if nothing else, Kirk could have beamed over with a phaser and taken a shot at the doggone thing. It might have exploded or prematurely detonated, but what did he have to lose? Neither of these was tried, so apparently the Genesis Wave, once engaged, set up some sort of interference that kept the transporter from operating (or, in the case of beaming the Genesis Device away, a force shield that would prevent it from being beamed). You'll remember that the Genesis Wave registered intensely on Spock's instruments, so it must have been very powerful.

3. When Spock died, why was his body not taken to Vulcan or Earth? Certainly a starship captain with a record as good as

Spock's would be quite important, deserving more than a "burial at sea." Also, why did Spock's coffin not bear any obvious identification of its contents?

It is quite likely that Spock left definite instructions that his remains be disposed of exactly as they were. Although he considers himself Vulcan, Spock really doesn't have many ties to that planet, and even fewer to Earth. So why would he wish to be interred in either place? Space was his home for many years; space would be the place he would naturally choose for burial. Too, Spock would be the very last to want a memorial service filled with pomp; I suspect he'd have been embarrassed (although pleased) by the simple service consisting of farewells from his friends.

Spock wasn't launched in a coffin *per se*, it was a photon torpedo casing. Kirk would have seen to it that some sort of identification was included with Spock's body, if for no other reason than to explain its presence to any possible future visitors to the Genesis Planet. Even so, we cannot be totally sure that Kirk intended the casing to survive entry through the atmosphere —it could well have been his intention to cremate Spock in an appropriate manner.

Diane Rosenfeldt, of Racine, Wisconsin, offers an explanation for why the casing didn't burn up. She surmises that the newly formed atmosphere of the Genesis Planet was too thin (at that time) to create the friction needed to incinerate the tough casing.

4. Who was Khan's wife? One would assume it was Marla McGivers, but one cannot be sure.

Oh, yes one can! Take a closer look at the pendant Khan wears—it is a *USS Enterprise* Starfleet emblem! Khan certainly held no love for Kirk's ship, so the only conceivable reason he would be wearing such a thing is in memory of his late wife . . . former Starfleet Lieutenant Marla McGivers.

5. How did the *Botany Bay* get on Alpha Ceti V, when in "Space Seed" we see it falling out of the tractor beam when Khan takes over the *Enterprise*?

The entire *Botany Bay* wasn't on Alpha Ceti V, only a number of items from it. Khan and his followers were living in converted Starfleet cargo containers, cobbled together to form "temporary" quarters, which were obviously left by the *Enterprise*. We can assume Kirk detoured back to the *Botany Bay* and cannibalized anything that could be useful or valuable to the exiles. It makes good sense: Why deplete the *Enterprise*'s stores any more than necessary when a number of items could be salvaged from the

Botany Bay derelict? Kirk was going to give Khan and his people a chance—but he wasn't about to give them the shirt off his back.

Teresa Cleveland, of Green Valley, California, wonders why Saavik has humanlike eyebrows. This might not seem like such an important thing to worry about, but many, many Star Trek fans (myself among them) feel that Saavik is potentially one of the most exciting and intriguing characters to come along in years, so we naturally want to know everything we can about her. So to the Great Eyebrow Question: Although upward-tilting eyebrows are a distinctive feature of all the Vulcan or Romulan men and women we've seen, it is possible that not all members of these races naturally have them. Saavik's eyebrows are highly arched, and we've seen quite a bit of variation in thickness, etc., so she's not too far from the Vulcan/Romulan norm. And it could very well be that Saavik has a touch of human blood somewhere in her ancestry. That's an interesting thought!

Margaret Lewis, of Richardson, Texas, also has some questions about Saavik. Margaret wonders if Saavik can perform the Vulcan neck pinch and if she possesses the same amazing mental capabilities as Spock.

Saavik should have at least the potential to perform the mind meld and other Vulcan mental feats, and we can be sure that Spock carefully instructed her in the techniques. (You'll remember that Miranda Jones had a natural telepathic ability that was controlled and enhanced through training on Vulcan.) Spock would have attempted as well to teach her the neck pinch. We don't know how much of it is physical, and how much is due to Vulcan disciplines—Kirk, despite Spock's patient efforts, couldn't learn to do it—but chances are that Saavik quickly and efficiently learned the pinch. Don't be surprised if you see her pinching with the best of them in *Star Trek III* . . . provoking a rueful sigh from Kirk.

But Saavik *is* a Romulan/Vulcan hybrid, and this is a good time to propound some theories about the differences in Vulcan and Romulan mental capabilities. From the example of the Romulan commander in "The *Enterprise* Incident," it seems that Romulan and Vulcan psychic abilities operate in almost exactly opposite fashions: A Vulcan's powers are greatest and most efficient in the absence of emotion, a Romulan's greatest in the presence of strong emotion, like passion or anger. Remember that it wasn't until the female commander got a little hot and bothered that she moved her hand to Spock's face in the meld position? And although a Vulcan can share consciousness during a meld and is able to delve into another's mind and discern information, it seems that Romulans can only share raw emotion, and that intellectual faculties do not come across clearly. (The commander could not, despite the closeness she and Spock shared, discern his "treachery.")

So although Saavik would probably be able to perform the same psychic gymnastics as Spock, her technique would be radically different, for she would either have to utilize the vast amount of emotional data flowing into her mind in some way, or else she'd have to use a strict discipline to damp it out, which could very well lessen her effectiveness. Whatever shape and form Saavik's mental abilities take, we can be sure that they will be uniquely her own.

Margaret and many others also wondered why Cadet Peter Preston was not identified as Scotty's nephew in the movie. This question brings up an often irritating point about film or television versions versus their novelization counterparts. In the case of both Star Trek movies, a couple of the live-action episodes, and the animated episodes, the prose adaptations were much more detailed in every way. The reverse was true of James Blish's adaptations of the original episodes—Bantam's strange insistence upon cramming as many episodes as possible into each volume forced Blish to compress and sometimes even truncate stories. On the one hand, we have all this extra, in-depth information; on the other hand, things were often overlooked or simply cut. In both cases, the additions or omissions cause "mysteries."

In the process of editing *Wrath of Khan* (as was done with *STTMP*), many nuances of characterization and quite a bit of action ended up on the cutting-room floor. So, like the famous never-seen scene of Kirk's meeting with Admiral Nogura, we simply must assume that Kirk and Co. were informed of the relationship between Scotty and Peter *offscreen*. This would account for the grief that Kirk and McCoy feel at Peter's death (and that wonderfully controlled grimace from Spock at the sight of Peter's mangled body), as well as for the overriding concern Scotty shows for one of his trainees. (No matter how fond Scott was of all his cadets, he'd hardly have left his post in time of emergency and then staggered blindly to the bridge instead of sick bay for just any of them.) Like the deaths of the scientists on Regula I, the revelation that Peter was Scotty's nephew was something we didn't see, but we *know* it happened nonetheless.

This is a good time to make another distinction about the filmed versions and adaptations. Much of what is contained in the book adaptations is *background*, and has little bearing on the actual events of the story. For example, in Vonda McIntyre's *Wrath of Khan* novelization, we learn much about Saavik's history, about the hobbies and personalities of the Regula I scientists, and about the unique and loving relationship between Saavik and Peter. None of this is important to the basic storyline of *Wrath of Khan*, however. The information that Peter is Scotty's nephew is important, for it *could* have had a bearing on Spock's death. How? Well, perhaps if Scotty had not been shattered by grief, he might have been thinking quicker and been able to jury-rig the warp drive, sparing Mr. Spock from the fateful trip into the chamber. This is pretty far out, to be sure, but we can assume that the determination of all the major characters to defeat Khan was heightened by Peter's death, and that may have made the difference.

As usual, I digress. Margaret also had two other questions: what it was that Spock told McCoy to "remember," and where Khan heard the Klingon proverb.

I'm going to take a pass on the "remember" question. Frankly, I'm not willing to tackle that one! I'm trying to persuade Walter and G.B. to present "an official *Trek* guess" about what it meant and what will happen to Spock, and if I'm successful, it'll appear at the end of this article. (Go ahead and look, but if it's not there, don't blame me.)

As for the Klingon proverb, prior to *Wrath of Khan*, Khan's time in space was limited to a couple of hundred years snoozing aboard the *Botany Bay* and a couple of weeks (at most) on board the *Enterprise*, so it's not too likely he ever ran across any wandering Klingons with whom he swapped proverbs over a bottle. Obviously, only two solutions are possible: Khan, an ultra-speedy and voluminous reader, could have run across the proverb in a section on Klingons when he was (rather foolishly) given access to computer records on the *Enterprise*; or Kirk could have ordered that one of the small, portable, but extremely powerful computers carried on the *Enterprise* be added to the survival gear given Khan and his followers when they were exiled. In a society such as Star Trek's (and, increasingly, our own), a computer would be considered as necessary for survival as food, water, and fire. We can be sure that Khan would have drained the computer of every bit of information, which could have included the Klingon proverb (and the other space/future-oriented knowledge he displays). In either case, Khan's prodigious memory could be trusted to recall the perfect axiom for any situation. If nothing else, the man had style!

Keith McHugh, of Fresno, California, sends in the kind of letter I love to get—not only did he praise my work, he sent in a list of questions and supplied answers himself! Even when I don't agree with solutions such as Keith's, or if I think a little more elaboration is necessary, such a letter is a welcome treat, and serves to get my overworked gray cells cooking again.

Keith (like many others) wondered why most of Khan's followers looked so young. His solution is a pretty good one: He theorizes that the genetic manipulation that made them "supermen" also slowed their aging processes. It is a good, solid answer—*except* (as Keith pointed out) it fails to explain why *Khan* seemed to have aged the complete fifteen years, if not more. Well. Khan was one of the first (if not *the* first) of the genetic manipulates. Even in "Space Seed" he appears appreciably older than the rest of his crew. So it is possible that Khan's "engineering" was not as extensive as those born later, and that he ages normally, although he would not suffer from senescence as radically as a "normal" human would. Another explanation could be that Khan simply shows his age more than his followers do—it was *his* will, *his* determination, that allowed even a handful to survive, and the strain might have caused him to age prematurely. We've all heard the old wives' tale about hair turning white overnight, and we certainly know that worry and strain can put gray in our hair and lines on our faces much faster than mere age can, so why shouldn't Khan show the effects of his trials? Remember, aside from a few buxom and fair-skinned females lounging around the Bridge of the *Reliant*, most of the men appeared to be in their early thirties or so. If they were only in their early twenties at the time of "Space Seed," then they didn't age too much slower than normal.

Keith also offers his explanation for the appearance of the *Reliant*. Keith says (and rightly so, I think) that the *Reliant* is a *light cruiser*, as opposed to the *Enterprise*-class heavy cruiser. It makes sense, as the *Reliant* is smaller in overall configuration. It probably doubles as a scout, which would make it faster and more maneuverable than the *Enterprise*, although the *Enterprise* would probably have greater firepower and a greater cruising range. So let's go whole hog and say that the *Reliant* is one of the *Columbia* class of starships (nice, fitting name, wouldn't you agree?) and is a standard Starfleet model. It is new since the time of the series, but has apparently been in service quite a while, since no one aboard the *Enterprise* remarks anything unusual about its appearance.

Susan Biedron, of Chicago, wonders about the time span between *Star Trek: The Motion Picture* and *Wrath of Khan*. Okay. If we consider the first year of the television series as Year One, then the end of the original mission took place in Year Five. Kirk says he's spent two and a half years as chief of Starfleet Ops in *STTMP*, so figuring in about six months R&R, *STTMP* took place in Year Eight. Khan says he and his followers have been on Ceti Alpha V for fifteen years, so that would make *Wrath of Khan* take place in Year Sixteen. So eight years passed between *STTMP* and *Wrath of Khan*. That's more than enough time to explain the seemingly radical changes we saw in some of the characters—but to explain *why* these changes took place (or, in some instances, why there were no changes) is an article in itself.

The figures are simple, but complicating and confusing things is the tendency of many fans to pretend that *STTMP* never happened at all! (Or, at the very least, to relegate it to the status of "imaginary story" or "alternate-universe story.") As I feel that *everything* officially sanctioned by Paramount (no matter how many errors or inconsistencies it may contain) is part of the Star Trek canon, I find it impossible to agree with these fans. Besides, part of the appeal of Star Trek is its very realistic and endearing occasional inconsistencies. Life isn't always wrapped into neat packages—why should we expect that the almost-real life of Star Trek should be?

Susan also wonders who will become Kirk's first officer now that Spock is gone. She adds, "Technically, I would assume it would be Chekov, since he was second in command on the *Reliant*." No, I don't think so, Susan, but before I venture my guess, let's go back and look at the circumstances of that last voyage.

It was, if you'll recall, a *training cruise* for the benefit of the cadets and Lieutenant Saavik, who had probably just graduated Command School. Spock was captain of the *Enterprise*, but he was also serving as an instructor, and for all we know, the *Enterprise* could have been more or less permanently assigned as a Command/cadet-training vessel. This would account for something that disturbed many readers, Spock's commanding a ship after so many years of protesting he didn't desire command, for teaching would fit right in with Vulcan principles and such a command would be nothing like deep-space exploration. (Maybe that's why Spock seemed relieved when Kirk took command.) For all intents and purposes of the mission, however, Saavik was second in command as part of her schooling, and Kirk was aboard only for inspection and observation.

But who *was* Spock's second in command? It wasn't Sulu, for his comment about "good to be back" tells us he was berthed aboard another ship. It wasn't Chekov, for he was on the *Reliant*. Scotty was still down working happily with his bairns. And there was no one else of command rank aboard the *Enterprise*. So that leaves only one possibility: *Uhura* was Spock's second in command. She returned to her old post at Communications for the purpose of the training voyage, and once the emergency began, it was only logical that she stay there, for none of the cadets had the necessary experience or training to do the job and Spock was acting as Kirk's exec.

Kirk will naturally keep Uhura as his exec now that he's again in command of the *Enterprise*, and to round out the bridge crew, let's suppose that she'll man the helm, Saavik will navigate, David Marcus will sign on as science officer (and he may not have to join Starfleet to do so), and we'll see a couple of new interesting characters manning communications and the weapons console. (Arex and M'Ress, anyone?) Sulu and Chekov? Why, Sulu should be captaining his own ship with Chekov as his first officer—reuniting them and making use of their years of side-by-side experience on the *Enterprise*. They'd probably be a smooth-working team second only to the legendary Kirk/Spock combination.

Kim Webb, of Columbia, Missouri, also wondered about the age discrepancy of Khan's people, and added a question about Joachim. She points out that Joachim is a Spanish name and the actor who played him in "Space Seed" (Mark Tobin) was fittingly a dark, Latin type. But in *Wrath of Khan*, Joachim is played by Judson Scott, who is a blue-eyed blond, as are most of Khan's gang, which was supposedly composed of a mixture of Earth races.

It would be easy to say that raw chance dictated that only Anglo-Saxon types survived on Ceti Alpha V, but common sense dictates against that. For one thing, the odds would be zillions to one against that happening, for if Khan's crew even roughly paralleled Earth population mixes, Anglo-Saxon, Caucasian types would be in the minority. Even if it were true, we'd still be left with the problem of Joachim.

Since we've assumed earlier that Khan's followers were of a slightly more "advanced" type of genetic engineering than was he, it is possible to theorize that they would have an inbred ability to adapt their bodies to changing climatic conditions. Chameleonlike, they are able to become (on a genetic level) whatever they need to be to survive. In extremely cold conditions, they might gain vast amounts of body fat; in an aquatic environment, they might develop the ability to swim long distances and sound like whales or dolphins. (There would be limits, of course. They could not transform into Vulcans were they placed on that planet, but they just might sprout pointed ears!) Conditions on Ceti Alpha V obviously demanded that they metamorphose into blondish, Anglo-Saxon, Caucasian types, and that is exactly what they did.

Doug Sills, of Lilburn, Georgia, has a question about the ship's phasers in *Wrath of Khan*. He wants to know why, if sensors travel faster (ahead) of the ship while it's in warp, the *Enterprise* sensors couldn't detect Khan's incoming fire and automatically erect the ship's screens. Okay. We've all seen dozens of episodes where Sulu would say, "Screens just went up, captain. Something's out there." And in *STTMP* the computer detected the "incoming fire" from V'Ger, and V'Ger's plasma bolts traveled far in excess of a starship's speed. But you'll also remember Kirk often orders "full shields" when that happens, so we can assume that only a portion of the deflectors go up automatically at the approach of a foreign object. In *Wrath of Khan*, it was the full-strength shields that were "down," and the partial shields that were erected automatically at the approach of the *Reliant* (and those that the crew put up at Yellow Alert) weren't nearly strong enough to withstand Khan's fire at such close range. (As for sensors and phasers traveling faster than the ship, that is because they travel at the speed of light *relative to the speed of the ship* no matter how fast it is going in or out of warp drive.)

To finsih up with this section, I have to admit that for the first time in this series, I am stumped! Many, many, many letters—two at random were from Ann Ice, of Crystal River, Florida, and Barbara Corrigan, of East Derry, New Hampshire—wanted to know how the hell Khan recognized Chekov when Pavel didn't even join the crew until the second year of the mission.

Had "Space Seed" been the final episode of the first season, I could have fudged a little and said that the newly commissioned Ensign Chekov had just reported aboard the *Enterprise* when

Khan took over, and would have been among those Khan saw. That at least would have explained why *we* didn't see Pavel around before that. But . . .

There's really no solution to this mystery. All we can do is take Chekov and Khan at their words, and assume that Ensign Chekov *was* on board the *Enterprise* at the time of "Space Seed." We just didn't see him, that's all. We can't even make a case that perhaps Chekov was on board for a special training mission or somesuch, for Khan clearly identified him as part of the crew. It's frustrating and illogical, but there's no way to make any explanation work satisfactorily. This is one we'll just have to live with, troops. Now if only the doggone producers of *Wrath of Khan* had put *Sulu* on the *Reliant*, maybe we could all sleep nights!

Although *Wrath of Khan* has been the focus of attention these last few months, we've received many other mystery questions as well:

Regina Marracino, of Lewisville, Arizona, has an interesting speculation: Why, she asks, since we know so little about Spock's early life, couldn't he have been married and have a child?

That's the kind of thing it's fun to write fiction about, but it's not really a mystery. The evidence we are given in a number of episodes tells us that Spock is, and always has been, single and without child. He had not even gone through *pon farr* until the events of "Amok Time." We've no cause to doubt this information, and it would have taken some really bizarre and almost unbelievable circumstances for such a thing to have occurred. Sorry, Regina, no chance.

James Rone, of Columbia, South Carolina, has a question about "City on the Edge of Forever." He wants to know why, if history had been changed by Edith's life being spared, her obituary appeared on Spock's "stone knives and bearskins" tricorder image. The images Spock so painstakingly drew from the tricorder were recorded from the Guardian's presentation of history, which was at "incredible speeds" and apparently infinitely more detailed than we could see. You will also recall that Spock took recordings both *before and after* McCoy went back into time, so he had both timelines stored in his tricorder, and he was able to display both Edith's obituary and the record of her meeting with President Roosevelt. Sifting these images and their meaning out of the flood of images from the Guardian is what gave Spock so much trouble.

Barbara Overton, of Las Vegas, Nevada, asks why Starfleet

was modeled on the Navy and not on the Air Force, as space travel would seem to be a natural progression from air travel.

Our Air Force chain of command is modeled on the Army, as it was part of the Army (the Army Air Corps) for many years. But naval chain of command and rankings are more appropriate for Starfleet, as it is a fleet and performs the duties (defense and exploration) of a navy. Besides, Starfleet does not correspond exactly to our naval rankings or chain of command, but is instead sort of an amalgam of several services and traditions. Most likely, Starfleet did not grow out of any of our current services, but instead was created by the Earth government when it was realized that a quasi-military organization would be needed to defend Earth and perform many of the duties that NASA (and other space-exploration bureaus) are in charge of today.

Along with her comments on *Wrath of Khan*, Diane Rosenfeldt also wanted to know why Spock would be attracted to "the shallow, selfish, wimpy" Droxine in "The Cloud Minders," and why the only time we've been treated to voice-over access to Spock's thoughts, "the magnificent Vulcan intellect is lost in contemplation of what a nifty chick she is." I think Diane is overreacting here. True, many fans feel that other women in Spock's life have been more deserving of his attentions, but we have to look at it from Spock's viewpoint. He was attracted to Droxine, that is undeniable, but why? Couldn't it have been that he saw something *more* in her than the shallow facade of a Cloud Minder? Spock is human enough to be intrigued by a challenge; and having Droxine realize that her society's system is wrong and channeling her undeniable intellect into something more constructive than hedonistic art would be quite a challenge indeed. Also we have to remember that Droxine was very lovely, and a case could be made that her fragile beauty is somewhat reminiscent of Vulcan females. Whatever Spock's reasons, they were justifiable to him, and we have to bow to his logic. And, after all, he didn't exactly turn cartwheels, did he?

Unfortunately, that's all the room we have for mysteries this time around. As always, we are very appreciative of all of you who take the time and trouble to write. I'm looking forward to the next article, so keep those questions coming in!

What's Going to Happen to Spock?

Editors Walter and G.B. won't allow me to call this "an official *Trek* guess," but it is pretty much a synthesis of the ideas, notions, and opinions of myself, Walter, G.B., and several local fans we talked to:

Mr Spock will literally return from the dead because of several factors influenced by:

1. His well-known propensity for "playing a hunch."
2. His unique Vulcan physiology and mental abilities.
3. The *aftereffects* of the Genesis Wave.

Spock's decision to risk his life restoring warp drive was a logical one, and we may assume he was fully cognizant of the fact that his chances of survival were practically nil. But Spock would also have taken into account the many times he, Kirk, McCoy, and other members of the crew had been rescued from death before. Such thinking wouldn't have been logical and wouldn't have affected his decision to go into the chamber, but it *would* have caused him to take one last gamble: He paused to briefly mind-touch McCoy and whisper, "Remember."

On a billion-to-one chance that somehow he—or his body—could be restored, Spock formed a temporary mind-link with McCoy. Once the necessary job of restoring warp drive (and the *very* necessary job of saying goodbye to Kirk—after all, there might not be a rescue this time) was completed, Spock transferred his consciousness—his essence, if you will—into a portion of McCoy's mind.

This is entirely possible, for it was done before: The alien Sargon transferred Spock's consciousness into Christine Chapel's mind in "Return to Tomorrow." True, Spock's mental powers are not as great as were Sargon's, but impending death would have lent a desperate strength. The transfer was made, making doubly ironic McCoy's final comments about Spock.

Although Spock's body was killed by the massive radiation, we know that a number of cells within it would have escaped damage and remained alive. Just as a number of cellular and biochemical functions continue for some hours after death in a human, so they would in a Vulcan. The period of time in which such functions continue and cells remained alive would probably be much longer in the hardy Vulcans, so it is a sure thing that quite a few healthy and active cells remained in Spock's body at the time he was launched to the Genesis Planet.

When she and Kirk are in the Genesis Cave, Carol Marcus says that although the matrix formed in a day, the plant life grew later *at a greatly accelerated rate*. So obviously one of the *aftereffects* of Genesis is the stimulation of cellular growth, whether on material formed by Genesis or put there later.

So this aftereffect would work on Spock's corpse, accelerating the cellular growth within his body and causing it, in effect, to heal and repair itself. Spock will not be recreated by the Genesis Effect, nor will he look different, be of a different age, etc. He will simply be restored to health and vitality.

Of course, without the consciousness stored within McCoy's mind, all a healthy Spock body can do is lie there. It would have to go into suspended animation because it would eventually starve to death—unless, of course, it first suffocated within the sealed torpedo casing. But we have seen Spock slow his bodily processes before; there's no doubt his body would automatically do so to the greatest possible extreme in the absence of consciousness.

So all that remains is for Dr. McCoy to beam down to the Genesis Planet, open the casket, reach down with his hand in the meld position . . .

"THE WRATH OF KHAN": IN PRINT/ON SCREEN

by Diane Rosenfeldt

As is no secret to anyone, Star Trek II: The Wrath of Khan took fandom by storm. Almost equally popular, however, was Vonda N. McIntyre's novelization of the film. In the following article, Diane discusses the many differences between the two and the possible reasons therefore. Along the way she manages to get a number of her own pithy comments and opinions in, and we know you'll enjoy those too.

Even the most regrettable Star Trek episodes had Moments—memorable dialogue or situations—that made them bearable, if not worthwhile. Such moments were as diverse as Spock's "Forget," Kirk's explanation of Fizzbin, and Uhura's reaction to the appellation "fair maiden." *Star Trek: The Motion Picture* was worthwhile for auld lang syne, but disappointing for a Moment Watcher. In *STTMP*, Kirk and Spock, in the few years supposedly between the movie and the original mission, have discovered private demons that render them practically strangers to us, to their friends, and to each other until their respective exorcisms occur. The situation all but precludes the affectionate ribbing and gestures of caring that made up so many of the best Moments in the series. Admittedly, Gene Roddenberry's novelization of *STTMP* explained their obsessions and the psychic pain they suffered, but when watching the film, we have to guess why they act as they do. The film is further undermined by serious pacing problems and a one-note plot. In many ways, *STTMP*'s story is best suited to book form.

Star Trek II: The Wrath of Khan has no such problems. Furthermore, Vonda McIntyre has achieved that all-too-rare occurrence: a film novelization that augments, clarifies, and illuminates the film to the extent that the two should be experienced—and discussed—in tandem.

In *Wrath of Khan*, the characters are back "in synch." Each has his or her own concerns, but they haven't grown apart despite changes of circumstance, and are happily reunited on the cadet training cruise. Now-Captain Spock has apparently learned a lasting lesson—from V'Ger or elsewhere—and he's mellowed to the point of open (for a Vulcan) affection for Kirk. Kirk (again a deskbound admiral) is afflicted with middle-age malaise on the occasion of his birthday, feeling superannuated and somewhat superfluous. McCoy, as ever, is the twenty-third century's answer to Marcus Welby. Even as he exacerbates Kirk's problem with an unwelcome gift of reading glasses, he also knows the cure: Jim must reassume command, a directive later echoed by Spock. Scotty, between "bouts" of shore leave, has been instructing cadet trainees in the operation of his bairns. Chekov is first officer of the *USS Reliant* under Captain Clark Terrell; now-Commander Kyle is communications officer. We learn little about the remaining members of the crew in the film; the novelization (which appears, from some minor—and major—alterations, to have been based on an earlier script) provides us with a scene or two about each character, hinting at his/her current life (including Chapel and Rand, who are lost altogether in the film).

Cadet Peter Preston and Lieutenant Saavik are also examples of two major differences between the film and the novelization. Peter is seen only twice briefly in the film, and so we do not understand why Scott mourns him more than the many other brave boys populating sick bay at that moment. Peter is, the novelization tells us, Scotty's nephew. Preferring to carry his own weight, Peter was dismayed that Scotty revealed their relationship to Kirk. As a result, he and Scott are having a "difficult period," an estrangement that makes Scotty's grief all the more wrenching. Peter also has a tenuous crush on his math tutor . . . Saavik.

It's rather unfair that throughout the history of Star Trek the few resident women haven't had enough to do; it's also unfair that the one woman in *Wrath of Khan* who gets the spotlight is a stranger. Undeniably, however, Saavik is the filmmaker's single best new idea. Unfortunately, a bit of her essence is lost in the film along with her history, but in the novel, McIntyre brings her to fascinating life. Saavik is a brilliant, outspoken, unselfconsciously lovely, and (though inexperienced) unfailingly competent Vulcan. She also possesses courage, loyalty, and an intriguing hint of volatility.

This trait is explained in the book by the fact that she's not a true Vulcan. She was one of a group of half-breed offspring of Romulans and (sexually coerced) Vulcans found on a deserted Romulan colony world by a Vulcan expedition, of which Spock was a member. It was only as a result of his intervention that his fellow Vulcans agreed to rescue these reminders of Vulcan disgrace and death, and for the past several years, Spock has been Saavik's teacher, mentor, guardian—in essence, her parent.

This relationship reveals as much about Spock as it does about Saavik; he's guided her in her studies on Vulcan, aided her as only *he* could to cope with her half-breed heritage, and acclimated her to living and working with humans. Having helped to curb her Romulan temper through Vulcan disciplines, Spock assigned her to tutor Peter so that she could learn the positive virtues of human friendship from the ebullient youth. Spock is wise enough to know that his way can't and shouldn't be hers, and he's trying to show her how to find her own way. Conversely, his contact with Saavik may in part be responsible for the change in him. These circumstances, unrevealed in the film, give Saavik's situation an added poignancy—within a few days' span she loses the only two people in the galaxy for whom she gives a damn.

Interesting characters also abound on space station Regulua I—Del and Vance, the resident computer whizzes and Lewis Carroll freaks; a pair of Deltans; several others. McIntyre explores their backgrounds at some length, then details the horror of their deaths at Khan's hands. The movie neglects all but Carol and David Marcus, the masterminds of Project Genesis. The evolution of David's relationship with Kirk, from its suspicious, troubled beginnings to mutual respect, is one of the several interesting narrative threads.

Khan was a happy choice of villain. V'Ger, for all its potential for harm, was a machine, totally amoral, doing its worst because of faulty programming. Khan, on the other hand—twisted, bitter, and possessed of the arrogance of the *Ubermensch*—adds welcome dimensions of unpredictability and the capacity for true evil. (And could V'Ger have gotten away with such tasty utterances as "From hell's heart I stab at thee"?) In Khan's case, too, an interesting relationship from the book is no more than hinted at in the film—that between him and his second in command, Joachim. Joachim is to Khan much as Spock is to Kirk—deploring his excesses, even questioning his wisdom, yet serving with the utmost loyalty and even love. Yet, ultimately Joachim has no more success in preventing Khan's all-out vendetta than Spock has ever had in curbing Kirk's impetuous, albeit brilliant, command "hunches." In both the film and book, Khan is formidable, but it is in this relationship, in his ability to command the fealty of decent men like Joachim, that we see the greatness that could have been within his grasp. It's as well it wasn't, however—as an unbalanced throwback to a more violent age, with his archaic notions of power and retribution (and his convenient lack of the usually attendant sense of honor), Khan is a nifty high-style menace.

The film is terrific, fast-paced, and crammed with scenes guaranteed to warm a Trekker's cockles; its excellence isn't compromised by the "missing" scenes cited above. Most were probably deleted for sheer lack of time to deal with them, or because their inclusion would have affected mood or pacing. For instance, the subtleties of the Spock/Saavik/Peter thread could not be briefly conveyed. Nor could the fact that McCoy was an old friend of Clark Terrell's, which in the novel heightens the drama of Bones having to helplessly witness Terrell's self-immolation. Similarly, the passage in the novelization describing Spock's observations and reflections as he's bombarded with radiation would be difficult to translate to film without seriously impairing its emotional impact. These omissions give rise to *further* omissions which, given a chance, could "play" well onscreen. Two of the most notable of these feature Saavik:

1. In the book, Spock helps carry Peter to sick bay. When he returns, Saavik is relieved to see that the blood on his tunic isn't his, not knowing that it belongs to her other friend. When she finds out, she feels in danger of shaming herself and her mentor with an emotional outburst—until Spock mercifully invents an errand so she can leave the bridge. Saavik arrives at sick bay too late. Locking herself in a conference room, she succumbs to rage and grief, then returns to duty.

2. Saavik, having guessed Spock's intent in leaving the bridge but dutybound to remain at her post, wants him to know, at least, that a new planet has been born of his sacrifice. Kirk cuts off her message, reacting in *his* grief, and in ignorance of the extent of her knowledge. Spock, of course, understands. Saavik

spends the night in the stasis room, keeping vigil over the bodies of Spock and Peter.

A few changed scenes "play" better in the film than their counterparts do in the book. These basically involve situations that in the novel seem unlikely or uncharacteristic:

1. In the book the scene in which Spock relinquishes command to Kirk comes *after* Kirk has given an emergency order on the bridge. This, despite the circumstances and intent of the order, gives Kirk an air of highhandedness and makes Spock's abdication of command ring a bit hollow. As the filmed version stands, both men act graciously, Kirk only accepting command (however much he may want it) at Spock's insistence that it's Kirk's "first best destiny." It's one of the movie's warmest moments.

2. In the novel, Kirk doesn't know what eyeglasses are. Earth in the twenty-third century is still a lot like our present-day world—people look and dress recognizably, there are "no smoking" signs on starship bridges, and controlled substances are still in use. Glasses, however rarely used, wouldn't be unheard-of.

3. Also in the novel, Kirk doesn't know that David exists. The emotional bond between Jim and Carol is obviously a lasting one, and by all indications they've been in touch since David's conception. Kirk would have been uncharacteristically obtuse if he hadn't guessed. As it is, it's surprising enough that David doesn't know.

Within the narrative of *Wrath of Khan* are several clever, even inspired, touches: The *Kobayashi Maru* wargame scenario, with its emphasis on the "no-win" situation, illustrates the fact, despite his glib sermon to Saavik on the subject, that Jim Kirk has never faced up to the possibility of defeat any more than Saavik has. This is confirmed by the fact that he took the test three times, finally cheating to win. When Spock faces his own *Kobayashi Maru*, Kirk is suddenly forced to *confront* his mortality as well as his friend's.

The reading glasses provide not only a few laughs, but also a nice visual motif for Kirk's feelings toward aging. The use of *A Tale of Two Cities* is very apt (amazingly, director Nicholas Meyer says it was chosen at random); the beginning, "It was the best of times, it was the worst of times," epitomizes Kirk's active *Enterprise* years. And the ending—"It is a far, far better thing I do than I have ever done"—is, of course, appropriate to

Spock's situation as he assumes the self-sacrificing Sydney Carton role.

The Genesis Device is also an interesting concept. Its ability to rearrange the molecular structure of any chunk of matter and make it life-bearing makes it an intriguing solution for the homeless and hungry of the universe. But even when used benignly (as pointed out by—who else?—Dr. McCoy), its complete destruction of any existing life makes it a double-edged sword. It ultimately proves to be just that, but the *other* way around; escape from its malevolent use costs Spock's life, but the world it creates gives Kirk—and us—hope for Spock's resurrection.

Spock's death is easily the most controversial event in the history of Star Trek; it also has been the subject of a certain amount of media hype. The rumors flew for months, fed by vague pronouncements from studio reps and actors alike, culminating in Trekkers of all persuasions lodging protests of varying virulence—letters, even threats, or just private resolutions not to see the film. It was a surprise to find that fans as well as critics approved it wholeheartedly. The reason for this, perhaps, is that for all the audience manipulation (and the whole death sequence is as manipulative in its way as was anything in *Love Story*), the event is treated in a fashion consistent with all characters involved. Spock, as a fictional creation, is right up there with Sherlock Holmes, King Arthur, and the Three Musketeers. Their literary demises were reflections of their lives and deeds; Spock's cannot but be the same. The producers of *Wrath of Khan* have done a bang-up job of fulfilling this edict by adhering faithfully to the demands of (if nothing else) the laws of decency:

1. Spock's death is meaningful. For him to have succumbed to an act of random violence or an accident, however common those are in Star Trek's universe, would be simply unbearable.

2. His death arises from a conscious choice—like so many other altruistic, but potentially lethal, choices he's made in the past.

3. His decision is logical. Nobody else aboard, except possibly Saavik, could have lasted long enough to do the job.

4. Kirk is with him at the end; goodbyes are said. This scene is laden with dramatic and emotional impact. There's a lot of pain of various kinds involved: physical pain for Spock, as his Vulcan body finally betrays him; mental pain for Kirk, as he realizes he's powerless to save Spock; and mental pain for us, as we watch all this. There's also nobility and total selflessness on Spock's part, and profound shock and grief on Kirk's. The

physical barrier between them adds extra nuances: It is ironic that Spock, having finally won for himself, from himself, the right to open friendship with this human, is denied the last comfort of his, or any, hand. Also, because of the clear wall, the two men are seen throughout the scene as mirror images, virtually matching gesture for gesture, and thus emphasizing our already established and much analyzed perception of them as two aspects of one total person. The third part of the Friendship, McCoy, is present but not participatory; perhaps his regulatory influence has no place in these proceedings.

Catharsis is made complete with the following scene of Spock's funeral service. Spock's remains are moved to the launch to the accompaniment of Scotty's bagpipes keening ''Amazing Grace''—a phrase which describes Spock perfectly: his perpetual gallantry and generosity of nature in abnegating all personal ambition to put his superior gifts at the disposal of his commander; his unshakable loyalty; his respect for all living things; his integrity of word and deed; the quality of what Jim Kirk, in the novel, thinks of as his ''questing spirit.'' As the torpedo arcs into space, and the orchestra takes up the theme, the mood is at once elegiac and elevated, a celebration of an exemplary life.

5. Finally, and best of all, it's probably not permanent. Thanks to the Genesis Device, we may be experiencing a fascinatingly radical ''What If?'' scenario with no lasting ill effects—a sort of Shore Leave. In this the film makes a final deviation from the book; in the novel, nobody has any kind of conviction that Spock, in an accessible form, still exists. Saavik, during her vigil, feels what may be a mind touch *or* an illusion born of wishful thinking. And the route of the coffin is described as a carefully plotted decaying orbit around the planet, ending eventually in incineration. This *looks* like the intent in the film, too, but since Kirk seems to feel there will be something to return to, he must have sent it *to* the planet. Some of the Star Trek novels have postulated a psychic bond between the two men that would make either aware of the other's cessation (much as Spock was once aware of the ''death'' of the *Intrepid*). An attractive and plausible concept, but the film claims no such linkage. Kirk's firm resolve to return seems based mainly on hope, and a tenuous one at that: If he were sure the Genesis Device would work on Spock, he wouldn't leave the area. Of course, we're left to sweat out the details, but it's pretty evident that Spock, in some form (let's hope it's Nimoy's) will turn up again. With this assurance firmly stated, we could wish for Kirk to be a little *less*

optimistic, in order to heighten suspense for the next film. (The effect of a totally unexpected mind call, like the one Spock received from him in the Roddenberry novelization of *STTMP*, might be satisfying.) At any rate, the image of the unharmed torpedo housing, gleaming in the new sun with verdant life springing up all around it, is a powerfully poignant and hopeful one.

The technical and visual aspects of the film can be summed up as "neat but not gaudy." Quite correctly, the focus is on people, not hardware, which is kept unobtrusive and subordinate. One neat technological advancement since the series is the ability of people being transported to move and talk. (Consider Dr. McCoy's discombobulated atoms fidgeting apprehensively through space, leaving the message "I don't trust this thing" bouncing through the cosmos.)

The sets are quite nice, and a few are standouts: the Genesis Cave, a shimmering combination of set and effects; Khan's grungy digs; and, best of all, Kirk's Earth apartment. A few deft touches reaffirm three years' worth of character development in one glance. It's very modern, gleaming, yet comfortable. The items of adornment—pieces of armor and weaponry, models of tall ships and various antique sailing instruments—mark Kirk as a bit of a throwback himself. Obviously the perfect nemesis for Khan.

The costumes are also well done. The new *Enterprise* uniforms are universally flattering (especially the officers')—much classier than those of the series or *Star Trek: The Motion Picture*. The outerwear looks right; the accessories seem comfortable and functional. The clothing of Khan and his people is quite witty; the fragments of ragged clothing in the macho-hippie-barbarian mode and the jewelry made from random bits of space junk give the gang an appropriately piratical air.

Undeservedly brief comments on some technical matters: The visual effects, model work, and process shots rarely call attention to themselves, but when they do they're fine. The Mutara Nebula backgrounds are beautiful and mysterious, great for the silent battle of wills taking place. The model work during this final showdown, while not of the slambang *Star Wars* variety, is very effective, especially the shot in which the *Enterprise*, like Jaws, rises up behind the *Reliant*. The music, like the visuals, is effective without blatancy. The film itself is best described as an "intimate epic," and the music fits it—dignified and majestic when necessary, but not bombastic. Finally, it's uncertain whether the Ceti-Alphan lizard thing and its larvae come under the heading of props, effects, or makeup, but whatever they are, they're revoltingly realistic!

Many fans were apprehensive when it was learned that the second Star Trek film would be made without the active participation of Gene Roddenberry or any of the writers from the series— apprehension increased when it was announced that Harve Bennett would be the producer. However, he's done an exemplary job, especially in his selection of an old episode as a starting point. (As with *STTMP*, any storyline devised would be reminiscent of series situations—*why not* make it intentional?) And Jack B. Sowards has written a delightful, *right* screenplay, capturing the relationships with the best of the series' writers—where was he during the wretched third season?

Nicholas Meyer, coming in "cold" to direct the film, had one major advantage: Being unfamiliar with the Star Trek canon, he could see, without the passions and biases of many years' association, the strengths and weaknesses of what had gone before. His job was to make established, beloved characters ring true for a highly knowledgeable, critical, and vocal audience. (Established characters are not unknown to Meyer, who has two fine Sherlock Holmes books to his credit, and his only other film, *Time After Time*, is a fantasy about two other well-known historical figures, H.G. Wells and Jack the Ripper. It's fitting that the man who told us what *really* happened during those "post-Reichenbach" years should be the the one to send Spock over the falls, so to speak.) Meyer's work has always featured warm relationships, and *Wrath of Khan* is no exception. The fellow-feeling among "our" crewmembers is so immediately apparent that the *audience* practically purrs. Meyer has quoted Robert Bresson: "My job is not to find out what the public wants and to give it to them; my job is to make the public want what I want," and he adds that "the issue is not what we do, but whether we do it well. If we do it well, they'll buy it." In point of fact, he *has* done what he wants, he *has* done it well, and we *do* buy it, probably because he's managed to maintain the integrity of the characters' personalities even as he causes them to live, learn, change, and grow.

The Star Trek films have the advantage of an ensemble company many of whose members are already accustomed and attuned to each other. The regular cast is still capable of pleasant surprises, of course, and there are nonregulars for novelty. Many of the original cast still have roles that are frankly rather thankless.

It's no disparagement to simply say that they do their usual fine job, and to commend them for their graciousness in returning to make the twenty-third century feel like home.

Of these, Walter Koenig has a nominally expanded role which amounts, in actuality, to repeated screaming and collapsing. However, he manages a nice touch while under Khan's control, when the finger he uses to terminate a transmission seems also to switch off the insincere smile pasted on his features. During the final battle, too, his Chekov displays a suitable dedication and stoicism.

The supporting players are uniformly good. Judson Scott, an elegant young classical actor unbilled as Joachim, manages (in a few brief scenes and without much to say) to convey some of the qualities ascribed to the character in the novel. Paul Winfield brings to the small but important role of Clark Terrell the dignity and gallantry inherent in Starfleet's best; he's a man very much like Kirk. As Carol Marcus, Jim's old flame, Bibi Besch is obviously the kind of woman worthy of a man of Kirk's caliber (as he is worthy of her). Kirk may have had his little flings with ladies of a very different type, but if it were at all in his nature to settle down, Besch's warm, *intelligent* womanliness would be what he'd seek.

As their son, Merritt Butrick ably combines Carol's intelligence with Kirk's hotheadedness. In a couple of short scenes he shows us, by stages, the confusion of a youth who must learn to accept as father a man whose life-style and motives he despises and distrusts; the growth of a grudging respect for the man; and finally outright pride in the person Kirk has become. He's very believable as the kind of young man Kirk must once have been.

Kirstie Alley's Saavik is a prize. If Butrick is a reborn Kirk, Alley is young Spock to the life, with her air of intelligence and quiet competence. Even in the film's curtailed scenes she conveys some of the same conflicts Spock must have faced as a half-breed. This is nicely played in the funeral scene: Her upbringing and training make an emotional display out of the question, but her volatile Romulan half needs *some* release. Her compromise: a single tear. Also, as befits Vulcans (with the notable, and glaring, exception of Stonn), Alley has more sex appeal in one mobile brow that Persis Khambatta's Ilia had in her whole complement of pheromones. (Saavik's existence also allows us our first exposure to spoken Vulcan—which resembles a severe head cold in Gaelic.)

Ricardo Montalban had a different dilemma than most of the

other cast members. Instead of having to stay within the confines of a well-known character, he had to submerge his most famous creation, the suave Mr. Roarke, to recreate one fifteen years old. His challenge was twofold: to play Khan fifteen years older *and* to play him insane—a megalomaniac turned madman. In this performance we see many years' worth of bitterness kept somehow in check instantaneously transformed into a sort of killing frenzy at the mention of Kirk's—*Admiral* Kirk's—name. His more psychotic episodes take on a weird ritualistic quality. As the film progresses, it's clear that he now has no aim in life but to ruin Kirk; all Joachim's efforts to rechannel that bloodlust are for naught. At times Khan seems sustained solely by the strength of his hatred. It is an arresting performance.

In his time, Dr. McCoy has served as savior, shrink, conscience, and clown. In *Wrath of Khan* his function seems to be that of rock-steady anchor and sounding board for the more volatile—and troubled—Kirk . . . a role to which DeForest Kelley is eminently suited. The laid-back, reassuring aspect of his presence is easy to take for granted; McCoy is more noticeable when he's being irascible, sarcastic, or excited. He's *still* more than willing to dispense contraband booze and pithy, though unwanted, advice to Kirk, or to take up the cudgel on behalf of illogic against Mr. Spock; but as Kirk moves from crisis to crisis, Kelley's Bones is comfortingly, solidly There. No more is needed.

It's also hard not to take for granted Leonard Nimoy's work as Spock. Spock's dilemma is that his human half is more than willing to indulge in emotions; where most Vulcans must master one set of deviant impulses, Spock must keep track of *two*. His control, as we've seen, is often less than perfect. It is a tough distinction to conceptualize, much less act out, but Nimoy has always succeeded, often triumphing over material seemingly aimed at undermining his carefully built characterization.

What does the passage of fifteen years do to such a man? In Spock's case, it seems to have given him peace. Since *Wrath of Khan* is obviously a sequel to the series rather than to *Star Trek: The Motion Picture*, it's hard to tell how much (if any) influence the events of *STTMP* have had on Spock's character in *Wrath of Khan*. It seems pretty evident that his guardianship of Saavik and its attendant responsibilities, rather than the experience with V'Ger, are what have brought about the subtle changes in Spock—made him able, for instance, to give Kirk a present without making up an elaborate excuse, as he might've in the past; or to enable him to say, "I am your friend." (In the novel, he says this to McCoy as well, although the doctor is unconscious at the time.)

In other ways, however, the new Spock is still the old Spock, particularly in regard to his sense of humor (which throughout Star Trek has always been evidence of how human he really is). We see this best after Kirk expresses his fear that "these kids can't steer" and has emerged on the bridge with that very much in mind. Spock immediately takes this in (that's one nice thing about established characters: we know That Look), blandly orders Saavik to "take her out," and stands back to enjoy the sight of Kirk as six feet of screaming nerve ends. ("Damn leprechaun," thinks McCoy in the novel.) Spock's motives are semi-pure after all—he wants Saavik, after her disastrous *Kobayashi Maru*, to redeem herself in Kirk's eyes and in her own.

We know the look, too, as he leaves the bridge that last time—with the barest flicker of expression Nimoy telegraphs Spock's total grasp of the situation and his acceptance of the consequences. This Spock is, if possible, even more admirable than before. By the time he breathes his last, ravaged but ever stalwart, we feel terrible—for him, but also for Kirk, to have had such a friend and lost him. The subtleties of Nimoy's lovely performance, alas, aren't likely to be fully appreciated outside the circle of Star Trek aficionados.

An admission: I loved Star Trek from the start, but it took me a long time to develop any liking for William Shatner *or* for Kirk. They both seemed to epitomize the traditional macho values I found unattractive. I disliked Kirk, in fact, long after I learned to admire and appreciate Kirk/Spock. This prejudice has faded only slowly and incompletely. In light of this, Shatner's performance in *Wrath of Khan* is a revelation. I really like *this* Kirk. His promotion has been a disastrous mistake in all but one respect: He's had time to reflect and doesn't much like the conclusions he's reached. He's afraid he's lived his life wrong; regrets wait around every corner—his desk job, Carol, David, Khan. Though his friends know he can still cut it as a starship captain, *he's* not so sure anymore. In short, he's vulnerable, and it makes all the difference in his character.

Kirk runs the gamut in this film—gains family, loses friends; feels old, and is "reborn"; he experiences every possible emotion. Shatner is equal to it all, and in a much quieter way than heretofore. His Kirk has lost the swagger and bombast, found poise and an attractively rueful sense of humor. His attitude toward Saavik—as compared to what his reaction would have been in the old days, when every female was a personal challenge to his virility—is amusing. He doesn't automatically turn on the hormones any more, but he's not above a polite ogle and an attempt at small talk. He's later heard, during a moment of dire peril, to mutter a "Damn!" when he notices Saavik noticing the glasses. Older, yes, but far from old. Some of his best scenes involve his dealings with his old friends, and, inevitably, the strongest of all is his last with Spock. Throughout the scene his face is a heartbreaking mask of grief, shock, and love. It's ironic that Shatner's character is the one obsessed with age. Of all the principals, he shows the fewest effects of time and gravity.

Wrath of Khan is a terrific movie; capturing the style of the series and the characters. Vonda McIntyre's novelization of the film is also terrific—her style is super. She manages to incorporate verbatim script dialogue with her own lucid, perceptive prose style. As Jack Sowards captured the characters verbally in his script, McIntyre portrays their mental and spiritual essences with affection and accuracy in her novel.

FATHERS AND SONS AND THE "NO-WIN SCENARIO"

by Larry Sisson

In Wrath of Khan *we see the two sides of man, represented by Kirk and Khan. We have no difficulty in discerning which is good and which is bad. But, as Larry Sisson points out in this article, their relationship is more involved and interconnected than just that of enemies representing the sides of good and evil in a battle. Larry also examines the roles played by friends and family in the never-ending battle between the forces represented by Kirk and Khan.*

Star Trek II: The Wrath of Khan is an action picture, advertised as "a battle between good and evil . . . a warrior and a madman." It is the story of Admiral James T. Kirk's renewed conflict with an old enemy, the obsessed, vengeful Khan. But there is more to *Wrath of Khan* than intergalactic chases and exploding spaceships: The film also tells the story of fathers and sons, wherein the dramas of authority and independence are enacted. Central to all of these themes is Admiral Kirk, who for the first time in his life must confront mortality and loss, in a tragic test of his heroic character.

Khan was introduced in the 1967 Star Trek episode "Space Seed." The *Enterprise* discovered a drifting spaceship containing eighty or so men and women suspended in "cryogenic freeze." All were products of genetic engineering—physically stronger and intellectually more facile than "ordinary humans" like Captain Kirk. They are led by Khan Noonian Singh, a powerful prince of the 1990s who had hoped to take political control of the warring Earth nations. Instead, he and his loyal followers were forced to flee the planet when the tide began to turn against his dictatorial schemes.

Unaware of Khan's identity or activities in the 1990s, Kirk has him resuscitated. But revitalized in the twenty-third century, Khan feels no less hungry for power on board the *Enterprise* than he did three centuries earlier on Earth. He independently "reactivates" his followers and attempts to take control of the starship, but is thwarted by Kirk and his crew, who deposit him on a remote, uninhabited planet. With no means of departure and no ready-made civilization to conquer, Khan's autocratic appetite is placed in check.

Effectively marooned by Kirk, Khan's followers begin an effort to tame their primitive world. As we learn in *Wrath of Khan*, however, a neighboring planet explodes six months later, leaving Khan's own planet a dry, windswept dustbowl. Members of this hardy group begin to perish in this suddenly harsh environment, some of them (including Khan's wife, former *Enterprise* crewmember Marla McGivers) killed by the planet's only indigenous survivor of the explosion, a repugnant sand creature that enters the human ear and takes up parasitic residence in the brain, causing insanity and then death.

For fifteen years Khan has been stranded in this hellish environment. Once a prince, now forced to combat the relentlessly savage elements for mere survival, he blames Kirk for his plight. For although Kirk knew nothing of the wreckage of Khan's previously habitable planet, he "never bothered to check on our progress." When two unsuspecting Starfleet officers stumble on Khan's group, he gains control of a starship and sets out across the universe, madly obsessed by his quest to avenge himself on Admiral Kirk.

Meanwhile, it seems that the past fifteen years have taken a wasteful toll on Kirk as well. Having accepted promotion from captain to admiral, thus forsaking active starship command for deskbound duty on Earth, a despondent Kirk becomes concerned with how rapidly the years are passing. The empty luxuries of his rank and surroundings give him no consolation. He feels old and alone, with little hope of regaining the vitality he once knew as commander of the *Enterprise*.

Kirk's longtime friend and frequent spiritual counselor, Dr. McCoy, advises him to return to active command before he "really" gets old. Kirk rebuffs this suggestion, saying that "galloping around the cosmos is a game for the young." But during an inspection of the *Enterprise* and its youthful crew of cadets (in training under the half-Vulcan Captain Spock) an emergency situation arises causing Kirk to once again assume command of the starship.

The emergency is, of course, Khan's doing. His first project for luring Kirk into combat has been to raid a scientific outpost which holds a life-creating device called Genesis. Kirk responds to the outpost's distress call, thus taking Khan's bait and suffering the first blow in their protracted battle. Kirk's resourcefulness and greater tactical experience prevail over Khan's "superior intellect," however, and the war seems to be won. But Khan still has one more card up his malevolent sleeve: a delayed explosion of the Genesis Device which the *Enterprise*'s battle-damaged engines cannot outrun. There appears to be no escape for Kirk and his crew, as critical ship-propulsion elements are situated in a radioactive chamber and repairs seem impossible.

Meanwhile, at his station on the bridge, Mr. Spock privately surmises that owing to his sturdier Vulcan physiology he alone might be able to enter the chamber and restore the ship's failed engines before succumbing to the fatal radiation. Unnoticed by Kirk, he leaves his post and performs this act of self-sacrifice, enabling the ship to escape destruction.

Thus runs the rousing main action of *Wrath of Khan*. But also at work in the film are several subtler conflicts and resolutions, best understood as an examination of the different relationships between fathers and sons.

The first and least complex of these relationships develops in the early part of the movie, when Kirk is inspecting Captain Spock's crew of young cadets on the *Enterprise*. The admiral doubts gravely the trainees' ability to "steer" a starship; like the father who worries about his child's first drive out of the garage and around the block, Kirk frets when Spock instructs Lieutenant Saavik to pilot the ship out of space dock. Yet, "regulations" and his own (temporary) lack of confidence keep Kirk an observing bystander. Then Khan's raid on the outpost drastically alters the situation. This emergency, along with the promptings of the emotional Dr. McCoy and the logical Mr. Spock, compel Kirk to resume his authority as leader of this crew of "children." Reluctant necessity restores a parent-child relationship; as Spock suggests, commanding a starship is Kirk's "first best destiny . . . anything else is a waste of material."

In another, heretofore secret parental area, however, Kirk's "destiny" has not fared so well. Awaiting him at the scientific outpost are scientists David Marcus (Kirk's biological son) and Carol Marcus, designer of the Genesis Project and David's mother. At Carol's request, Kirk has stayed away from their son and kept his "romantic" identity hidden; now the two must meet under unpleasant circumstances.

David at first misunderstands and thinks it is the military-minded Kirk who is trying to take the Genesis Device from them. When Kirk arrives at the outpost, David instantly attacks him with a knife; Kirk subdues him, but Carol must intervene before the (still-secret) father-son violence is calmed.

As the film progresses, David learns his estranged father's identity, and becomes more familiar with Kirk's true character as he watches him duel Khan. By movie's end, after the death of Mr. Spock, father and son effect a meaningful reconciliation. But in an interesting "inversion" of the relationship, it is David who takes the lead in establishing emotional contact and respect: "I'm proud, very proud, to be your son." Kirk, uncomfortable and elusive until this declaration, confirms the sentiment with a speechless embrace. Here, David acts in fatherly fashion, and Kirk responds like a son: With the aid of this temporary reversal, the relationship is restored.

Still more complex is the connection between Kirk and Khan. At first (in "Space Seed") their conflict is almost predictable: the older, stronger Khan tries to subjugate the "upstart" Kirk, much as a domineering father might attempt to quell the challenge made by an insubordinate son. But the "inferior" captain is resourceful enough to withstand Khan's offensive and banish him to a planet where his tyrannical inclinations can do no further harm. Thus is the "evil father" disciplined by the "virtuous son."

Suddenly, however, the battle is renewed. The strife in "Space Seed" must seem in retrospect a cool prelude to the all-out warfare that materializes in *Wrath of Khan*. Khan, driven nearly insane by his fifteen years of banishment on Alpha Ceti V, is more determined than ever to be revenged upon his old enemy Kirk. Like the central characters from three of the books he has carried with him since the 1990s—*King Lear*, *Paradise Lost*, and *Moby-Dick*—Khan rages against the elements and his fate in the endless sandstorm of his environment; he feels himself "cast out" by Kirk and civilization, "exiled" in a wasteland; he fixes all his fury on one being, Kirk, and swears that he will have his vengeance. Once again the son must prepare for the father's onslaught, for only a fight to the death will sate Khan's wrath.

But if Khan is something of a "father" to Kirk (albeit a malicious one), he is also a "son" to him; here, *Wrath of Khan* takes one of its most fascinating turns. In "Space Seed," Khan is near death in his failing cryogenic unit when Kirk discovers him. The captain has Khan revived and thus "gives birth" to his eventual enemy, whose actions in *Wrath of Khan* might be seen as those of an especially rebellious fifteen-year-old. Khan is thus not only a rampaging elder who must be overthrown, he is also a childish tantrum-thrower who must be authoritatively disciplined. He is both imperious father and naughty son.

Kirk, too, is cast in this dual light. As "son," he valiantly challenges Khan's malignant authority, and relievedly welcomes David's "fatherly" overture. But as "inattentive father," Kirk has "neglected" both Khan and David Marcus over the past fifteen years, and the hostility with which they each at first greet him is somewhat justifiable. Unlike Khan, however, Kirk's solutions to these problems with his "relations" need not end in destruction: To his foe, Khan, who will accept only ruination, Kirk can give only ruination; but with his son, David, Kirk enters into a redeemed and redemptive accord.

Thus are old scores settled, old difficulties resolved. But in *Wrath of Khan*, Kirk not only takes care of "unfinished business," he is also catapulted into the future. The catalyst is his friend and perennial "second in command" Mr. Spock, whose example and companionship launch Kirk into a more "actualized" present, with real possibilities ahead.

In the series, Kirk and Spock operated week after week in extremely close tandem. Their efficient, inspired partnership fostered a deep friendship to which the coolly logical, "unemotional" Mr. Spock could never admit. But it was largely Spock's propinquity which helped make Kirk into such a dynamic and sensitive leader.

In the fifteen years since their original tour of duty together, however, new responsibilities have pulled the two officers somewhat apart, and the aging, isolated Kirk seems the worse for it. Yet he nevertheless encounters a Spock who again complements him in the precisely appropriate ways. Concerned that his assuming command of the *Enterprise* might injure Captain Spock's dignity, Kirk hears only reassurance from his old friend: "You are my superior officer," Spock says, "but you are also my friend. I have been, and always shall be, yours." This sort of adventuresome human contact (missing from much of Kirk's life of late) helps restore the old relationship to its previous splendor.

With the admiral at the conn, Mr. Spock remains peripheral to much of the film's main action; it isn't until the final battle with Khan that he and Kirk fully join forces on the bridge. As the commanding officer, however, Kirk bears all responsibility for the mission, his ship, and its crew, so when the fighting reaches its climax and the *Enterprise* seems unable to escape destruction, Kirk is understandably distraught. The situation appears hopeless.

Such a dilemma might be termed a "no-win situation," and Kirk's ability to confront such a condition honestly is as important a theme to *Wrath of Khan* as is the battle with Khan.

As the film opens, Lieutenant Saavik is "in command" of the *Enterprise* and confronted with the *Kobayashi Maru* simulation. This crisis is part of any would-be starship captain's training. Kirk himself underwent the trial, achieving (on his third try) an ingenious solution to the problem by reprogramming the test computers and thus avoiding failure.

But the drill is not meant to be "passed" or "failed": it represents a "no-win scenario" designed to test the character of the captaincy-cadet. Kirk "passed" the test by using his cunning and in effect "changing the conditions of the test," a pattern which he often successfully repeated as captain of the *Enterprise*. Later in the film, he says, "I don't believe in the no-win scenario," probably because he never has had to confront one honestly. But by the film's end, with the *Enterprise* seemingly at Khan's mercy, and escape attained only through the sacrifice of Kirk's closest ally, the "no-win scenario" has shown itself to the admiral in all its fierce severity. This time, it is not a simulation; there is no way to "change the conditions of the test." Kirk at last must face real failure and loss.

As Spock lies dying in the engine room, Kirk rushes unbelieving through the ship—no matter how logical, the "father" could never have permitted the sacrifice of his "son." By acting independently, without a "direct order," Spock has made safe the most valued "possession" of his superior officer—command of the *Enterprise*. But Kirk is devastated. Spock asks him not to grieve, again repeating his vow of friendship. Then, as a son might seek his father's approval, Spock, who has never been tested in the "no-win scenario," straightens his uniform and asks his admiral, "What do you think of my solution?" The two share a parting gesture of love and respect, and Spock dies.

Thus does Kirk at last come face to face with mortality. This time, there is no way out; without losing Spock, the *Enterprise* could not continue its voyages—just as sometimes a painful loss is necessary to the ongoing "enterprise" of living. At precious cost, Spock's last act has made possible Khan's defeat, as it has facilitated the reconciliation between Kirk and David. Spock's self-sacrifice also serves to revitalize the moldering, aging admiral, who at last has been through a "no-win scenario" and *survived*. No longer "old and alone," he stands on the bridge with his closest remaining friends. "All is well," he says, and when Dr. McCoy asks him how he feels, he replies, "Young . . . I feel young."

Every father is also a son, just as every son carries at least the potential for fatherhood; each is implied by the other, in tensions or gratifications. Through the complex workings-out of the intertwined and inverse father-son dynamics in *Star Trek II: The Wrath of Khan*, rejuvenation comes to James T. Kirk, the film's central character. With the death of Mr. Spock, the "most human" of all the souls he has known, Kirk confronts grievous loss and his own mortality, and is "made human" again. By passing through a "no-win scenario," Kirk comes to terms with the energizing and sometimes devastating consequences of human relationships and responsibilities. This was no drill.

SPOCK . . . MEET SPOCK

by Rowena G. Warner

One of the very first articles discussing the death of Spock to arrive at our offices was this one by Rowena Warner. It is a highly personal essay, obviously written soon after viewing the film when the shock that Rowena (and all of us) felt was still great enough to come strongly through in her words. Yet even so, Rowena was able to examine the Vulcan's character in light of this new development with a dispassion that can only be termed . . . logical.

> "I want, by understanding myself, to understand others. I want to be all that I am capable of becoming. . . . This all sounds very strenuous and serious. But now that I have wrestled with it, it's no longer so. I feel happy—deep down."
> —Katherine Mansfield (1889–1923)

That sounds like Spock.

I speak of him in the present tense because I firmly believe he will "return from the dead"; after all, such a concept is not difficult to visualize.

But it's not his death I would like to talk about—it is his life.

While waiting with undisguised anticipation for the premiere of *Star Trek II: The Wrath of Khan*, I kept wondering: What will Spock be like? To paraphrase the Wicked Witch of the West, this matter would have to be handled del-i-cately—too much emotion and you might wind up with a psychotic Vulcan; too little emotion and his mind-boggling experience with V'Ger was for naught.

After viewing the movie, my first impression was: I like this new Spock, but I feel as if I need to become reacquainted with him. As is so often the case, my first impression was inaccurate. This is not a *new* Spock at all, but merely the result of a logical evolutionary process which has taken place, the evolution of the "self."

His encounter with V'Ger might be considered a revelation; however, it was not a revelation of answers, but of the question "Is this all there is?" Spock had to find his own answers, and in *Wrath of Khan*, he is beginning to do so.

Why has the Spock character become so popular? Why do we humans feel a kinship to this Vulcan? Because Spock is no more an alien to us than we are to ourselves. The constant battle between his Vulcan and human halves is a personification of our daily battles with different aspects of our own personalities. From his encounter with V'Ger, Spock has learned a most valuable lesson: To "be all there is" invokes much more than just the use of logic; it involves the kaleidoscopic combination and full potential of all aspects of one's personality and is applicable not only to Spock, but to us humans as well.

Spock has spent his entire life attempting to mold himself into a category labeled "Vulcan" and in striving to do so was endeavoring to exorcise any personality traits which did not fall within that definition. In his burning desire to find the correct answer, it never occurred to him to step back and study the race he was attempting to emulate. If he had done so, Spock would have realized there was no easy solution, nor a simple choice. For instance, take into consideration T'Pau, Stonn, T'Pring, and Sarek—all Vulcans and yet each unique. The human counterparts—Kirk, McCoy, you, and I. Each of us is human, yet diversified in our thoughts, ideals, and actions. Therefore, Spock is unique, not because he is a human/Vulcan hybrid, but because of the simple fact that he exists, and it was through V'Ger that he finally understood: In reality, there is no *one* choice that can be made.

We are all of the stuff of the universe: greatness, mediocrity, idealism, apathy, hatred, love. Through his mind meld with V'Ger and his subsequent search for answers, Spock has now come to realize there are infinite choices, endless alternatives to ponder and select; and in *Star Trek II* he has obviously begun to make such selections—"You are also my friend. I have been and always shall be yours." He has always been aware this friendship existed, but it took a matured Spock, a being who no longer had a battle waging within, to admit such friendship—not only to Kirk, but to himself.

In *Wrath of Khan*, Spock tells Kirk, ". . . were I to invoke logic . . ."—an important phrase, for it demonstrates that Spock has now accepted his ability to choose between Vulcan logic and human emotion. This is *the most important* decision Spock has ever made.

People speak of Spock as a Vulcan with no emotions; a talk-show host once described him as being incapable of love. Such people understand Spock as little as he understood himself. He has always possessed the ability to love or hate, to become angry or sad, to experience the feeling of happiness. Spock, however, was a deceiver, not only of others, but—most important—of himself. Spock could not follow the dictum "To thine own self be true," for he was endeavoring to follow the Vulcan teachings, the teachings of others, and therefore was ashamed to admit, even to himself, that he could love.

So how could an intelligent and logical creature commit such a grave error? Spock's earliest memories consist of his father's, his teachers', his society's emphasizing "logic" as the only alternative. For a race which is supposed to be advanced in its thinking, such an ideology is rather narrow-minded and primitive. Logic should be taught as a viable alternative, not as a rigid discipline. In Vulcan society, logic works as the dominant characteristic; however, this race obviously has not learned that many subordinate characteristics exist that can be accepted and integrated with no adverse effects.

Perhaps Spock can teach *them*; he may one day become the first of the new Vulcan Masters. He has been, is, and always will be a Vulcan; but Spock is a new breed, not because of his racial mixture, but as a result of his new pattern of thought. The young Vulcan who once endured the jibes and taunts of his peers can now look upon those peers and feel pity, for they are not all they are capable of becoming.

Let's consider for a moment how Spock might have arrived at his answers. What other questions did he need to ask? "Who am I?" "What am I capable of becoming?" And probably the most important of all, "What is right for me?" I feel that Spock needed to find the answer to this question above all others. Most of his life, he had been instructed as to what path he should follow; the rigid Vulcan training left very little room for free thought. But now, Spock is able to make that decision for himself, and who would know better than he? If mistakes are made, they will be made by Spock, not as the product of someone else's beliefs, and it is also Spock who will learn from such mistakes and plan his next step accordingly.

Yes, he is slowly determining the answers, but will that make him less interesting to those of us who are still groping for the questions? Hardly! On the contrary, the Vulcan will be even more intriguing because he has now acquired the most revered of human characteristics: unpredictability. In any given situation, one can only guess whether he will react with cool Vulcan logic, "irrational" human emotions, or perhaps a combination of both. Now that would indeed be fascinating!

One thing I believe we will not witness again is the lack of confidence he displayed while in command of the Galileo Seven mission—"I have made the correct and logical decisions, and yet two men have died." Spock is now able to reflect upon that incident and accept the inevitable—no matter what decisions are made or what actions are taken, the results are not always what one would desire. Perhaps this is a lesson Spock could teach his superior officer and friend.

What of Mr. Spock's relationship with the newest member of the *Enterprise* crew, his protégé and "daughter," Lieutenant Saavik? It is evident she does not possess Spock's ability for controlling emotions; however, I received the strong impression that he is not pushing her toward such control, but instead is offering his guidance. Obviously, he does not intend to repeat the mistakes made by his father.

This relationship is quite interesting because it is the first true glimpse we are offered of Spock's matured character—"Lieutenant, have you ever piloted a starship out of space dock before?" He knew darn well she hadn't! (In all honesty, it was not a major assignment, and had she issued an incorrect order, he was right there to countermand it.) The importance of this scene, however, involved a display of several new personality traits of Spock's: an ability to play a joke on someone (in this instance, a very nervous Admiral Kirk); the time-honored custom of a "father" desiring to display the talents of his "offspring"; and the "fatherly" mistake of not taking into consideration the uncomfortable position in which he was placing Saavik.

I could detect very little difference in Spock's attitude toward

McCoy, except perhaps a more congenial approach to their arguments, which, I have a feeling, will someday drive the good doctor into a frenzy. It's difficult to carry on a serious argument with someone who sits there and gently chides you in a most benign manner.

What of Spock's mind meld with McCoy and the whispered "Remember"? I have several theories regarding this, but the answer is probably quite simple—a touch of minds and the thought, "I am your friend, and because of that friendship, you could not have stopped me."

Spock has come a long way from the young Vulcan who was grief-stricken because he could not tell his mother, "I love you," but that maturity has little to do with his ultimate decision in *Wrath of Khan*. Spock has always possessed the capability (indeed, it sometimes seemed an urge) to sacrifice himself for his friends. Whether he justified this particular sacrifice through the use of logic or emotion is irrelevant; one fact is clear: It took guts! I can't help but wonder how many of us, when faced with our own personal *Kobayashi Maru*, would have the courage to arrive at that solution.

"Love" and "friendship" are merely words, but Spock did more than just emit the sounds—he taught us their true meaning.

He has changed in many ways, but Spock is still very much a Vulcan, which is why, as I listened to Kirk's eulogy, there were tears in my eyes and laughter in my throat. I realize Kirk was attempting to give his friend the highest possible compliment—"Of all the souls I have encountered, his was the most . . . human"—and it was a very touching eulogy, but I could not help but envision an indignant Spock turning over in his torpedo. "I hardly believe that insults are within your prerogative as my commanding officer."

Now that I feel I have become "reacquainted" with my favorite Vulcan, I am looking forward to *Star Trek III: The Search for Spock* with even greater impatience. If my understanding of the Genesis Device is accurate, it does not institute the evolutionary process which ultimately results in Man; therefore, when Spock "returns from the dead" he will be alone on the planet. It is going to be quite fascinating to follow his pattern of thought. Will he perhaps feel resentment because the "ultimate sacrifice" was not really "ultimate" after all? Will he be able to accept the solitude and loneliness which will once more become his companion? How Spock answers *these* questions and the manner in which he faces this new turn of events is going to be intriguing, to say the least.

I must admit, I am envious of Spock. He has not found *all* the answers; indeed, he had not even asked all the questions, but he is now on the right path to understanding himself and thereby understanding others. In his continuing quest, Spock has learned that "No man is always"; he must continue to grow and adapt to his constantly changing environment, not to become one of the people around him, but to become compatible with them.

As I watch *Star Trek II: The Wrath of Khan*, I sincerely believe Spock now feels happy—deep down.

THE WRATH OF KHAN—REVIEW AND COMMENTARY

by Walter Irwin

Walter is the first to admit that in his enthusiasm at seeing Star Trek on the big screen, he might have gone a little overboard with his superlatives in a review of Star Trek: The Motion Picture *a few years back. Promising to control himself "this time," Walter sat down immediately after seeing* Wrath of Khan *and typed out the following review. Yes, the superlatives are there, but this time Walter offers no apologies. And we think you'll agree he doesn't need to.*

The most telling moment of *Star Trek II: The Wrath of Khan* occurs during the first encounter with the Khan-commandeered *Reliant*, when Admiral Kirk offhandedly comments to Lieutenant Saavik: "You've got to understand how things work on a starship."

Kirk obviously understands very well how things work on a starship, and even more obviously, he has learned from his mistakes prior to *Star Trek: The Motion Picture* and done his homework.

Producer Harve Bennett and director Nicholas Meyer obviously did their homework as well. *Wrath of Khan* stands ably on its own, providing a tangible link to the series and its theatrical predecessor. (Although *Wrath of Khan* owes little or nothing in the way of character development or continuity to *Star Trek: The Motion Picture*; one could infer that Paramount prefers to pretend that the first film does not exist.)

Wrath of Khan is a wonderful movie . . . and it is also true Star Trek. One can easily see on the screen the sheer pleasure and dedication of everyone involved with the project; an aura of camaraderie and fun that has been missing from Star Trek since the earliest episodes of the first season. Much of this credit can be given to producer Bennett and screenwriter Jack Sowards, whose expressed desire to return Star Trek to its ''roots'' resulted in an exciting, literate, and witty script. But the bulk of the film's success is due to Nicholas Meyer, whose straightforward and unpretentious direction of the material and characters restored Star Trek to its former greatness.

The story is a simple one. Exploring various planets for a site suitable for testing Dr. Carol Marcus's experimental Genesis Device, Captain Terrell and Commander Chekov of the USS *Reliant* mistakenly beam down to Ceti Alpha V. There they are captured by Khan Noonian Singh and his remaining followers and forced to cooperate in the capture of the *Reliant*. Khan then flies off with the dual purpose of taking the Genesis Device and destroying his old nemesis, James T. Kirk.

A straightforward, exciting, and suspenseful premise—just the kind of thing Star Trek, the television series, excelled in. But, as in the series, we get more than just an adventure story. Along the way, we are given insights into the problems and psychological quirks that are always part of us: aging, death, vengeance, and, as always, friendship. The moral lessons and observations are gently and subtly worked into the plot—in many instances, they advance the plot—and never do the characters lapse into preaching or stridency. Remaining true to their original series archetypes, Kirk, Spock, McCoy, et al. render their opinions and beliefs in an honest and caring fashion. As a result, none of the strain which could occasionally be seen in the actors' performances in *Star Trek: The Motion Picture* is visible here; they not only enjoy what they're doing, they believe in it as well.

William Shatner is particularly good. His performance in *Wrath of Khan* is his best work in quite some time. (The only thing he's done lately even approaching it in quality is the controversial ''good old days'' scene in the *T.J. Hooker* pilot.) Although the James T. Kirk we first see in *Wrath of Khan* is an unhappy and confused man, still he is confident and competent, still very much the Jim Kirk we remember and admire from the series. Shatner limns this dichotomy of character very well; we totally believe that Jim Kirk is a man at midlife crisis, but we also immediately know that it is a crisis of circumstance, not confidence.

Once back in the center seat (this time by invitation!), however, it is as if the intervening years have not passed for Jim Kirk—or William Shatner. The familiar poise, the unconscious leaning forward in the seat as if to control the mighty starship by his own will, the sharp-eyed glances around the bridge, missing nothing, and the crisp, confident tone of voice tell us immediately that James T. Kirk is once again captain of the *Enterprise*. Although he makes an early error in judgment, it is Kirk's experience— and his bravado, bluffing, and careful planning—that allows them to escape destruction and bring an end to Khan's machinations.

Leonard Nimoy's Spock is, as always, excellent. It is a tribute to his acting skills that Nimoy is able to breathe new life into a character he has so often publicly expressed a reluctance to portray again. This time, however, he had help from the script—in *Wrath of Khan* Spock is again that appealing mixture of aloofness and warmth that so endeared him to the television audience. Thanks to his encounter with V'Ger, Spock has "loosened up" considerably, now freely able to express friendship and affection for Kirk, even able to permit himself a small joke about his lack of ego. (And didn't we, who have so often seen examples of the stubborn Vulcan pride, get a good laugh out of that one!) One of the most enjoyable things about *Wrath of Khan* is that it once again gives us a Spock that we can *like* . . . and, it is plain to see, a Spock that Leonard Nimoy can like as well.

Throughout the film, Nimoy easily and rather casually offers us a Spock who is very much a man happy with his lot. Nimoy even looks younger, a result perhaps of his having come to grips with the fact that he, regardless of protestations and denials, will always *be* Spock—just as Spock has finally come to grips with *his* dual nature. In both instances, the pleasure of this acceptance shows up onscreen.

We also see a new side of Mr. Spock in *Wrath of Khan*—the patient and caring, almost fatherly, mentor to Lieutenant Saavik. It is obvious that Saavik is Spock's "baby," the young and inexperienced officer who he hopes will someday prove his successor. It is his mission not only to teach her to be a competent and superior Starfleet officer, but to give her the gift of comfortably working and living with humans—something which Spock had to learn on his own. Because of this guidance and advice Spock has given her, Saavik will experience far less of the rejection and pain he suffered; her life will therefore be that much easier, happier, and productive. Such concern may have been logical, to be sure, but we can plainly see the emotion involved as well—Spock *cares* about Saavik very much.

Perhaps it is this involvement with Saavik which has brought Spock to total realization of himself. (We know from Vonda McIntyre's novelization of the film that Spock has been looking after her for some years.) "Fatherhood" may have been the final ingredient in the recipe for this content Spock we see in *Wrath of Khan*. For perhaps the first time since the events on Omnicron Ceti III, Spock is a happy man.

Thus, his death is all the more devastating. When we hear Scotty tell Kirk that the energizer chamber is flooded with radiation and that the warp drive cannot be restored until someone can get in and fix it, we *know* what's going to happen. Spock knows it as well. And if he had not been so busy and so involved in the battle with Khan, Kirk would have known it too. He certainly had no trouble figuring out what happened when he saw Spock's empty chair. . . .

The death scene is masterful. Shots of the newly aborning planet are sharply intercut with shots of Kirk racing along the corridors to engineering; new life intercut with impending death, a victory negated by the death of a loved one. By the time Kirk arrives in engineering, we are as apprehensive as he, and as devastated when he is held back by McCoy and Scotty, and we hear Bones's solemn "He's *already* dead, Jim."

For a moment, we are shocked. *Already dead*? Has Spock died offscreen, cheating us—and Kirk—out of the farewell that would be so difficult to watch and yet impossible not to look at?

No. Spock still lived. Kirk knew that Spock would hang on, would *refuse* to die until he was at his side. We knew it as well. Even in his agony, Spock forced himself to his feet and straightened his uniform. Straightened his uniform! What else could tell us more about Spock? On the verge of death, Spock paid his respects—to his captain and his friend, to his heritage and his dignity, to Starfleet and all it had given him—with this simple gesture. It is a subtly played, heartbreaking moment, one which forces us to be all the more affected when Spock's will finally fails him and he collapses against the Plexiglas wall. It is a shame and very disturbing that many members of the audience do not understand the significance of this gesture and break into sudden laughter.

Both Shatner and Nimoy play the death scene very well. It would have been all too easy to let the moment slip into scene-wrenching histrionics, but both men obviously appreciated the import of what was happening. It is also satisfying that the moment was used to reiterate the previous scene, wherein Spock professed his friendship for Jim, as well as the "logical" premise that "the good of the many outweighs the good of the few—or the one." This is, perhaps, one of the strongest statements of what Star Trek is all about that has ever been made. It is hardly original, hardly new, but all the more powerful because both men so evidently believe it.

The only complaint that can be made about the death scene is that Dr. McCoy was left in the background. It would have been nice to see Spock tell his friends goodbye at the same time; after having shared so much together, they deserved to have that final moment together as well as an affirmation of the Friendship. But fate—and, it could well be, Spock—had other plans. We didn't need to see a closeup of Bones's face to know he was weeping . . . weeping for Spock . . . and for Kirk.

As in many of the television episodes, DeForest Kelley didn't have nearly enough to do in *Wrath of Khan*, but he was a constantly visible and comforting presence throughout the film. (This is especially gratifying when one considers that early reports about the movie had the good doctor playing little more than a cameo role. Obviously, as Bennett and Meyer delved deeper into the Star Trek mythos and history, they realized the importance of Leonard McCoy—and DeForest Kelley—to the integrity of the concept. The movie simply would not have worked without him.)

It is no disparagement of Kelley's talents to say that he could play McCoy in his sleep—the doctor is part and parcel of his own personality, much more so than Kirk is of Shatner's or Spock is of Nimoy's. Unlike the other two, who portray vital and physically active characters, Kelley must use his voice, a wry twist of that marvelously expressive face, or his deep, soulful eyes to delineate his characterization. The laconic doctor is not an easier character to play than Kirk or Spock, just a different sort. And it is a character that DeForest Kelley is very comfortable with.

In *Wrath of Khan*, McCoy, like Spock, is a man happy with his life and station. He has finally accepted that his life is in space, and he has—at long last—left his ghosts behind him. His biggest worry seems to be about Kirk (Spock shares this concern: as we've always known, he and the doctor are more alike than either of them would ever admit), and he speaks his piece on the subject so bluntly that Kirk admonishingly teases him, "Say what's on your mind.'' McCoy is right, of course, and his concern causes him to lapse into repetitive needling—something we've rarely seen him do, even with Spock, for his insight into the human psyche (especially Kirk's) is usually unfailing, and he knows just how far he can go without crossing the line. His failure to see that line in regard to Kirk tells us just how concerned he was.

Fortunately (as in *Star Trek: The Motion Picture*), Kelley has some of the best lines in the script—including a few that *aren't* in the script. Apparently, some of those caustic comments like "*We* will" are pure DeForest Kelley. And it is only right and proper that the one comment that sums up the fans' feelings for Mr. Spock is delivered by the emotional and humanistic Dr. McCoy: "He's not really dead, you know . . . not as long as we remember him.''

Speaking of scripts, the first draft of *Wrath of Khan* prominently featured a young Vulcan *male* named Saavik! Fortunately, somewhere along the line the decision was made to perform a quick sex change, and we are now blessed with the fascinating character of an enticing female Saavik, as excellently performed by newcomer Kirstie Alley. It is amazing that one as young and inexperienced as Ms. Alley can more than hold her own with such veteran scene-stealers as Shatner and Kelley, but Kirstie does just that. Saavik is a rarity in continuing fiction; she emerges as a full-blown characterization—a young woman who is sure of herself and her goals, but (as the young Spock must have been) very confused as to just how she will achieve those goals in a Starfleet rampant with illogical, emotional humans.

But, as we have learned, Saavik is not a full-blooded Vulcan—she is half Romulan. As such, she is not a hybrid *per se*, as is Spock—she would most likely be able to interbreed with either human, Vulcan, or Romulan—but she would still have many problems resulting from her dual heritage. Perhaps even prejudices . . . Romulans are, after all, the ''enemy,'' and it is entirely likely that there are more humans in the mode of Mr. Stiles (''Balance of Terror'') in and about Starfleet who will make life very difficult for Lieutenant Saavik in the future. But they had better be careful, for Saavik is not the type to take much of anything from anyone . . . even an admiral.

Immediately the film begins, we see that Saavik is no cold, emotionless robot; her muttered ''Damn'' when the *Kobayashi Maru* is shown to be carrying passengers is quite eloquent and revealing. But she has studied Vulcan techniques and has a certain amount of control over her emotions. We get a definite feeling that Saavik understands some human emotions more than others—and shares them as well—and it is primarily the more subtle emotions which escape her. She can't fathom teasing; camaraderie (as opposed to loyalty) is something new to her; and she obviously believes in that old wives' tale that Vulcans never bluff. But she is trying and she is learning. And it's no shame, for there are many humans, in our time and in Star Trek's, who will never even make that effort to grasp and enjoy those subtler emotions.

Besides her skillful acting, Kirstie Alley brings a smoldering sensuality to Saavik that is quite intriguing. (Not since Uhura crooned her blues to the accompaniment of Spock's harp has any female in Star Trek been so sexy.) One senses that Saavik would be quite a passionate lover—and on the other hand, she would be a vicious and tenacious fighter. Any male member of Starfleet desirous of checking out the former would be well advised to consider the latter!

Physically, Alley is perfect for the part. Her body movements and expressions are perfect; she has that same seemingly rigid yet curiously supple control of her body that Nimoy has. (It has been reported that Alley pretended to be a Vulcan during her girlhood, and sought to copy Spock's bearing. The Second Generation of Star Trek has truly come into being!) But it is the small things she does that round out the character so well. For instance, after she has grabbed David when the Genesis Device is beamed out by Khan, she releases him with a quick, almost repelled motion. It is as if she cannot bear to touch a human—or as if she cannot bear to touch *anyone*. Many mysteries are yet to be revealed about the enticing and exciting Saavik.

It is comforting to see that Saavik, as the first new continuing character to be added to the cast in many years, fits so well into the Star Trek universe. Like our other old friends on the bridge, we know that Saavik will never bore us. We will always be learning something new about her, and in the grand Star Trek tradition, in the process we will learn something about ourselves as well. Kirstie Alley's Saavik is a welcome and enriching addition to the cast.

Merritt Butrick, on the other hand, still remains a bit of a cipher to us. Although Butrick has a "dream role"—James T. Kirk's only son—we actually learn very little about David Marcus during the course of the film. Confined to mouthing dire warnings against "the military" for the most part, Butrick has scant opportunity to display his acting talents. Even in the finely written "reunion" scene, Merritt seems rather stiff and uninvolved, but we cannot lay total blame at his feet. For an actor to give a convincing performance, he must be able to get into the skin of his character, and Merritt Butrick was seemingly as perplexed by David Marcus as were we. Butrick may be a fine actor (surely he would not have been cast in a film such as *Wrath of Khan* if he did not impress the producers with talent and presence), but we had little opportunity to see indications of it in *Wrath of Khan*. We would like to know much more about David Marcus; we would like to see more of Merritt Butrick. But will we?

The role of David Marcus was a patent attempt to introduce a new character and give him immediate identification and acceptance with the audience—after all, how could any true-blue Star Trek fan *not* like Captain Kirk's son? But just dropping him in on us (and worse, dropping him in on Kirk!) was unfair; it was especially unfair to do so and then not provide us with sufficient background on his character or sufficient screen time to get to know him. We care about David Marcus because he's Kirk's son, but we've yet to see any good reason why we should care about him as an individual. It is possible that David will return in the next film (although the lukewarm reception to his character and Butrick's "Luke Spencerish" good looks makes it questionable at best), and if he does, the producers owe it to us to provide him with a larger, more interesting and involving, and more revealing part. Butrick is a likable fellow, but as one fan said recently, "Nobody's in love with him yet."

Because of the lack of involvement we felt with David Marcus, it is indeed fortunate that the planned romantic interest between him and Saavik was dropped during editing. It would not have worked in any case—Saavik was quickly, but firmly, established as being totally career-oriented, independent, and a bit of a shy recluse. She is also trying very hard to be a Vulcan and a Starfleet officer. None of this is conducive to romance; even less so when we realize that the David Marcus we saw in the movie didn't so much as cast a lingering look in Saavik's direction. Such a relationship is possible, of course, but not for a very, very long time. And it would have to have more of a basis than the desire of Paramount's publicity department to spew out stories luridly describing the "love affair" between Kirk's son and Spock's "daughter." That kind of nonsense we can very well do without!

Bibi Besch turned in a fine performance as the brilliant, but earthy, Carol Marcus. Now this is a character we would feel comfortable with; she would fit right into the *Enterprise* gang. If you ask where, then think again how natural she looked standing at Dr. McCoy's side during the film's final scenes. It wouldn't be such a bad idea to have a new doctor come aboard to fill Christine Chapel's shoes and give Bones a hand . . . and it would be nice to see Jim Kirk have a wife. At least it would rescue him from the position of being the Starship Stud.

It is strange that Carol Marcus was immediately acceptable to us whereas David Marcus was not. True, Ms. Besch is an accomplished actress, but her role was not that much more challenging or lengthy than Butrick's. Perhaps we fans can more easily believe that Jim Kirk would have an affair with this lovely, brilliant, and strong-willed woman than we can believe that he would go for many years without even hearing that she had a son—his son. True, Jim Kirk is notorious for loving-and-leaving, but in his position as chief of Starfleet Operations, he would, at one time or another, at least have come across Carol's name, and the fact that she and her son were involved in Starfleet research, however secret it may have been. But then, maybe Kirk was too concerned with the consequences of "opening old wounds." As with his total disregard of events on the *Enterprise* in the years preceding *Star Trek: The Motion Picture*, he may have closed his mind totally to any news of the one "true love" of his life. If Carol Marcus was truly that woman, Bibi Besch makes us believe it. Her Carol is one strong lady, able to stand toe to toe with James T. Kirk, give as good as she gets, and yet still remain completely feminine and appealing. Hers is one of the most complete female characters we have seen in Star Trek, and that simple fact may be why she is so readily acceptable to us.

New faces drop in during the course of *Wrath of Khan*, but so do old ones. Did you happen to notice our old friend Winston Kyle serving aboard the *Reliant*? It was certainly a pleasure to see John Winston again (even if only in profile), and he looked fit and well. (Which should certainly make reports of his death, like Mark Twain's, greatly exaggerated.) Let's hope now-Commander Kyle will be transferred back to the *Enterprise* by the time of the next movie, and we will once again see him at the transporter post where he served so well for so many years.

Other old faces include the crew. Unfortunately, Nichelle Nichols and George Takei as Uhura and Sulu had little to do. Competent professionals that they are, however, they manage to instill their small parts with the same charm and likability they had in the original series, and we are pleased to see them again. It is a shame, however, that the editing of the film cut the small scene wherein we learn that Sulu has been given a captaincy of his own.

Walter Koenig's Chekov fared much better. As the hapless first officer of the *Reliant*, Koenig got a chance to stretch his acting muscles a bit. He was especially effective in the scenes where he realizes the cargo containers they discover are part of the *Botany Bay*, and his reluctance to kill Kirk at Khan's command is also very well done. It was nice to see that Chekov has advanced and matured well beyond the callow navigator stage, and his reassignment to another ship was a believable and natural outgrowth of series "reality."

James Doohan turned in his usual competent performance as Scotty, but his part seemed strangely truncated. Also, no mention was made in the film of the fact that young Cadet Peter Preston was Scotty's nephew, as was stated in the script and early publicity. This omission effectively destroyed much of the pathos designed to be felt when Peter died. (Because of this, Ike Eisenmann's role of Peter was cut as well, leaving him little more to do than smile chipmunkishly and lie around covered with gore.) This little bit of insight into Scotty's family and background would have made us care a little more about the chief engineer, and it is a shame that it was excised. (We did, however, get to hear the "in joke" about Doohan's heart attack. Small favors.)

Rounding out the characterizations were Paul Winfield as Captain Terrell, and Judson Scott as Khan's henchman Joachim.

Winfield, a very fine actor with a great diversity of past roles, managed to give us a Clark Terrell who was almost completely realized in only a very few scenes. Terrell is one of the career officers, the backbone of Starfleet, and commanding the *Reliant* is probably as far as he will ever rise in the ranks. And he knows this. The mission to discover the suitable site for the Genesis Experiment is typical of the type of missions Terrell is given; we can see his resignation in the slump of his shoulders and the bored expression on his face. But Terrell has not allowed his ship to slacken; the bridge of the *Reliant* is clean and efficient, he and his men are competent at their posts, and Terrell still has that spark of independence that makes for a good starship commander. And his loyalty is without question—he kills himself rather than destroy an admiral, a man he has never even met!

Winfield acted Clark Terrell with such skill and depth that one can only feel that he is a Star Trek fan himself. So it is all the more of a shame that his character did not survive the film, for he would have made a fine addition to the continuing cast . . . perhaps as that security chief/weapons officer who has always been so sorely needed to round out the bridge crew.

By the evidence, we can guess that Judson Scott is *not* a Star Trek fan. It was reported that he was unsatisfied with what remained of his role after the final cut, and asked that his name be removed from the credits. If this was the case, it was an unfortunate mistake, for not only has *Star Trek: The Wrath of Khan* made quite a bit of money worldwide (it never hurts an actor to be associated with a blockbuster movie), but his performance is very effective. As the rational Joachim, Scott more than holds his own against the flashy histrionics of Ricardo Montalban's Khan. Scott deserves to go on to bigger and better parts, but by disassociating himself from *Wrath of Khan*, he has made it more difficult for himself to do so. A shame.

And so to Khan. Khan Noonian Singh. Although he appeared in only one episode of the original series, he has lived fondly in our memories for these many years. It was a masterstroke on the part of the producers to bring him back as the villain in this film; not only is he an intriguing character, but he is perhaps the best example of the "anti-Kirk." Like our captain, Khan is powerful, intelligent, charming, and single-minded to the point of obsession, but unlike Kirk, Khan bends his powers toward personal gain and aggrandizement. Khan feels that the good of the one is more important than the good of the many. In his rage and grief, he becomes like unto the Satan of "Paradise Lost"; a man in battle with the forces of good, a man obsessed with destroying the individual he sees as the one thing blocking him from fulfilling his destiny. "He tasks me . . . he tasks me, and I shall have him!"

It is apparent that Ricardo Montalban, after so many years of smiling his way through episodes of *Fantasy Island* and shilling Cordobas, had the time of his life playing Khan again. In a performance that is overblown, but still splendidly controlled and built, Montalban rivets our attention each time he appears onscreen. So intense is Montalban's Khan that the viewer cannot help but become involved in his overwhelming hatred for Kirk and his lust for vengeance. Each of us felt a mixture of repulsion and admiration for Khan in "Space Seed"; he was so attractive and charming, so powerful and noble. But in *Wrath of Khan*, the charm is gone, the nobility besmirched. Khan is no longer attractive in the least, on the contrary, he has become a nightmarish figure of terror and death. Following the classical pattern, the once-noble figure has been twisted by forces beyond his control, warped by his own inner weaknesses. Montalban understood this, and he provides us with a Khan radically different from the one in "Space Seed." It is a brilliant example of the maturation —or, more accurately, the disintegration—of a character.

But, repugnant as he is, Khan is just plain old fun to watch. Montalban understood this as well—he provides us with an old-time villain, the kind we can gleefully boo and hiss; the kind of villain who chews the scenery unmercifully while mouthing poetry and thinly veiled threats. It has been many years since such an enjoyable nemesis appeared to be a thorn in Kirk's side, and the fact that we know and once appreciated the "superior mind" that has become so twisted by hatred makes him all the more interesting and exciting to watch. Montalban reportedly obtained a tape of "Space Seed" and watched it several times to reimmerse himself in the role of Khan, and his efforts were more than worth it.

Apparently someone at Paramount decided to bring *Star Trek II: The Wrath of Khan* into theaters at a running time of exactly one hour and forty-five minutes, come hell or high water. In several instances (such as those mentioned above) the film was harmed by this decision. It is never quite clear when David Marcus learns that Kirk is his father; it is also not clear exactly when Khan attacks Regulus I. It is always an advantage for a film to move quickly, but a few more minutes spent on characterization and exposition would have made *Wrath of Khan* a better movie.

Too, there are several discrepancies in the film. We wonder how Terrell and Chekov, trained and experienced spacegoers, can make the almost unbelievable mistake of landing on the wrong planet; even if that planet had shifted *exactly* into the orbit of Alpha Ceti VI, they should have noticed the absence of a planet in the system. This is sloppy scripting—coincidence and contrivance of the worst kind—and to make matters worse, there was not even the most flimsy or glib explanation given for the error.

The special effects in *Wrath of Khan* have been disparaged in some quarters, but this reviewer found them to be more than adequate, and in many instances very effective and realistic. Also helping the film were the varied types of special effects used. The computer animation of the Genesis Tape was particularly nice; it looked like something we would really see on a starship. Other effects, such as the creation of the Genesis Planet and the Mutara Nebula, combined animation, models, and "cloud tank" mattes to form more than adequate backgrounds.

The *Reliant* was lovely to see. Combining the best of the *Enterprise*'s classic features into an entirely new configuration, it was sleek and compact, a perfect example of the various kinds of starships the Federation would utilize. It was totally familiar, but strange at the same time, with its bright rear lighting, its unorthodox placement of engineering and phasers; it was a canny combination of the known and the unknown, serving perfectly as a vessel to convey the unpredictable Khan.

Effects reprised from the series and the first movie were phasers, photon torpedos, and the transporter. Yet, each of these effects was slightly different, again giving us a feeling of time having passed, of advances and changes being made. The new transporter effect, which allowed the characters to move and speak while in the midst of beaming, is a little hard to get used to, but it allows for more freedom of action and gets rid of the distracting "freezing" of the characters that often marred the series. The gradual disintegration of Terrell when he used his phaser on himself was far more frightening than the flare effect used in the series; and the effect of the large ship's phasers slicing into the hulls of the ships was also exciting and realistic-looking. (The destruction of the *Reliant*'s nacelle and the resulting shower of debris, electric arcs, and static charges was much more effective than the cheap "sparklers" or blaze of animation utilized in the original episodes.) The photon torpedos still look a bit "cartoony," but it was a nice touch to see that one of them could miss its target and fly on by to expend its energy elsewhere.

The engine room, a standing set from the first film, was made more interesting by the addition of several more control consoles and the deadly radiation chamber. The effect of the radiation from the warp-drive bypass upon Spock was also quite good; it was accomplished by the use of simple lighting and a wind machine.

New to *Wrath of Khan* was the torpedo room, a redress of the docking port from *Star Trek: The Motion Picture*. The tracking shot along the torpedo launching track as the crewmen lifted away the protective grids and the sleek, deadly torpedo was lowered into place was one of the most exciting of the film. It gave an immediacy to the proceedings that no amount of shots of fingers pressing buttons or flashing lights could have.

The *Enterprise*, the drydock, and the redressed and inverted space station were all miniatures from *Star Trek: The Motion Picture*, but each was used to good effect in this film. Several shots of the *Enterprise* in Earth orbit and in drydock were stock footage, but this too was used effectively and sparingly. The "warp effect" was changed somewhat; the "boom" when the ship entered warp space was eliminated, and we saw no shots of the ship leaving warp space; but the addition of the effect to give an impression of constant acceleration when the ship was escaping the Mutara Nebula was most welcome, and served to heighten relief at the narrow escape. Also reinstalled in *Wrath of Khan* was the dull roar the mighty warp engines make as the ship moves through space. Used only in the earliest episodes, the noise was forgotten very quickly; the official explanation was that there is no noise in space, but in actuality, the dubbing in of the roar was an additional expense of time and money, one of the many small touches dropped as the series progressed and the expected high ratings failed to appear, causing the network and Desilu to spend less money on each episode. Having that roar in the background as the *Enterprise* makes a flyby enhances the "reality" of the scene and increases our enjoyment.

The battle of the two starships was exciting and superbly choreographed. The only complaint that can be made about these scenes is that they sometimes looked a bit too two-dimensional, but every effort was made to avoid (or at least disguise) this, including front-projected lighting effects within the nebula and the use of a constant perspective. It was not a problem at all when the ships were seen in orbit or passing through space; such shots were also enhanced by the new, "deeper" starfields.

The only disappointing effects shot in the film were those inside the Genesis Cave. It is difficult to understand why these failed; they are simple matte shots, the kind used with great success for many years. Perhaps too much was attempted in too little time; no one part of the cave (with the exception of the rocky cave entrance where Kirk and party camped) was clearly visible, and the long shots were murky, giving little indication of the vastness we were told about. A potentially fine effect, the one cavern wall covered with cascading waterfalls, was almost completely lost because of lack of color definition and contrast. It is probably not the fault of the effects people—they did a fine job on the rest of the film. But the Genesis Cave was so important to the plot, a tangible demonstration of the power of the Genesis Device, that more time should have been spent showing it to us.

Mention the new uniforms to a Star Trek fan and you are likely to find yourself in an argument. Oh, not about whether or not they look good, but what they may symbolize to that fan. The uniforms are soundly condemned by many as being "too militaristic." Well, Starfleet, like it or not, *is* the military. However benign and altruistic its mission, Starfleet is a peace-keeping and exploratory force with military chain of command and traditions. To complain that the uniforms worn by members of this force are "militaristic" is silly—it's like complaining that William Shatner's uniform in *T.J. Hooker* makes him look too much like a cop. Those who complain that the uniforms are not within the spirit and intent of the original series are wrong. As Carol Marcus said, "Starfleet's kept the peace for a hundred years." It is ridiculous to assume that any organization could operate so effectively if it denied its military backgrounds and mission. For Starfleet or any member of it to pretend that it is not a military organization—or for us to pretend that it is not—would be totally untrue and a great disservice to the enduring concept so carefully and lovingly crafted by Gene Roddenberry and Gene L. Coon so many years ago. And what does it matter anyway? We like Kirk, Spock, McCoy, and the rest regardless of what they're wearing—we like them for what they *are*, not for what they look like. Contrary to legend (and contrary to what many fans seem to think), clothes do *not* make the man.

Whatever connotations you choose to place on the cut of the cloth, it cannot be denied that the new uniforms are very effective. The primary rust-brown color does not clash with the starship interiors (and certainly does not blend into the background like the uniforms worn in *Star Trek: The Motion Picture*). Too, the design is flattering to almost every figure. A bit of variety is seen in the cut of various uniforms: the nifty landing-party jackets, the "pullovers" worn by the cadets and supporting personnel, and the revamped and more colorful engineering and security armor. Made from natural materials and having just enough differentiation in design and accouterments, the uniforms work splendidly as something we can definitely "believe" in.

Other clothing worn in the film worked quite well, although we got to see all too little of it. Kirk's and McCoy's suits looked comfortable and expensive, just the kind of thing two mature and unself-conscious senior officers would wear when off duty.

Saavik's loungewear was a nice touch: the functional but feminine cut perfectly reflects her personality. And it was nice to see that Spock still owns and wears his traditional Vulcan robes. These were the same ones that appeared in the first movie, but he certainly looked more comfortable in them this time! Perhaps in the next film we'll get a look at the off-duty wear of some of the supporting characters. What do you want to bet that Sulu's favorite clothing is more than a little reminiscent of an eighteenth-century swashbuckler?

Take them as you will—the uniforms, the off-duty clothing, the weaponry, the sets—*everything* in *Wrath of Khan* has a purpose. Nicholas Meyer was speaking of the plot when he said that "this film is of a piece," but everyting in *Wrath of Khan* is carefully constructed to return Star Trek to its origins; to recapture the spirit of the glory days of the first seasons, but yet with a new freshness and vitality. It worked, but it was mostly the characterizations that made it work. Each and every person in *Wrath of Khan*—yes, even including Khan himself—had a mission, a purpose, a sense of worth. We saw, for the first time in many years, men and women doing something because they believed in it, because it was *right*.

As always, the success or failure of a Star Trek tale rests on Kirk and Spock. It is inescapable; they are the movers and shakers and how they act and react determines the course of the story. Fortunately, Spock and Kirk were both quite different men in *Wrath of Khan* than they were in the first movie. They were both forceful and capable, Spock in particular. A few years ago, it would have been inconceivable to have Spock commanding a training cruise—almost as inconceivable as it would have been to have Jim Kirk admit, confront, and accept the fact of his own mortality. The solid, reassuring presence of both men added immeasurably to the film. Not for many years have we seen Spock, Kirk, and McCoy so sure of themselves, so at home on the bridge and with each other. This is why the movie succeeds—this is why fans are proclaiming it as "true Star Trek." Everything we love and admire about the series was included and enhanced in *Wrath of Khan*; everything we cherish about the characters was expanded and reaffirmed. Harve Bennett, Nicholas Meyer, and the cast and crew achieved something beyond their wildest plans and imaginings—and, to be honest, beyond ours as well: *Star Trek II: The Wrath of Khan* is an excellent movie, and more important, it is excellent Star Trek. It is an honor to Gene Roddenberry that the series he created has finally become such a rich and alive entity that it can go on without him; it can reach new heights and achieve new growth without his personal guidance. Star Trek has achieved a life of its own, and we *know* that no one is more pleased than Gene Roddenberry!

But what of the future, now that Star Trek has reached this landmark? What next? And the question that everyone wants answered: What is going to happen to Spock? He will return, that much is certain. It was practically flashed on the screen in the mode of the James Bond films—"This is the end of *The Wrath of Khan*, but Spock will return in . . ." And Kirk's musings, the long, lingering, loving scenes of new life on the Genesis Planet, and McCoy's unintentionally prophetic statements practically chart out the course of the next movie. (Which will, according to Paramount, be somewhat unsubtly titled *In Search of Spock*.)

All of the elements for a logical revival of Spock were carefully planted *throughout* the movie; we can only hope that they will be brought into play and were not just red herrings. Such continuity would be pleasing, for we have been told that an entire series of Star Trek movies is planned, each one to lead logically and chronologically into the next. It is only by establishing such continuity and credibility that Paramount can ever hope to bring in the "new generation" of Star Trek characters and events. If this is done with care and sensitivity, if it is done within the spirit and framework of the original concept, and if it is done with consideration and appreciation for those whose efforts have made Star Trek such an enduring success, then, and only then, will we fans accept changes and departures and not be angry at the "loss" of our beloved series regulars. Instead, we will have the pleasure of watching them move on to other things, other careers, and look back on their tenure on Star Trek fondly, without any rancor or bitterness to spoil our memories.

Thank you, Harve Bennett, Nicholas Meyer, and the production crew, for a great movie! Thank you, Gene Roddenberry, for getting it all started! Goodbye, Spock—for a little while. Welcome, Saavik—stay awhile. And to Kirk, McCoy, Scotty, Sulu, Uhura, Chekov, and Kyle—good to have you back home, guys!

"HE'S DEAD, JIM": ON SPOCK'S DEMISE

by Mark Alfred

Why did Spock have to die? What were the events leading up to this momentous decision by the producer, writers, and director of Wrath of Khan? *The entire story may never be known, but in this article Mark Alfred examines some of the public statements and events that may shed some light on the truth.*

Even before production began on *Star Trek II: The Undiscovered Country* (the original title of *Wrath of Khan*), the rumors began: Spock was going to be killed off because Leonard Nimoy was tired of playing the Vulcan.

Ever since 1975 and the publication of Nimoy's book, *I Am Not Spock,* it had become apparent to fans that a strange, dichotomous love/hate relationship existed in Nimoy's mind between himself and the character of Spock. On page 150 of the Ballantine edition of *I Am Not Spock*, Nimoy states, "This is a character built on Star Trek. . . . I can feel the influences all around me." In the opinion of some fans of Nimoy and Star Trek, it seemed that on the one hand the actor was glad about the wealth and prosperity brought him by Spock, but on the other hand he was becoming jealous, even resentful, of Spock. Might he not take the final step of one day seeing to it that he be freed of Spock forever? Might he request of screenwriters that in any revival of Star Trek, Spock be allowed to die in a particularly dramatic episode?

In 1976, a theatrical film was first projected, and the entire crew of the *Enterprise* including Nimoy as Spock, was to be included. A year later, in the summer of 1977, Paramount laid plans for a fourth commercial television network, and plans for the Star Trek feature film were scrapped in favor of all-new episodes to be the cornerstone of the proposed network. During preproduction, however, Gene Roddenberry ran into a very big problem—Leonard Nimoy would not be returning. He had other commitments which made it difficult, if not impossible, for him to participate in the series; he also expressed a desire for his "own, Spockless" career. So a new character, a twenty-two-year-old Vulcan named Xon, was proposed to man the science station, and an actor was selected for the role. (He was David Gautreaux, who was later to play Commander Branch on the doomed Epsilon Nine station in *Star Trek: The Motion Picture*.)

Plans for the network, and the Star Trek series, fell through, and the next stage came on November 11, 1977, when it was announced that Star Trek would become a theatrical motion picture, and all members of the bridge crew, including Leonard Nimoy as Spock, would return. This project, unlike the others before it, became an actuality, and as we all know, the character of Mr. Spock survived *Star Trek: The Motion Picture*, despite many rumors to the contrary.

The success of *STTMP* spawned yet another sequel, and as filming began on *Star Trek II*, the closed set caused the rumor mill again to grind out new speculations. As the secrecy around the movie intensified, hysteria and apprehension grew among fandom. Some said that Nicholas Meyer, the film's director, would go so far as to film two endings—one in which Spock died, and one in which he lived to trek another day. Fans began writing to Paramount and to various professional and fan magazines, one fan even going so far as to suggest that Mr. Spock, should Nimoy tire of the role, be allowed to "evolve" to a higher plane of existence, or leave his consciousness behind, "melded" with that of another Vulcan. In April 1982, *Starlog* magazine reported Nimoy as having told *Variety*, "I'm looking forward to talking about doing *Star Trek III*. That should answer the questions about the survival of Mr. Spock. Besides, nobody dies in science fiction—look at Alec Guinness." Still, *Moviegoer* magazine ran a photo from the upcoming film and supplied the caption: "Star Trek II: Death of a Vulcan?"

On Saturday, May 8, 1982, in Overland Park, Kansas, a few fortunate souls attended a sneak preview of *Star Trek II: The*

Wrath of Khan. (Reports claim George Lucas had asked for a title change, complaining that the planned *Vengeance of Khan* sounded too much like *Revenge of the Jedi*.) An Associated Press story dated May 10 stated that the attendees "left Saturday night debating whether the half-Vulcan hero Mr. Spock had died—or it just seemed that way." Later in the same article, Paramount executive Gordon Weaver said, "Spock actually dies, but there's enough in there to lead one to believe he'll be back." Weaver also said that audience reaction to the sneak would determine whether or not the ending would be "altered."

Such vacillating comments did not please director Nicholas Meyer. A week later, in a *Los Angeles Times* story headlined "Star Trek II Director Says Mr. Spock Dies; Studio Waffles," Meyer made it plain that there was, and always had been, only one ending to *Wrath of Khan*, and that ending included the demise of Spock. "I did not shoot multiple endings of this film," Meyer said. "No other ending was written, no other ending was shot, and no other ending was contemplated. It would have been impossible, because this movie was all of a piece." Meyer further stated that the studio's attempt to boost publicity by suggesting multiple endings was "a disservice to the convictions and the integrity of the people who made the movie. It makes me seem either disinterested or callous."

Vonda N. McIntyre's well-wrought novelization of the film, released by Pocket Books on June 2, made it certain. On page 208, the good Dr. McCoy utters those most infamous words: "He's dead, Jim."

So, it's finally true. Spock is dead. Not the victim of brain-napping females, or in a Vulcan healing trance, nor lost inside a cosmic amoeba, nor abandoned on a desert planet in a burned-out shuttlecraft, nor sharing consciousness with Christine Chapel, nor even in hiding contemplating his Vulcan navel on the high plateau of Gol on Vulcan. Spock is dead.

But what of Nimoy's talk of doing *Star Trek III*? What about his statement that "nobody dies in science fiction"? And what about Weaver of Paramount, who told us that "Spock actually dies, but there's enough in there to lead one to believe he'll be back"?

What are we to say to these things? What are we to think? Spock is dead—long live Spock?

Despite Nimoy's oblique reference to Obi-Wan Kenobi, let us rule out any such role for Spock in *Star Trek III*. If Spock is to appear in the next movie, it should be as flesh and blood, not as a wraith. It would also be unacceptable for Paramount to "cheat" and have subsequent Star Trek movies take place prior to the action of *Wrath of Khan*. At the moment, most fans feel that Spock will somehow be rejuvenated as a by-product of the Genesis Effect—the powers of creation bringing him back to life before the laws of entropy could exert themselves, before the Genesis Wave subsides. This would tie into Kirk's statement that he "must" return to the friend he left behind.

But what about the soul? If there is no living consciousness, no soul remaining, then the Genesis Effect would have produced only a healthy, mindless Vulcan shell.

Recall, however, the events of "Return to Tomorrow": When Hanoch decides to keep Spock's body, he destroys the receptacle containing Spock's consciousness, forcing Kirk to admit, "We must now kill his body." But after Hanoch has been tricked out of Spock's body, it was revealed that Spock's consciousness had been transferred to the body of Christine Chapel, where it had lain dormant until his body was again available.

Remember how, when each millisecond was necessary to save the ship and the captain he loved, Spock took the time to place his hand on McCoy's head in the "mind meld" position and say a single word: "Remember"?

Could the essence of Spock, his soul, be residing within Leonard McCoy just as it once did within Christine Chapel? And could that essence be restored to a Vulcan body made healthy and whole by the Genesis Effect?

What do you think? Is this what will happen in the first half hour of *Star Trek III*? We will have to wait and see if Nimoy and Paramount can agree that Mr. Spock will after all return.

But, like so many others, I must admit that as the camera panned across the Genesis Planet at the end of *Wrath of Khan*, I half expected to see the casket open—and footprints leading away from it. . . .

NOT A EULOGY FOR SPOCK

by Matt G. Leger

We received a number of articles dealing with Spock's death. Because of space limitations, we could only print a few of them. Our criteria were simple: the most honest and feeling articles would get priority. Matt's is one of these; longer and more involved articles could not match it for depth.

In the latest chapter of our beloved myth of screens both large and small, *Star Trek II: The Wrath of Khan*, Mr. Spock—first officer of the USS *Enterprise*, friend and ally of Admiral James T. Kirk and Dr. Leonard McCoy, legend of the Starfleet, and hero to two decades of Star Trek fans—dies.

He perishes as we all knew he one day would, sacrificing his life to save those of his shipmates. As in episode after episode of the original series, and even in *Star Trek: The Motion Picture*, he plunges in where others dare not, with typical Spockian daring and bravery, and that touch of Vulcan egotism that convinces him that he and only he can survive the danger and save the day. ("As you are so fond of observing, doctor, I am not human.")

And now, all over Trek fandom, people are hanging their heads and shedding tears and perhaps are even in states of total disassociation. Fannish pens are no doubt scribing elegies, eulogies, paeans, and laments to express a sense of bereavement. This is understandable and expected; fans of all ages, colors, and creeds have taken the character into their hearts.

Even I—I, who have always prided myself on thinking realistically, on never losing touch with reality, on being in control—felt my heart leap as I watched Spock's poignant, heroic effort to drag his radiation-ravaged body the final few steps to say goodbye to Kirk. As Spock raised his hand to the captain's for a final touching of minds with his *t'hy'la*, I wanted to scream, "No, by all that's wonderful in this universe, he can't die!"

But Spock was only a celluloid creature dying a celluloid death; a fabrication of the labor of scriptwriters, the talents of an actor, the artistry of makeup men, and the skill of costumers. For this fictional character, I felt grief and rage and sorrow.

Yet, how strange is that? Is it stranger than comic-book readers protesting the death of Jean "Phoenix" Grey in *X-Men*? Stranger than people betting their homes and savings on who pulled the trigger on J.R. Ewing in *Dallas*? Stranger than women by the thousands falling in love with Luke Spencer of *General Hospital*?

Quite often in the history of entertainment, the cleverness and creativity of a storyteller has so captivated us as to make us believe that fantasy is reality, and that imaginary people are as alive as we. That we should be moved by the death of an imaginary alien on a fictional spaceship does not display immaturity or shallowness of character on our part, but rather the superior craftsmanship of the characters and story.

It is certainly acceptable and even healthy for those of us who have come to love Spock and what he stands for to spend a period in mourning and contemplation. As the Vulcan himself said on a similar occasion, "Each of you must evaluate the loss in the privacy of your own thoughts." But to do so for too long or too intensely is to miss the entire point of the ending of *Wrath of Khan*.

Death in any event is regrettable; death without meaning or purpose is wasteful and even more tragic. If, however, someone dies for a purpose, as a result of trying to achieve a worthwhile goal, then those who are emotionally shattered by his death can more easily accept the loss. Spock died for such a purpose, a purpose much larger than only the deliverance of the *Enterprise* and her crew.

Spock's death must have had a profound effect on all those who witnessed it. The young command cadet Lieutenant Saavik saw the ultimate expression of a Starfleet officer's devotion to duty and the Starfleet ideals of self-sacrifice and preservation of life; the example will probably influence her entire future career in Starfleet. Engineer Scott and Dr. McCoy were shown the full measure of their Vulcan friend's feeling for them; he would rather attempt a million-to-one shot than allow either of them to commit suicide. (And if Bones is half the man we know him to be, he is thoroughly ashamed of his earlier "inhuman" swipe at Spock.) But the person by far most moved and altered by the tragedy—and the one through whom we watching the film are sent a message—is none other than Admiral Kirk.

Throughout the film, in Kirk's own words and those of others around him, we are shown that James T. Kirk believes himself to be charmed, that he is confident of always thwarting fate, that he refuses to acknowledge the eventuality of "no-win scenarios." This facet of Kirk's psychological makeup is brought home most vividly in the exchange between Kirk and David Marcus in the hours after Spock's death:

David: "Saavik was right. . . . You've never faced death."

Kirk: "Not like this. I've cheated death, tricked my way out of death—and patted myself on the back for my ingenuity. I know nothing."

Spock's sacrifice forces Kirk to finally sit down and confront what he has resolutely avoided dealing with for most of his life. True, he has dealt with the deaths of crewmen and friends in the past, but up to now he has never faced up to the terrible reality that at some time in his life, death must touch him even where he dreads it most fiercely, in his most vulnerable spots—lovers, children, and first officers. And, in the end, we realize that Jim Kirk is stronger as a person and a commander because of it.

At another point in the film, we are told that Kirk is starting to feel the weight of the years on his shoulders, that the malaise of midlife is creeping up on him (a malaise aggravated by Bones's unfortunate timing in presenting him with a pair of antique spectacles for his failing vision). The catharsis of Spock's death and the events surrounding it—the creation of a new planet in the wake of the explosive overload-detonation of the Genesis Device— serve to bring Kirk to the realization that every day, every second, the universe is made new in some way; that even in the ashes of destruction, things can live and grow and thrive. So the death of his friend gives Kirk the ability to feel young again; in Carol Marcus' words, "As young as when the world was new."

And here is the message for us, the audience, especially those of us who are fans: Spock has said that change is the essential process of all things. Should that not hold true for what we have known for the last fifteen years as Star Trek? If all things must change, is it so unreasonable to expect that Star Trek must change as well?

The sad fact is that the ever-advancing ages of the original cast, the changing attitudes of audiences, and the demands of believable storytelling must eventually conspire to end the vision in many fans' minds of the "old crew" somehow defying time and probability to roam the stars forever. Spock's death should provide a catharsis for us fans as well; it should be the first step to our realizing and accepting that the time must all too soon come when, if the legend is to live on, the play must have new players. As Admiral Kirk said, "Galloping around the cosmos is a game for the young."

Too, the "new crew" need not completely supersede the old. Joyce Tullock has likened the "Friendship" of Spock, McCoy, and Kirk to components of a human being—logic, emotion, and ego, respectively. The loss of Spock creates a gap in the Friendship that, in one sense at least, can never be truly filled by another; but we have seen at least once before ("The Tholian Web") that the triad cannot be made any weaker by the death of one member, and can even be made stronger in some ways by it. McCoy and Kirk will indeed carry on quite splendidly without Spock, for his logic and wisdom will always be with them, maintaining the "balance" Ms. Tullock speaks of as firmly as though he were still physically present.

In time, the personification of logic can be presented anew by Lieutenant Saavik (with her half-Vulcan heritage to quash any rumors of romance), or by David Marcus (he is a scientist, remember, and his feelings about the military may just have been changed radically by his experiences), or even by some totally new character yet to spring from the replenished Star Trek well of creativity. Such a new personage might well merge with the other two to form a new and more vital entity, having in its being both the fire and compassion of the old and the strength of the new—remember V'Ger?

This, then, is not a eulogy for Spock, but a song of celebration. A song of the new beginning, full of the hope and promise that made Star Trek live for us all, and that is embodied in the words with which the first film ended: "The Human Adventure Is Just Beginning."

And to those who would still immerse themselves in grief and despair for Spock, I commend to you Dr. McCoy's words at the end of *Wrath of Khan*, as he, Kirk, and Carol Marcus look upon the newborn world that is the Vulcan's final resting place: "He's really not dead, you know, so long as we remember him." As I heard DeForest Kelley speak that line, I could have sworn that I saw the blue eyes in that famous craggy face look straight out at the audience.

Or maybe I was just imagining it. . . .

A STAR TREK CHRONOLOGY

by Jeffrey W. Mason

As well documented as the Star Trek universe is, many discrepancies still abound. Among the most vexing of these is an incomplete and maddeningly inconsistent chronological history of the Federation and Starfleet. In this article, Jeff takes on the thankless task of trying to correlate the "past" events mentioned in the series, stories, and other sources in a manner both consistent and logical. As a small appendum to the article, Jeff has included a number of short personal chronologies of people important in the Star Trek chronology.

From "One small step for man . . ." to "Where no man has gone before . . ." represents a span of time that all Star Trek fans have wondered about from time to time. The questions raised in this article are: How and when could the universe of Star Trek have come about? In what years could the voyages of the Starship *Enterprise* occur? How do the characters of Star Trek fit into this chronology?

Scientifically speaking, the odds against a future exactly like that of Star Trek's universe are immense. Nevertheless, it is fun to speculate, and unless some great cataclysm descends upon mankind, it is likely we will reach out for the stars sometime within the next thousand years, if not sooner.

In attempting to set up a chronology for a Star Trek future, one must start at the point of origin. Gene Roddenberry is the "father" of Star Trek; it is he who created the concept in the early 1960s. In Roddenberry's original "series format," no definitive time frame was established for the series. It was merely noted: "The time could be 1995 or even 2995, close enough to our times for our continuing cast to be people like us, but far enough in the future for galaxy travel to be fully established."

One date is mentioned in Roddenberry's pilot script "The Cage," outlined for NBC-TV executives in 1964. In the story, the Keepers project an illusion of an Earth scene to Captain April, the time setting of which is A.D. 2049. Roddenberry noted that "the Keepers' illusions can allow April to live on Earth in his own time." Later, when Roddenberry began to fine-tune his "new baby" in preparation for the submission of three complete scripts to NBC, the time setting of Star Trek was moved up to the twenty-third century. But this was as specific as Roddenberry ever got, for the continuity and consistency of the television series did not depend on precise dates.

Thus, in order to establish the most logical chronology for Star Trek, one must look to other sources. The most definitive record of the Star Trek series is Bjo Trimble's *Star Trek Concordance*. The *Concordance* catalogues all seventy-nine episodes of the series (and the animated episodes as well), enabling us to create some boundaries for our quest (aided by verbatim dialogue from the series itself).

In the episode "Space Seed," the awakening Khan asks how long he and his crew have been sleeping. Captain Kirk replies, "We estimate two centuries." Determining that the DY-100-class "sleeper ship" was launched some time in the 1990s, this estimate would (plus or minus fifty years) indicate that the year was sometime between 2140 and 2240.

In "Tomorrow is Yesterday," a frustrated interrogation officer threatens to lock Kirk up for two hundred years; Kirk dryly retorts, "That ought to be just about right." Again, this indicates a time frame of circa 2160.

Finally, in the episode "Wolf in the Fold," the *Enterprise* computers reveal that the last in a series of Jack-the-Ripper-type murders has occurred in 2156, definitely establishing an exact minimum time boundary for the *Enterprise*'s adventures.

Thus, the *Concordance* provides us with a time range from which to "date" the voyages of the *Enterprise*: sometime between 2156 and 2240. Combining these figures with Roddenberry's dating, we can narrow the range to 2200 to 2240.

The next reference guide useful in fixing our chronolgy is Stan and Fred Goldstein's *Star Trek Spaceflight Chronology*. In this exacting work, the authors suggest that the first of the Constitution-class cruisers, the USS *Enterprise*, was launched in the year 2188. A later section mentions the Babel Conference ("Journey to Babel"), Dr. Daystrom's M-5 wargames disaster ("The Ultimate Computer"), the Organian Peace Treaty ("Errand of Mercy"), and other unspecific references to the voyages of the *Enterprise*. In the section entitled "An Overview: 2201—   " we find that the updated version of the cruiser *Enterprise* (as seen in *Star Trek: The Motion Picture*) is completed in the year 2215. Thus, it would seem from this work that the Star Trek voyages occur between 2200 and 2215.

Another work of value in establishing a Star Trek chronology is Paramount Pictures' *Star Trek Maps* and *Introduction to Navigation*. However, this source material disagrees with that mentioned earlier in this article. The latest date mentioned in *Star Trek Maps* is 2267. From this material it appears that the voyages of the *Enterprise* occur between 2261 and 2263. Dates for events during the *Enterprise* voyages are also given in the *Introduction to Navigation* manual, and they also fall between these years.

However, because of the weight of evidence established in earlier-cited source material, we must disregard the dating argument set forth in *Star Trek Maps*. Nevertheless, there is much valuable material in this work that makes reading it an enjoyable experience. The background on Federation planets and their colonization history was particularly helpful in establishing this article's chronology section.

Now we are ready to construct a chronology for the voyages of the USS *Enterprise*:

January 2188

The Constitution-class cruiser USS *Enterprise* is commissioned. Captain Robert April is assigned to command the vessel.

January 2190

A two-year shakedown cruise ends successfully. The first standard five-year mission of the *Enterprise* begins with April in command.

October 2191

In commendation of April's actions in preventing an interstellar war, he is named honorary Federation ambassador-at-large.

January 2195

The first five-year mission ends successfully. After seven years of commanding the *Enterprise*, April retires from active duty to devote his full-time efforts to diplomatic endeavors as a full-fledged Federation ambassador.

June 2195

Captain Christopher Pike assumes command of the *Enterprise* after serving for three years as captain of the destroyer *Fomalhaut.*

August 2196

After a difficult mission at Talos IV, Captain Pike recommends to Starfleet Command a strict quarantine of that planet

May 2201

The Orion Abolition Crisis delays the completion of the first five-year mission under Christopher Pike.

November 2201

After six months' leave and a major overhaul of the ship (including the installment of a new weapons system/phasers), the next five-year mission begins with Pike again commanding the *Enterprise*.

October 2206

The second five-year mission is interrupted when the Enterprise is summoned back to Earth. Captain Pike, upon the sudden and unexpected death of his predecessor, is named Federation fleet captain.

April 2207

After six months' leave, a new crew and commander board the *Enterprise*. Chosen by former captain Pike, James Tiberius Kirk assumes command, after serving for four years as captain of the destroyer *Hua C'hing*.

April 2207–March 2208

The voyages of the *Enterprise* as related in the episodes from the first season of the Star Trek television series.

April 2208–March 2209

Voyages of the *Enterprise* as related in episodes from the second season of the series.

April 2209–March 2210

Voyages of the *Enterprise* as related in episodes from the third season of the series.

April 2210–March 2211

Voyages of the *Enterprise* as related in the one and a half seasons of the animated Star Trek series.

April 2211–March 2212

Voyages of the *Enterprise* as related in stories of the *New Voyages* series, novelizations, and other fan fiction.

April 2212

The fourth five-year mission of the USS *Enterprise* is completed successfully under the command of James T. Kirk.

October 2212

Captain Kirk is promoted to admiral and named chief of Starship Operations. The *Enterprise* is mothballed temporarily, then undergoes eighteen months of refitting and redesign.

April 2215

Willard Decker, chosen by his predecessor to command the *Enterprise*, steps aside to allow Admiral Kirk to resume command of the now refitted vessel in a vital mission to intercept a giant alien machine approaching Earth. Upon the later disappearance of Decker, Kirk assumes permanent command of the *Enterprise*.

With this dating chronology established, we can now tie in all the source material mentioned in this article and establish a full chronology of the universe of Star Trek:

1968

The first orbital flight around Earth's moon is undertaken by American Apollo astronauts. The first lunar landing is accomplished in 1969.

1976

The American *Viking I* becomes the first unmanned probe to land on Mars.

1981

The American Space Shuttle flights begin.

1991

The first unmanned probe penetrates the atmosphere of Saturn.

1992

The American Space Shuttle flights end, the orbital missions having proved that man can successfully live and work in space.

1992–1996

The Eugenics Wars involve over forty Third World nations in combat. This "Third World War" results in the deaths of 37 million people in Africa and Asia.

1996

The DY-100-class vessel SS *Botany Bay* flees Earth carrying almost one hundred of the eugenically bred "supermen" led by the colorful dictator Khan Noonian Singh.

1998

The Goddard Moonbase is constructed as the first permanant outpost on another planet.

1999

The Asteroid Belt Lander discovers a number of bodies rich in minerals, sparking the birth of asteroid mining.

2001

The first unmanned probe lands on Mercury.

2003

The United Space Initiative, an international agreement, calls for the peaceful exploration and colonization of the solar system.

2004

A mass driver is first used at the Clavius mines. The construction of L-5 stations and colonies begins.

2007

Tsiolkovsky, the first L-5 city, is inhabited by 250 persons.

2008

The invention of the fusion torch accelerates the development of fusion power space propulsion systems.

2012

Marsbase One, the first interplanetary outpost, begins a radio search for extraterrestrial intelligence.

2014

The Space Homesteading Act is passed by the United Nations. The first manned mission to Jupiter's moons is launched. The first manned mission to Venus is launched.

2015

The first unmanned interstellar probe, *U Thant*, is launched from Earth. Two years later it discovers large amounts of antimatter in extrasolar space.

2018

The first pioneers leave Earth for the Asteroid Belt.

2020

Nomad, the unmanned probe of the Stellar series, is launched from Earth. The manned Earth-Saturn probe discovers evidence of ancient alien visitation on one of Saturn's moons.

2021

Evidence of extinct microscopic life found on Mars.

2026

Asteropolis, the Asteroid Belt's capital, becomes the focus of interplanetary mining activity.

2027

The terraforming of Venus begins.

2029

Radio signals are received at Farside Moonbase from a star near the galactic center, 15,000 light-years distant.

2032

The second generation of interstellar probes are launched from the moon.

2034

The United Nations Solar Fleet is established by international agreement and a Solar Base is constructed on Titan.

2036

Geon holes are discovered in the fabric of space-time. Eventually this discovery leads to the development of warp communications.

2040

The advanced fusion-drive Columbus-class vessels are first launched.

2041

The first manned interstellar journey is launched to Bernard's Star. The ship is called the *Adameve*.

2042

The *Icarus* manned mission leaves for Alpha Centauri.

2047

The Venus Terraforming Project succeeds in adapting that planet for human habitation.

2048

The first face-to-face contact with intelligent extraterrestrial life is established by the *Icarus* near Alpha Centauri.

2048

The theory of warp drive is first formulated by the Alpha Centaurian Zefrem Cochrane.

2055

An experimental warp-drive ship is tested near Pluto.

2059

The first warp-drive ship voyages to Tau Ceti, twelve light-years distant from Earth.

2062

The Fundamental Declaration of the Martian Colonies grants local autonomy to all inhabited regions in the Sol system. Zefrem Cochrane, the discoverer of warp drive, mysteriously disappears.

2065

The first contact with Vulcan occurs.

2066

The warp-drive ship UNSS *Bonaventure* is lost on its third mission.

2070

Ten Space arks leave Earth for interstellar space, never to be heard from again.

2071

The first commercial space lanes are organized as a joint venture of Alpha Centauri, Vulcan, and Earth.

2073

The first contact with Tellarites, a race that introduces Earth to the Rigel Trading Planets, occurs.

2077

The Alpha Centauri Conference convenes as Vulcan, Andor, Tellar, and Earth discuss an alliance.

2079

The first contact with the Rigel Trading Planets (Rigel II and IV) occurs.

2081

The Milky Way series of galactic probes are launched from Earth.

2087

The First Babel Conference establishes the birth of the United Federation of Planets. Original members of the Federation include: Alpha Centauri, Vulcan, Tellar, Andor, and Earth. Rigel remains outside the alliance until 2125.

2091

Starfleet Academy opens with a first class of three hundred students.

2092

The first contact with the Romulans occurs when an ore carrier (the USS *Muleskinner*) is spacejacked by pirates.

2093

The UFP launches the Horizon-class vessels, the second generation of warp-drive ships.

2095

Starbase One is constructed as the first common UFP contact point.

2097

The USS *Archon* is lost near the Beta III star system.

2102

The USS *Horizon* becomes the first ship to journey to the edge of the Milky Way Galaxy.

2103

Starbase One is destroyed by Romulan forces and a Federation military mobilization begins.

2106

War with the Romulan Star Empire begins as Romulan forces are confronted near Rigel.

2109

The Romulan War ends in victory for the Federation at a battle near the boundaries of the Romulan Empire. A peace treaty is negotiated over radio and a neutral zone is established along disputed territorial space.

2110

Deneb becomes the ninetieth member of the UFP. By 2113, Federation membership reaches one hundred.

2116

Izar becomes the 108th member of the United Federation of Planets.

2122

Subspace radio is introduced as a major improvement in warp communication.

2123

The first interstellar space liners, the Declaration-class vessels, are launched; the first of these is named *Enterprise*.

2124

The first evidence of extragalactic life is discovered when a mysterious unmanned probe is retrieved from deep space.

2125

With the accession of the Rigel Trading Planets, Federation territory is redefined. By interstellar agreement, the center of the UFP becomes a point on the galactic plane equidistant between planar projections of Rigel, Deneb, and Antares.

2129

The Vulcanoid civilization of Rigel V becomes the 227th member of the United Federation of Planets.

2130

The first serious violation of the Prime Noninterference Directive occurs when Captain James Smithson intervenes to prevent a nuclear conflict on Vega Proxima.

2138

The Beta Cersus interplanetary war creates a crisis in the Romulan Neutral Zone that threatens the peace negotiated by treaty.

2146

Richard Daystrom, renowned physicist and developer of duotronics, is born.

2147

The newly invented medical tricorder aids in quelling a plague on Rigel II.

2148

The Tritium class of third-generation warp-drive ships proves a failure and is soon removed from UFP service.

2151

The first contact with the Klingon Empire occurs.

2153

The USS Valiant is lost near the Vendikar star system.

2154

The Mann-class warp-drive vessels are launched; these become the first ships to achieve warp factor 4.

2155

The first unmanned probe into a black hole is launched.

2157

The advent of the Back to Earth movement coincides with the bicentennial of space travel.

2160

The Tarsus IV Colony is established; later the site of mass executions by Governor Kodos (2188).

2161

The first billion-ton super space convoys are organized.

2166

United Federation of Planets membership reaches five hundred with the admission of Theta VII.

2171

Richard Daystrom achieves his great duotronic computer breakthrough.

2174

An experimental transportation system, the "materializer" (later called the transporter), is perfected for human use.

2176

The dilithium crystal is discovered and first mined at the Rigel XII mining complex; it is soon put to use in warp-drive energy-flow mechanics.

2177

Dissolution is debated at the UFP's annual Babel Conference; Admiral Shepard and Carter Winston are instrumental in thwarting a dissolution vote.

2179

Subspace radio is uprated to warp-20 efficiency.

2180

The first contact with the Kzinti Patriarchy.

2184

Daran V becomes the 550th member of the UFP.

2187

The Memory Alpha Library Complex is established as part of the Federation Centennial celebration; it opens to the public two years later.

2188

The Constitution-class fourth-generation warp-drive ships are launched, the latest improvement in starship design and equipment. The first ship of the line is USS *Enterprise*.

2190

The USS *Wells* becomes the first ship to travel through time; it returns from a three-year voyage in thirty-three days.

2194

An alliance between the Klingons and the Axanar star system begins the Four Years War. Efforts by the Klingons to construct a starbase at Axanar are thwarted by Federation forces commanded by Captain Garth.

2196

The Talos IV star system is strictly quarantined by General Order Number Seven.

2198

The Axanar Peace Mission ends the Four Years War and establishes the current Federation-Klingon border.

2198

A new weapons system, the phaser, is introduced aboard all Federation vessels.

2201

Federation mandate outlaws the Green Slave Trade on Orion (Rigel VIII), precipitating the Orion Abolition Crisis (also known as the Rigellian Crisis).

2205

After a number of attacks on Federation colonies and isolated engagements with Federation vessels by the Kzinti, they are confronted by a Federation fleet and forced to sign a cease-fire, ceding their slave worlds to Federation protectorate.

2206

Flying space parasites destroy a number of civilizations, including the anthropoid inhabitants of Ingraham B.

2207

Omnicron Ceti III is colonized as a Federation Agricultural Settlement. One year later, discovery of deadly radiation forces relocation of the colony.

2208

The advanced, noncorporeal energy beings of Organia impose a peace treaty on Federation and Klingon forces.

2209

The intelligent humanoid civilization of the Maluria star system is annihilated by the renegade Nomad probe.

2209

Proposed UFP membership for Coridan is discussed at the Babel Conference; four years later Coridan joins the UFP.

2209

A secret alliance between the Romulan Star Empire and the Klingon Empire is signed. Possible aspects of the agreement include mutual defense and security and arms/technology exchange.

2210

A nova in the Minara system destroys three planets, including a Federation outpost on the first planet.

2210

Overpopulation on Gideon is drastically solved by the introduction of Vegan choriomeningitis. Over 97 percent of the estimated 500 billion Gideonites die.

2210

Energy beings known as Zetars partially destroy the Memory Alpha Complex.

2210

The Beta Niobe nova destroys the present-day planet Sarpedion; the population escapes to the planet's past by the use of time machines.

2214

Delta becomes the six hundredth member of the United Federation of Planets.

2215

The first vessel with advanced fourth-generation warp drive, the USS *Enterprise*, is launched ahead of schedule to intercept a giant alien machine approaching the Sol system.

Finally, let us turn to personal chronologies of important individuals in the Star Trek universe:

Khan Noonian Singh (1962–1996; 2208–   ) A genetically bred "superman" who ruled a quarter of the earth, from the Middle East to South Asia, during the Eugenics Wars of the 1990s. Awakened on his sleeper ship in 2208, Khan and his followers were banished to Ceti Alpha V.

Captain John Christopher (1938–1986) Twentieth-century United States Air Force pilot accidentally taken aboard the *Enterprise* when it was stranded in Earth's past.

Colonel Shawn Jeffrey Christopher (1970–2056) Commander of the first Earth-Saturn manned mission. Son of John Christopher.

Jackson Roykirk (1957–2022) UNSS scientist and engineer who designed the Stellar series, the first interstellar probes launched from Earth.

Zefrem Cochrane (2025–2064; 2210–   ) Brilliant theoretical physicist who pioneered the warp-drive theory. A native of Alpha Centauri. He mysteriously vanished for 150 years before being found alive and rejuvenated (by the energy being known as "the Companion") on Gamma Canaris N.

Harmon Axelrod (2038–2123) Diplomat and statesman who served as the first secretary general of the United Federation of Planets.

Richard Daystrom (2146–   ) Renowned physicist, inventor of the revolutionary duotronic computer system and the unsuccessful "M" computer series.

Carter Winston (2153–2206) Wealthy financier and philanthropist. His most important contribution was made at the Babel Conference of 2177 when his influence helped prevent dissolution of the UFP.

Admiral Shepard (2122–2179) Brilliant military strategist and diplomat. Aided Carter Winston in his efforts to maintain the Federation at the 2177 Babel Conference.

Ambassador Sarek of Vulcan (2105–   ) Astrophysicist and UFP ambassador. He participated in the Axanar Peace Mission and the Babel Conference of 2209. Father of Spock.

Amanda Grayson (2141–   ) Teacher and writer, the first Earthling to live permanently on Vulcan. She is the wife of Ambassador Sarek and mother of Spock.

Garth of Izar (2157–   ) Federation hero of the Four Years War who distinguished himself at the Battle of Cheron. He later became an instructor at Star Fleet Academy until a mental imbalance caused his internment on Elba II.

Commodore Robert April (2136–   ) The first captain of the Starship *Enterprise*; a Federation ambassador in later years.

Dr. Sarah April (2146–   ) First medical officer to serve on the *Enterprise*; developed many of the tools and procedures used in space medicine. Wife of Robert April.

John Gill (2140–2209) Earth historian and Starfleet Academy instructor. As cultural observer on the planet Ekos, he illegally sought to solve its society's problems by introducing Nazism, causing an interplanetary conflict in the M43 Alpha system.

Fleet Captain Christopher Pike (2158–   ) The second captain of the *Enterprise*. After he was injured in a space disaster, the Federation granted him permission to live on Talos IV, where he would have the illusion of health.

Commodore Matthew Decker (2159–2208) In command of the Starship *Constellation* at the time of its destruction by the Berserker, Decker gave his life in an attempt to destroy it.

Commander Willard Decker (2184–2215) Latest captain of the uprated *Enterprise*, he sacrificed himself to halt the threat of V'Ger. Son of Matthew Decker.

Lieutenant Ilia of Delta (2188–2215) Navigator of the uprated *Enterprise*; she was killed by V'Ger, but an android with her consciousness joined in Willard Decker's sacrifice.

Lieutenant Commander Gary Mitchell (2174–2207) Second officer of the *Enterprise*; served under Captain Kirk on the *Starstalker* and the *Hua C'hing*. Died during the *Enterprise*'s first visit to the rim of the galaxy.

Yeoman Janice Rand (2183–   ) Served as captain's yeoman aboard the *Enterprise*; later returned to the uprated *Enterprise* as transporter chief.

Dr. Christine Chapel (2174–   ) Served as chief nurse aboard the *Enterprise*; served as chief surgeon on the uprated *Enterprise*.

Lieutenant Pavel Chekov (2184–   ) Originally a replacement navigator aboard the *Enterprise*; promoted to weapons and security officer on the uprated *Enterprise*.

Lieutenant Commander Hikaru Walter Sulu (2179–   ) Chief helmsman on the *Enterprise*; served previously on *Paul Revere* and *Hua C'hing*.

Lieutenant Commander Penda Uhura (2179–   ) Chief communications officer on the *Enterprise*; previously served as communications instructor, replacement specialist on the *Atlantica*, and ensign on the *Adad*.

Commander Montgomery Scott (2160–   ) Chief engineering officer on the *Enterprise*; previously served aboard the. *Hua C'hing* and the *Starstalker* (which he helped design).

Commander Leonard "Bones" McCoy (2158–   ) Chief medical officer and chief surgeon on the *Enterprise* (also head of the Life Sciences Department); returned to active duty on the uprated *Enterprise* at Kirk's request. Unlike the other officers aboard, he does not consider himself a career military man.

Commander Spock of Vulcan (2166–   ) First officer and chief science officer on the *Enterprise*. Studied the *Kolinahr* discipline with the Vulcan Masters; left to rejoin the uprated *Enterprise*. Previous assignments include assistant navigator on the *Fomalhaut* and second officer under Pike on the *Enterprise*.

Admiral James Tiberius Kirk (2173–   ) The youngest officer ever to command a Federation starship. Served aboard *Chesty Puller*, *Farragut*, and *Jim Bridger*. Captained experimental vessel *Starstalker* and destroyer *Hua C'hing*. Promoted to admiral and appointed chief of Starship Operations; stepped down to resume command of the uprated *Enterprise*.

PLAUSIBILITY OF THE STAR TREK UNIVERSE AND TECHNOLOGY

by Rowena G. Warner

We've run literally dozens of articles discussing the hardware and science of the Star Trek universe, but Rowena's article differs in two important ways. First, she examines some of the devices and techniques of that universe from the standpoint of current knowledge and application. Second (and most important), Rowena is not a scientist or engineer. She discusses Star Trek science in the same layman's terms as would you and I, using the same general science background that you and I possess. The result makes for fascinating reading—and we believe you'll be seeing and hearing some of Rowena's "applied solutions" to Star Trek science popping up all over fandom quite soon.

While watching a particular scene from a Star Trek episode, have you ever wondered, "Is that possible? Is there any chance such a thing could happen someday?"

We've all asked ourselves those questions; this article will endeavor to set forth some possible answers. Science fiction, on the whole, deals in credibility—in many instances, the science fiction of yesterday is the science fact of today.

But what about tomorrow? Three hundred years from now, will we have warp drive? Discover parallel universes? Will we be able to select a color-coded card and have a fully cooked meal in less than a minute?

We will probably not know the answers to these questions in our lifetime. But all the theories, all the conjectures discussed in this article (whether those expressed by experts in a particular field, or drawn from imagination), are possibilities. Possibilities just waiting to be transformed into realities. There is only one unknown factor—man.

Warp Drive/Faster-Than-Light Travel

Critics of Star Trek have often cited this factor as an example of the series' lack of believability; they feel faster-than-light travel is impossible, as purportedly set forth in Einstein's special Theory of Relativity. However, if you examine this theory closely, you find that in a sense it does *not* prohibit faster-than-light velocity, but only velocity that *equals* the speed of light, stating that acceleration to that speed is impossible to achieve.

You might say, "What's the difference? If a ship can exceed the speed of light, at some point it would, at least for an instant, have to be traveling *at* the speed of light."

Not necessarily. Let's take, for example, an electron. If there is a change in its energy state within an atom, the electron can go from one orbit to another orbit apparently without passing through any of the intervening levels.

Taking Einstein's theory into consideration with regard to the *Enterprise*, we find that she cannot reach and exceed the speed of light simply by accelerating. As the *Enterprise* approached the light barrier, her mass would become infinitely greater, hence the energy required to accelerate would have to increase proportionately. Eventually a point would be reached, just a fraction less than the speed of light, when her mass would have become so great that if all the mass in our universe were converted to energy, it would still be insufficient to accelerate the *Enterprise* to and beyond that barrier. But if we look at this desired objective as just that—a barrier—then the propulsion systems of the *Enterprise* appear to be plausible. The fact that she has two modes of propulsion seems to suggest that by switching from impulse power to warp drive, a means has been found to "jump," "tunnel through," or suddenly "warp" the space around the ship, thus enabling it to enter into hyperspace and travel faster than light. This would in no way invalidate Einstein's Special Theory.

Subspace Radio Communication Received at Warp Speeds

If the *Enterprise* is traveling in excess of 186,000 miles per second, how can the ship receive subspace radio communications, since radio waves cannot travel faster than light travels? Unless the *Enterprise* was traveling on impulse power, radio waves could never catch up with her.

It would seem probable that in Star Trek technology, a way has been found to use something similar to "wave guides" for interstellar communication. Wave guides are rectangular tubes formed from aluminum or copper along which high-frequency radio waves pass. In doing so, the waves create electromagnetic patterns which also pass along the wave guides, but at speeds in *excess* of the speed of light. Since this is not energy or matter, but an "appearance," so to speak, it presents no contradiction to Einstein's theory.

We have not yet found a way to put these wave guides into use in interstellar communications, but it is highly probable that just such an apparatus will be in use within three hundred years. If the electromagnetic patterns could be "broadcast" at the same faster-than-light speeds at which they move along the wave guides, communication with a starship in warp drive would be no problem.

Matter-Antimatter Propulsion

Few details have been given concerning the *Enterprise*'s matter-antimatter propulsion system, and with good reason. The existence of antimatter has not been completely substantiated, although a few antimatter particles have apparently been produced in laboratories through experiments involving gamma rays. Also, a 1979 University of Mexico study of sensitive instrumentation aboard a high-flying balloon resulted in the discovery of what appeared to be interstellar antimatter particles.

An ordinary hydrogen atom consists of one neutron (no charge), one proton (positive charge), and one electron (negative charge). An antimatter hydrogen particle would contain opposite charges— one proton with a negative charge, and one electron with a positive charge (a positron). In theory, when an atom of matter come in contact with a like atom of antimatter, mutual annihilation results. Einstein stated that mass and energy are merely two sides of the same coin; therefore, when this mutual annihilation takes place the matter and antimatter cannot just simply disappear.

Instead, they are transformed into energy. When this is performed in a controlled situation, the resultant energy can be used for propulsion. In other words, the "fuel" can be produced precisely when and where it is needed.

How the ingredients for this "fuel" are obtained presents another problem. It seems logical to assume hydrogen atoms would be used, since these are the simplest form and in greatest abundance. A "scoop" could be utilized to collect these atoms while traveling through space. However, antiparticles present a much more difficult problem—antimatter, as far as we know, is very rare, if not completely nonexistent, in our universe. It's highly unlikely Starfleet has come across enough antimatter to power an entire fleet of starships.

But what about the dilithium crystals? What purpose do they serve and why are they so important?

In "Elaan of Toryius," Scotty reported that the dilithium crystal converter assembly was fused. When Kirk asked him if there was any chance to restore warp drive, he answered, "Not without the dilithium crystals, sir. We can't even generate enough power to fire our weapons." Obviously, these crystals are needed to generate power, or produce "fuel" for the matter-antimatter engines. Perhaps dilithium crystals possess a quality which can break up the molecular structure of an ordinary atom, reversing or "converting" the charge and thereby producing a mirror image of the atom—an antiparticle.

Or perhaps the dilithium crystals carry a negative charge or field, and when an ordinary hydrogen atom bombards this field, a "conversion" occurs—the proton becomes negatively charged and the electron becomes positively charged. (Remember your old algebra? Positive × negative = negative, and negative × negative = positive.) Over a length of time, this field or charge would become drained and new dilithium crystals would be needed.

All of this is, of course, pure conjecture, but it would seem to explain why the Klingons and the Federation take such great interest in those little crystals—warp drive would be impossible without their conversion capabilities.

In "That Which Survives," the problem experienced by the *Enterprise*'s matter-antimatter engines is theoretically accurate. In order for a matter-antimatter propulsion system to work properly and safely, a control would be needed to integrate both types of particles slowly and in the correct proportions to achieve a balanced annihilation. With this control fused, the flow of matter-antimatter particles would increase and annihilation continue at a greater rate, thereby providing continuously increasing energy and propulsion. If this had been allowed to continue, it would have resulted in a power overload and eventually an explosion.

Yonada—"For the World Is Hollow and I Have Touched the Sky"

This spaceship appears to be a variation of the "Dyson Sphere": Freeman Dyson discussed the concept that a civilization might choose to capture the radiation emitted by its sun by building a sphere around it made from the materials of a demolished planet. The principle involving Yonada is dissimilar in that an artificial sun was created, but all factors point to a planetary environment, not a spaceship environment. This would coincide with the Dyson Sphere principle.

The exterior of Yonada was formed from an asteroid (as Spock explained) which may have been hollowed out and the ship built inside. Conversely, the materials from an asteroid could have been used to build a sphere around a small existing planet and a limited amount of space surrounding it, along with an artificial sun. This concept is suggested by the fact that the old man climbed the mountain and "touched the sky." If the people of Yonada were actually living on the interior surface of an asteroid, he would have had to climb an extremely high mountain in order to touch the sky. But if a planet was suspended in the middle of the hollowed-out asteroid, he could easily have "touched the sky," probably only a few feet from his mountaintop.

We can probably assume the planet already had a breathable atmosphere and gravity, and it would retain these qualities if a sphere were built around it, so there would be no need for the production of artificial gravity or any life-support systems. This would seem likely when taking into consideration the antiquated nuclear-powered engines, since most of the available nuclear fuel would be needed for propulsion.

Ion Power—"Spock's Brain"

This is a conceivable mode of power; however, it could not be advantageously used to achieve a velocity near or exceeding the speed of light. A ship would need a mass ratio of 20 to achieve a velocity of only 3,860 miles per second. Apparently Kara's ship used a form of ion power which greatly increased propulsive power, giving credence to Scotty's comparison of ion power to an atomic pile a hundred miles wide.

Tachyons

If you have read *Spock Must Die!* then you know about as much as anyone does about tachyons. Our present technology identifies tachyons as theoretical particles which can only travel *faster* than the speed of light; if these particles slow down their mass will become infinitely greater until, in theory, they just cease to exist.

There is as yet no substantial proof confirming the existence of tachyons, but cosmic-ray experiments carried out in 1973 by Clay and Couch of the University of Adelaide produced results which could be explained by the existence of tachyons. Extreme care must be taken, however, to rule out all other possibilities before the existence of tachyons can be established as fact.

Invisibility Screen—"Balance of Terror"

This is, undoubtedly, one of the most difficult concepts to theorize about; no present-day hypothesis explains or allows for invisibility. However, we should begin by asking: What is invisibility? Simply, it is an object which cannot be seen by the eye; a state when light reflected from that object is somehow prevented from reaching an observer. But how is this achieved?

An immediate thought is of an artificially produced black hole, the gravity of which prevents any light waves from escaping. On closer examination, however, this explanation seems full of holes. If the Romulan vessel were at the center of this black hole, it would likely be crushed into a singularity. Also, it seems inconceivable that a black hole could be created or dispelled in seconds.

Another idea considers the possible establishment of an antigravity force field surrounding the Romulan vessel. It has been proved that gravity bends light waves toward the origin of the gravity; therefore, antigravity should, theoretically, repulse light waves or bend them away from the source. In this manner light waves would "bounce off" the force field, consequently rendering the vessel invisible. However, it is possible that the light waves bent back by the antigravity field would be reflected to the *Enterprise*, and the field itself would then become visible. Needless to say, this would not accomplish the Romulans' purpose, for Kirk could simply have the phasers trained on the visible field itself.

Several other theories are possible, including some means of spectroscopically altering the light wavelengths by shortening them into the ultraviolet region or lengthening them into the infrared region; this would effectively render the Romulan ship invisible, for the human eye (or the Vulcan eye, for that matter) cannot perceive light in these regions of the spectrum.

If tachyons, those faster-than-light particles discussed above, do exist, what effect would a dense field of them have on light waves entering the field? Would these light waves pass through the field, reflect off of it, or be integrated into the field itself?

Light also travels in particles, and these particles, when striking the tachyons in the field, could possibly fuse with the tachyons, thus forming an entirely new particle; a litachyon, perhaps. Since light travels at 186,000 miles per second, and tachyons, theoretically, can only travel faster than light, the average speed of a litachyon would be greater than the speed of light, and therefore it would be invisible to an observer. Accordingly, the tachyon field would prevent light from reaching and reflecting off the Romulan vessel and it, too, would be invisible.

Such a field could be heart-shaped, with the concave portion at the bow of the ship. This would allow radio messages to be transmitted without passing through the field. Also, the vessel would still retain mass and would still register on the *Enterprise*'s motion sensors. The Romulan vessel would not be able to see the *Enterprise*, since *all* light waves entering the tachyon field would be integrated into the field. The Romulans would have to navigate their ship by instrumentation only.

The Romulan vessel traveling through the tail of the comet would be analogous to passing a transparent sheet of glass through a pile of flour. The glass, although fairly invisible itself, still has mass and would change the physical structure of the pile of flour, thus leaving a visible trail.

This tachyon-field theory, of course, cannot be proved or disproved until the existence of tachyons is determined.

Silicon-Based Life Forms—"Devil in the Dark"

In contemplating what components might form extra-terrestrial intelligence, scientists have noted that silicon is similar in many respects to carbon, our terrestrial base, especially in its ability to link up and bond with other elements such as oxygen, as in rocks on Earth.

The probable reason our life forms did not develop as silicon-based is the abundance of water on our planet. To put it plainly, water and silicon do not get along. Therefore, we can theorize silicon-based life would evolve only on a planet with little or no water. Even the minute amount of liquid on Mars would probably be detrimental to the evolution of silicon-based life.

(Author's Note: Forgive me, but in dealing with this particular subject, I keep getting this mental image of Io, a satellite of Jupiter, because the first time I saw a picture of this moon, I immediately thought of the Horta. An amazing similarity!)

Surgery in the Twenty-third Century

If you recall in "City on the Edge of Forever," Doctor McCoy became quite upset over the thought of "cutting and sewing people like garments."

Obviously, in the good doctor's universe other means have been developed to treat wounds and to "close" after surgery. It is probable that very little surgery, as we know it today, has to be performed. Laser surgery has, no doubt, been developed to a fine art for use in the repair of damaged organs. However, for the removal of organs such as the appendix, or in the case of wounds such as Spock received in "A Private Little War," a means has obviously been found to close the incision or wound.

You may have heard of the development of a new plastic "skin" which fuses with the body's own natural covering; this may someday eliminate the need for skin grafts for burn victims.

In the twenty-third century, a more advanced version of this artificial skin, perhaps with its own dissolving adhesive, could be placed over wounds or incisions, speeding healing and eventually becoming part of the epidermis in that area. This would eliminate sutures and scars, and also be an effective deterrent against infection.

Also, as reported in the February 1981 issue of *Omni*, a variant of "superglue" is already being used in brain surgery; so, taking this one step further to Star Trek's time, an advanced facsimile of this superglue could be used to close wounds such as Kirk received in "Journey to Babel." The glue would be allowed to dry thoroughly and then a layer of the artificial skin would be applied.

Food Processors on the Enterprise

Is this seldom-seen technological process a gastronomical breakthrough we may all experience someday in the not too distant future?

The April issue of *Science 81* contained an article regarding freeze-dried pouches which are now being used by the United States Army. These pouches are light, are nonrefrigerated, require no preparation or cleanup, and cook in only five minutes. (With the advances being made in microwave technology, one day this cooking time could easily be reduced to a minute or less.)

Such technology would be greatly advanced by Star Trek's time, of course, and every type of vegetable, meat, fruit, etc. could be stored in very little space. The ship's computer, utilizing the colorful (and perhaps color-coded) chips we have seen so often, would select, mix, and cook the proper ingredients to prepare any meal desired by a crewmember. Upon completion of cooking (a very short time), the food would be deposited into a waiting bowl or plate. Presto! Meat loaf, potatoes, and green beans as good as Mother used to make—in a fraction of the time, and with no pots and pans to wash!

Time Warps—"The Naked Time"

In this episode Scotty put forth the idea that matter and antimatter cannot be mixed cold, but by following a theoretical emergency intermix formula, the engines "imploded" and sent the *Enterprise* into a time warp. What exactly does this mean?

Einstein felt that "time" should be considered as a fourth dimension. Many scientists today concur with this and often use the term "space-time continuum." Since space and time are inseparable, when we move "forward" in space, we also move forward in time; therefore, an "explosion" of some nature would thrust a ship "forward" in space-time (probably in a thousand little pieces!). Conversely, a controlled "implosion" would theoretically thrust a ship "backward" in space and time, hence the seventy-one hours the *Enterprise* crew had to "live over."

In this particular episode Spock made a remark which, on the surface, seemed completely illogical. When Lieutenant Sulu said, "My velocity gauge is off the scale," Spock replied, "We are now traveling faster than is possible for normal space." What? If it isn't possible, then how could they be doing it?

The velocity gauge on the *Enterprise* (or our present-day facsimile, the speedometer) is based on the amount of distance covered in a predetermined amount of time; e.g. fifty-five miles an hour, or 186,000 miles a second. Therefore, velocity is a combination of distance and time, and is no more separable than space and time. When Mr. Spock made his statement, he did so in relation to the velocity gauge, but in reality the speed of the ship had not increased, only the passage of time (they regressed seventy-one hours in a matter of minutes).

Let's say, for instance, that a person can walk from point A to point B in thirty minutes. He starts to walk this distance again, but this time (unknown to him) he is wearing a watch that is running slow. He completes his walk, checks his watch, and finds that only twenty-seven minutes have elapsed since his departure. He will naturally assume he has walked faster on the second trip, and it will be almost impossible for a person with an accurate watch to convince him otherwise.

So, although the *Enterprise* covered seventy-one hours of time in a few minutes, she covered very little distance in space. Taking the term "space-time" into consideration, let's say the *Enterprise* covered 250,000 kilometers of space in one standard second (slightly less than the speed of light). If it entered a time warp and the passage of time was exactly doubled, the *Enterprise* would cover the next 250,000 kilometers in .5 seconds. To an observer outside the time warp, the *Enterprise*'s velocity would not have increased one iota, but to Mr. Spock and everyone else on the ship, her speed would have doubled, and to them, she would then appear to be traveling at a velocity of 500,000 kilometers per second—"faster than is possible for normal space."

Parallel and Alternate Universes—"Mirror, Mirror"

One hypothesis postulates that two or more universes exist, possibly connected to ours by a black hole. The exit from our universe, a black hole, would lead to the entrance of the parallel universe, a "white hole," where matter and energy is gushed forth into that universe. Conceivably, we could enter a rotating black hole at an angle, and if we could avoid the singularity, we could pass through and be spewed out into another universe—a possible antigravity and/or antimatter universe. Unfortunately, unless black holes also exist in the parallel universe and white holes exist in ours (which at present is unknown), we could not return to our universe.

Imagine our universe as a balloon, and all of our existing matter as flat on the surface of this balloon. Because we have only three tangible dimensions, we cannot visualize what could exist in the space on the outside or the inside of the balloon. This is analogous to Dr. Carl Sagan's famous "flat people." They had no conception of height (or depth) because their universe consisted of only two dimensions—length and width. An object could be falling on their heads and they wouldn't know it, because they could not see or visualize "up."

If a parallel universe exists, it could be an antimatter universe as in "Alternative Factor" or a specific type of universe as in "Mirror, Mirror." This episode in particular is just a bit confusing, because nowhere does it specifically state that this is an antimatter universe; it is merely thought to be a parallel universe of some nature. If it *were* an antimatter universe, however, how did Kirk, Uhura, etc. escape instant annihilation the moment they touched a tangible object composed of antiparticles?

Theoretically, any mass of matter must combine with a replicated mass of antimatter—a mirror image. Obviously, the ordinary particles in Kirk's body would not be identical in molecular structure to the particles in the antimatter Spock's body; therefore, Kirk would not have had an interaction with the parallel-universe Spock. But if both Kirks had met—instant annihilation! Thus, the title "Mirror, Mirror" was appropriate in more ways than one.

This concept is also followed in "Alternative Factor." The Lazaruses never actually touched each other until they were in the "corridor" between the two universes—a neutral zone, neither matter or antimatter.

However, in theorizing that the parallel universe in "Mirror, Mirror" is an antimatter universe, it should be noted that not everything is antithetical—only the charge of the matter itself is reversed. Humanity, greed, kindness, barbarism, etc. are mental concepts and have no mass, and therefore no relationship to matter or antimatter. The Halkans, for instance, were a peace-loving society in both universes; the *Enterprise* crewmembers were good in one universe and evil in the other.

Another theory extrapolates the existence of billions of parallel universes, each one perhaps an instant before or after the others in time, extending infinitely in each "direction." Each second that passes is the passing from one universe to another; and each universe is dissimilar, however minutely, from the one which preceded it. Although this theory is not readily acceptable to many because it leads to the conclusion that Man's fate is predestined, it would explain the *Enterprise*'s voyages to the past in "Yesteryear" and "All Our Yesterdays".

Perhaps Star Trek's universe is such a parallel universe, billions of minuscule instants ahead of us. An exciting thought, isn't it?

BEYOND THE FINAL FRONTIER

by Eleanor LaBerge

The following article is a sequel of sorts to an earlier article of Eleanor's discussing Star Trek: The Motion Picture, *but to simply dismiss it as a rehashing of those ideas as applied to* Wrath of Khan *would be selling Eleanor short. As always, she seems to have found something within Star Trek that all of the rest of us somehow overlooked. By the way, those of you who enjoyed Eleanor's article on the music in* Star Trek: The Motion Picture *will be pleased to know she's working on a similar article dissecting the music of* Wrath of Khan *for* Best of Trek #7.

Every interpretation of Star Trek is like a doubly exposed negative. There is the actual television episode or motion picture, and also the image a superimposed vision creates. Some of us who comment on the world of Star Trek would like to believe ours is an objective analysis. Impossible! There cannot be an objective view of material such as this. Each one of us brings his or her subjective judgment and personal experiences to the commentary—not to mention our own alternate Star Trek universe. Part of the satisfaction of writing for *Trek* is the joy of sharing these personal thoughts.

In my article "The Beginning of a New Human Adventure" (*The Best of Trek #4*) I attempted to explore the Spock/Kirk relationship both in the series and in *Star Trek: The Motion*

Picture in terms of a philosophic stance—specifically Martin Buber's I/Thou and I/It definitions and the concept of Sören Kierkegaard's defining relationship. I felt that such an approach was valid. It did not seem to distort or strain the internal evidence of the film or the series. In *Star Trek II: The Wrath of Khan* the writers and director have presented material that justifies an even deeper look at personal relationships.

The beginning of the new human adventure on the big screen brought Star Trek within reach of significant character growth and development. In spite of its many shortcomings, *STTMP* was a challenge to future productions. *Wrath of Khan* has met the challenge and fulfilled Star Trek's potential with sensitive direction, a more than adequate script, outstanding special effects, and a musical score that should be nominated for an Academy Award.

Wrath of Khan is intelligently conceived and edited. Vivid action contrasts with dialogue that reveals character development as well as plot. The audience is not given time to sit in meditation as it did while passing through the costly special effects of *STTMP*. This new feature is action/counteraction; pause, thrust, and parry at its best. It is far more than an adventure-filled romp through the galaxy with old friends, and it offers much more than just the obvious plot of evil forces contending with the champions of truth and goodness: It is the chronicle of friendship and redemptive sacrifice, of death and rebirth.

In *Wrath of Khan* we are dealing not only with events but with deeply motivated characters who cause and react to them. Some profound changes have occurred in the lives of the *Enterprise* crew during the years following V'Ger. The euphoria of taking the *Enterprise* "out there" seems to have been a brief satisfaction for Kirk, and we learn that he has once again given in to whatever pressures first led him to accept promotion to the admiralty. Spock is captain of the *Enterprise*—not because he needs that role, but because it is the logical way to serve others. There are immediate contrasts between Admiral Kirk and Captain Spock. Spock is serene while Kirk is depressed and in turmoil; Spock is at peace while Kirk is angry with the natural and self-imposed limitations of growing older.

Let us consider *Wrath of Khan*'s Spock. At the end of *STTMP* Spock seemed to have realized the necessity and desirability of accepting his total self. In this second film that acceptance has become evident in his demeanor. We do not see a new "human" Spock, but a renewed character who has found the wisdom to accept himself as a unified duality. The agonized self-consciousness of earlier years is gone. His tenderness, affection, and concern for Kirk are direct and unashamed. No longer does he put up deflector shields of formality—''Jim'' is a name he uses on and off the bridge with as much ease as the proper ''admiral.'' He gives his friend a gift and spares him a jibe on its appropriateness by saying simply that it is for his birthday, ''surely the best of times.''

Spock now reveals warmth and humor. In his first exchange with Saavik he quips, ''Nobody is perfect.'' We suspect mischief when he permits Saavik to take the *Enterprise* out from its moorings. The direction? ''Indulge yourself, Mr. Sulu.'' These subtle changes in the way Spock deals with Saavik and humans show a far more mature attitude in relationships. This is the Vulcan/human ''whose task on Vulcan'' was completed.

''I am and *always will be* your friend,'' Spock repeats to Kirk in the film's significant lines. From their conversations one may assume that they have discussed relationships in general and their own in particular. Comments in regard to the good of the many over that of the few, and particularly the reference to the good of the *one*, reveal to us that their understanding of one another has reached the level at which individual needs may be acknowledged and spoken of openly. Who is the ''one'' if not Spock on the one hand and Kirk on the other? The reference would seem unnecessarily cryptic otherwise.

There are other differences in the way Spock and Kirk deal with each other. Kirk feels free, presumably as Jim rather than the admiral, to enter Spock's private quarters unannounced. He finds the Vulcan at meditation, but even then, knowing full well what a deeply personal experience Vulcan meditation is, he does not feel the need to make an apology for intrusion. Spock must have made it clear that he is always there for Kirk in unqualified friendship.

These examples seem to indicate that Spock has resolved his interior conflicts to a significant degree. In unifying the Vulcan/human factors in his temperament Spock has made a quantum leap to an understanding which admits (as Pascal termed it) that the heart has reasons the mind knows nothing about. There is an added dimension to this Spock who can admit that there is a step beyond logic: an acceptance that such a reality is of value.

As we look back through the television series, on through *STTMP* to *Wrath of Khan*, we see Spock formed in the subtle shades of a Renaissance painting: light and darkness, shadow and perspective, transparency and mystery. In *Wrath of Khan* we see the two peak experiences in Spock's life: his maturing friendship with Kirk and his death. Spock has reached a human and perhaps Vulcan greatness reminiscent of Heidegger's *Dasein*, the person who is *authentically* himself and whose choices are made from that one vital premise. In philosophic terms Spock in *Wrath of Khan* is Being-for-the-Other, the person caring with a solicitous concern that has as its goal freeing the other to be himself. In the existential sense Spock is Being-toward-Death, able at all times to accept his death and living in the midst of mortality in a way some philosophers insist is the most authentic form of living.

I think it is appropriate here to make a comment regarding Vonda McIntyre's novelization of *Star Trek II: The Wrath of Khan*. I was disturbed by what I felt was a lack of understanding of what had gone before. Spock is still holding back in the adaptation, avoiding touch because he finds automatic telepathic communication distasteful and disturbing, and cutting Kirk off short of tangible expressions of affection. Yet in many television episodes Spock does offer a helping hand to assist Kirk, Uhura, McCoy, and others. It is not something he does with apparent emotional stress. Hesitating to touch or be touched by Kirk hardly seems logical for Spock in view of the scene after his contact with V'Ger when he clings to his friend acknowledging that "simple feeling" was of greater value than all the accumulated knowledge in the universe. Such a turning point, such dramatic insight in Spock's life, is not likely to be discarded afterward. Nor would it seem logical to depict Spock as going through the same agonies of "who am I?" again and again. To reveal him, especially with Kirk, as vacillating between showing affection and being the reserved Vulcan is to show an individual who has not resolved the division in his nature. Spock's hesitations seem to be in discord regarding the one and the many with Kirk—a scene clearly emphasized in the novelization as well as in the film.

There is a contradiction between the book and the sequence of motion picture events, and I believe it is a critical point. In the decision to assume command, Kirk makes that judgment *before* consulting Spock in the book, while in the film he does so *after* coming to him, and then it is Spock who voices the desire and need Kirk will not acknowledge openly.

(Note: I found Vonda McIntyre's first *Timescape* book, *The Entropy Effect*, with its twists of time distortion and layers of surprises, complex and delightful. I was disappointed that the first book released after *STTMP* was one which did not take into account the growth and change in Spock. Nevertheless, it was entertaining. Her new characters were vibrant and in fact much more interesting than the *Enterprise* crew for the most part. In spite of the contradictions I see in Ms. McIntyre's amplification of *Wrath of Khan*, I am happy that she was given the project. Her creation of Del March and Vance, as well as the development of the Deltans, was excellent, as was her characterization of Saavik. However, in this article I have used the motion picture and only the evidence on the screen as a basis for my comments on *Wrath of Khan*.)

Let us now look at Kirk as we see him in *Wrath of Khan*. In his Bay Area home we see him surrounded by his many souvenirs—a contrast to the few adornments of Spock's beautiful but simply appointed quarters. Kirk is in possession of his antiques and the admiralcy, but he is earthbound. He feels neither joy in his surroundings nor satisfaction in his achievements. He seems lacking in hope for the future. Part of his interior frustration may stem from the fact that he knows he has made himself what he is now. Both McCoy and Spock tell Kirk that he is not what he should be, and we realize that somewhere between V'Ger and the time of *Wrath of Khan*, Kirk has lost the will to be himself, and he is dangerously close to despair.

It is impossible in this second Star Trek film to continue to analyze Kirk separately. His character is too closely bound to Spock, and to Khan. The three form a dramatic interpersonal triangle. Spock and Khan define themselves directly in relation to Kirk—Spock as his friend, and Khan as his enemy. Spock is and *will be* Kirk's *t'hy'la*, a state of being which will remain true in death as well as life. Khan is the antihero and as such finds meaning in life and death. Kirk treads the edge between positive and negative feelings about himself in his relationships both professional and personal, and cannot define himself wholeheartedly in any direction. He has no zeal, no enthusiasm, and no commitment—until Khan.

There are more significant parallels concerning Kirk and Khan. Escaping from Earth two hundred years before, Khan challenged death and won. Kirk has been a brilliant commander and has used his talents shrewdly even from his first encounters with the *Kobayashi Maru* test when he was a cadet. His intelligence and perhaps his luck have enabled him to win time after time against all odds. He is furious with himself that he was "caught with his pants down'' by Khan's clever attack. Similarly, it is as necessary for Khan to win as it is for Kirk. When Alpha Ceti V became a wasteland Khan was condemned to a no-win situation. The coincidental appearance of Chekov and Captain Terrell gave him an opportunity to become the master rather than the mastered. Kirk would have seized such an advantage had the necessity been his—however different the outcome might have been. Both Kirk and Khan have egos that form a dramatic contrast to Spock's humility and self-containment. Khan and Kirk are closer in temperament than we might like to admit. Kirk seemed to be on a private Alpha Ceti V, a wasteland of his own choosing. The resulting despair from having denied his real needs compares to the furious hopelessness of Khan—though in a far less harsh setting, of course. Both their situations were a waste. The confrontation between the two of them is a defining relationship. How ironic that Khan's relationship to Kirk is the catalyst that leads Kirk back to being his true self. Spock pointed out the waste of Kirk's ''first, best destiny,'' but Spock was not violent and violence was necessary to shock Kirk back into living his life.

Considering Khan from a philosophic point of view brings out other interesting points. Khan had known the I/Thou relationship —he loved his wife intensely, and when he lost her, hate filled the void. He existed in a state of personal and spiritual crisis. Khan was not in a situation nor on a world he could accept. There was no meaning on Alpha Ceti V. He was condemned to survive in an environment so hostile man was no more than a displaced life form that would inevitably disappear. When the possibility of rescue came there were undoubtedly those in the *Botany Bay* group who would willingly have put those horrors behind them. Khan could have chosen to do precisely this. Instead, he rejected the opportunity for freedom in the physical as well as the philosophic sense and in doing so he rejected the whole person he might have become.

At the beginning of their confrontation it would seem that Khan had an advantage in that he was wholeheartedly devoted to the pursuit of his goal. Khan's revenge was no impersonal I/It battle, it was a deeply personal commitment to destroy Kirk and all Kirk held of value. Again the contrast to Spock: Khan was willing to destroy himself and all his followers to win and beat Kirk; Spock was willing to destroy himself to save Kirk and the *Enterprise* crew. For the one it was destructive suicide and for the other, redemptive sacrifice.

Khan may seem to have crossed the line between sanity and madness, but he possesses free will. There is no time at which he does not have the ability to stand outside his hate and choose life for himself and his followers. Those who are led by Khan are victims of a distorted purpose: Their adherence to a pledge made on another world and in another reality. Theirs is a tragedy similar to Earth's Jonestown. We cannot view what Khan's madness does to his faithful disciples and judge the possibility as mere fiction. By the end of the film Khan has, in a sense, become nonhuman. (He reminds me of Dostoyevsky's Smerdyakov in *The Brothers Karamazov*.) All his ultimate choices are toward destruction. How appropriate, by contrast, is Kirk's tribute to Spock as the most "human" soul he has ever known.

Khan's cryptic "dear friend" in reference to Kirk leads to more speculation. Khan knew Captain Kirk on the *Enterprise* as a leader he could admire and despise at the same time. Kirk was, even then, the adversary Khan had to destroy. Facets of Kirk's humanity meant weakness to Khan, but the grudging admiration for Kirk, who had beaten him years before, brought out a passing, almost accidental exclamation, ". . . dear friend . . ." This ambivalent phrase is neither sarcastic nor illogical. Khan needed the one enemy to purge his being of the intense anger he felt in the Alpha Ceti V situation. His *Kobayashi Maru* was replayed every day that he and his pathetic group had to exist upon the wasted planet's surface. He could neither conquer that wasteland nor change it. It defeated him day by day in all but his tenuous hold upon mere physical existence. It had come close to killing his spirit as it had killed the woman he loved, and for this Khan could not forgive nor relent. The hope of vengeance was itself a "dear friend," and the reality of carrying it out inspired a resurgence of creative energy. It was not aimed at the survival or greater good of his company, but at destruction itself. Paradoxes again. Khan saw revenge as his achievement of "good," thus converting evil into goodness by his perverted perception. Death was the result. Spock transformed the evil of death into a goodness that gave life and rebirth. The greatest irony of all is that the ultimate effect of Khan's revenge upon Kirk brings about his enemy's salvation.

Kirk must face the greatest loss of his life at a time when the conflict with Khan has drained him, and at a time when he has had to face and resolve another interior conflict: the fact that he has let another opportunity pass him by—the life he could have lived with Carol and David. But however much he might regret such a void in his life, he would not have chosen this path and is honest enough to admit it. Spock's death thrusts upon Kirk the most profound choice of his life. He must either come to a *metanoia*, a change of heart, or choose despair. He must somehow reject the latter and realize that hopelessness would negate all that Spock has done for him and others. As we see the stunned, grief-stricken Kirk beside the lifeless body of his friend, the feeling of loss is chilling. At this point we can imagine Kirk crying out from the depths of his soul in the words of Shakespeare:

"For from this instant
There's nothing serious in mortality.
All is but toys. Renown and grace is dead."

Spock's courage as Vulcan and human confronted and conquered death far more truly than if he had somehow preserved his life while defying the deadly effects of the radiation chamber. Spock lived a life of transcendental significance. As a Vulcan his "seventh sense" was in constant union with the "All." He drew personal power from direct union with Being Itself and faced the end of his physical existence as an experience he was compelled to choose in order to attain a greater good. Spock, always reaching for his personal answers, found the ultimate choice by relationship. To choose the good of the many over the few was a logical, Vulcan act, but to choose the good of the *one* was relationship—personal, human, defining relationship. It was a choice made because Spock was and *would be* Kirk's friend. "It is a far, far better thing I do than I have ever done . . ."

In his final conscious moments Spock reaches for Kirk from the death side of the barrier and by sheer force of will makes his last affirmation of friendship.

Over the years many crewmen and others close to him have died, but Kirk never seemed to have made the all-important step beyond the I/It limitations in those days. He could take refuge from pain in his career and in his total commitment to the great love of his life: the *Enterprise.* He faced *objectified* death. In all his close calls, including what we see in *Wrath of Khan* when the mind-controlled Chekov and Terrell face him, death is a challenge to be outwitted or overcome. Death was also inevitable for Edith Keeler, but facing that fact as somehow predestined in Kirk's universe took away some of that pain. Death claimed Miramanee, but only after Kirk's memory had awakened. His fully conscious self met this death from the viewpoint of another reality. It was not the *whole* Kirk who faced the death of his brother or even of Reena. He came close to losing Spock upon several occasions, but they were always reunited against all probability. There had been no other person with whom a unity of mind and soul was so profound as that which he experienced with Spock. Kirk was close to the defining relationship with Spock, and it was Spock's death that finally brought that realization to him.

David possessed the insight to realize Kirk's problem. When his son challenged him, Kirk at last turned permanently away from the confines of the I/It stance toward the full experience of the defining relationship. He accepted Spock's death along with the pain and the challenge, and thus he made his friend's sacrifice redemptive in the fullest sense.

There is a provocative tableau in the film as Kirk embraces his son. They assume the same physical position that Kirk and his alter ego assumed in "The Enemy Within" when Kirk accepted and embraced the "Other." This does not tell us that David is evil in any way, but that Kirk is now able to form a personal relationship and embrace the risks of I/Thou interaction. This is perhaps the greatest gift Spock has yet given him: the ability to risk whatever is necessary to love another person, a rare gift "for the best of times and the worst of times."

In *Être et Avoir*, a play by Marcel, is the line ". . . to love a person is to say 'you shall not die.' " The same author insists that the love of friendship must lead "beyond" to the unknown dimensions of a universe of which we comprehend only that very little which fits into our organized structure of thought. The *Wrath of Khan* shows us that death may not be the ultimate evil. It is not Sartre's futility that Khan brings upon Kirk. Spock's death limits his physical life, but not his being. Spock is the opposite of the position that death never gives meaning but rather deprives it of all significance. Kirk carries the heavy burden of loss, but now he experiences a new unity with Spock. He comes to the intuitive knowledge that there is something beyond the apparent finality of death's total separation. Kirk accepts the gift of renewal and can now make a commitment to his own future. He will return to this place of Genesis, but for now he has "promises to keep and miles to go before he sleeps."

The Star Trek fan is privileged to see the series' maturity. If this phenomenally successful concept is to be worthy of its potential, the original characters could not be stretched out indefinitely like Tolkien's ringbearers or the eternally youthful heroes of a comic strip. We have been brought to a moving and climactic moment, and all of us who share in it will "remember."

The battle fought in *Wrath of Khan* effected a profound change in Star Trek as we have known it. The fan must face Spock's death as Kirk must face it. It remains for us, as well as Kirk, the omega mystery.

There are many doors that might be opened in the future. Will we go full circle and witness Kirk's death? Or has there been a forecast of things to come in the fact that we saw Spock's casket whole and not disintegrated by its entrance into the planet's atmosphere? Has there been an effect of the Genesis Wave that is unsuspected, a rejuvenation that is possible within a certain time frame between death and the Genesis formation? Has Spock passed through the darkness of death to be reborn in the light of a new creation? After the catharsis we have gone through in accepting Spock's death, it is staggering to imagine the shock, the incredulity, the *joy* of finding the casket empty and Spock *alive*. How such a parable of death and transfiguration might be presented could well be the most controversial and serious challenge in the history of motion picture fiction.

Whatever inner space the producers will set a course to intercept, it is clear that we may expect surprises in *Star Trek III*. In the next production we may witness resurrection and rebirth, or death and burial. We may welcome back an old friend or say farewell to another. *In either case*, it remains for us to realize that the Star Trek life force of defining relationship is not limited by time and space; it reaches beyond the final frontier.

A SAMPLING OF TREK ROUNDTABLE

The vast majority of mail coming to Trek Roundtable over the past few months has of course concerned Wrath of Khan. *The letters in this sampling reflect this, naturally, but we've also tried to include a fair number of letters which don't address themselves directly to* Wrath of Khan. *As always, we urge you to write and join in the continuing dialogues of the Roundtable.*

Regenia Marracino
Lewisville, Ariz.

I would like to know what kind of outcry has arisen about Spock's alleged death in *Wrath of Khan*. I know loyal Spock fans (myself, for one) are raising Cain. I wanted to see that movie so badly, but I *definitely* did *not* want to see Spock die in it. But I did and I cried. But deep inside I *know* that Spock's not dead. Why? First, his coffin did not burn up in the decaying orbit around Genesis—it wound up without a scratch in a beautiful glade on the new planet; second, Kirk stated that he was definitely coming back to Genesis; and third, since Genesis took dead matter and made live out of it, well, it's only logical for Spock to be "reborn." God help ST if he's not!

I am in the process of reading *The Best of Trek #2*, and was appalled to discover that some fans believe that Spock and Kirk have or had a sexual relationship. *Pon farr* or no *pon farr*, I can't see Kirk giving himself to Spock to save his life. He'd probably find a girl and lock her and Spock in Spock's quarters for a while. (Just kidding, but there's more logic to that than the idea of Kirk's having relations with Spock. That really is a cosmic joke!) Let Christine Chapel save Spock. I would, any day of the week! I really don't see how that beautiful spiritual and intellectual friendship can be defiled by adding the physical, too. Makes me want to cuss in Vulcan . . . if I knew any.

I also read that the animated series was a flop because fans didn't like not having it all "original," character-wise, that is. Or did I misunderstand? I personally loved it. I love Arex and M'Ress, too. I was glad to see that they stayed around in some of the stories.

I am also in the process of reading *The Best of Trek #3* (I keep one at home and one at work). I really enjoyed "A Sampling of Trek Roundtable"; and I notice that most of the fans really know the stories, shows, well, *everything* inside out! And while I love Star Trek and Spock, I guess I always watched it and read it with rose-colored glasses on. I never looked for anything to criticize. It was perfect . . . flaws and all. I never gave a thought about the transporter and the inconsistencies connected with it. Well, it's good to know there are those who are so into ST that they pick up errors like that. But I think I'll just stick to enjoying it and defending it and loving it.

A little about me? I'm thirty-three, married, two children, and a legal secretary. I love reading, good movies, Star Trek, animals, needlecraft, music, and writing (not in that order). I think William Shatner is a most gifted and versatile actor . . . up there with Martin Sheen in my eyes. I also love Clint Eastwood in *Dirty Harry* movies and anywhere else! And Charles Bronson and Harrison Ford. I never saw *Star Wars*, *The Empire Strikes Back*, or any other SF like that. (I think I'm about the only one who didn't.)) I never cared much for SF. I think I may have to change my mind there!

Linda Knight
Walla Walla, Wash.

I have loved Star Trek since the very beginning, but until recently I have never written to any magazine or subscribed to any fanzine. I am not even a member of any Star Trek fan club. Believe me, this is not a confession of a "closet Trekkie." All my friends and family know, only too well, how I feel about Star

Trek. It is just that recently, with the release of *Star Trek II: The Wrath of Khan*, I really feel the need to talk to someone who understands what I am going through. It is hard to put into words and very hard to explain to friends why I am so hung up on a canceled TV show.

I remember a few years ago several Star Trek cast members were going to appear on the *Tomorrow* show. I was so excited about it I could hardly contain my enthusiasm. A close friend of mine could not understand this and cut me down for it. I just told her she did not understand. Then, with a tone dripping with disgust, she replied, "I guess not." What can you do? It is hard to be a Trekkie at times.

Why am I so caught up in Star Trek? Why do I feel so personally involved with the movie? It is ridiculous! I mean truly odd. Why do I resent *E.T.* because it is so popular? I loved *E.T.* but I cannot help wishing it had been released this winter so that *Star Trek II* could have been number one or number two this summer. I know that *Wrath of Khan* is a smash at the box office, which makes me very happy; however, the popularity of *E.T.* no doubt diminished its impact. Why do I let that bother me?

I was on pins and needles every time I saw or read a review of the movie. I work nights, so when I read that *Sneak Previews*, with film critics Gene Siskel and Robert Ebert, was going to review the movie, I, of course, had to videotape it. I was anxious all that night wondering what they thought of it. I knew Roger would like it; he is an admitted fan of the show and he liked the first one. A true Trek fan indeed; he was one of the very few critics that did. I know this sounds silly, but I was so nervous I had to turn the sound down and fast-forward to the end where they show whether or not they recommend a movie. I had already seen the movie twice and had loved it, but I am a Trekkie; I liked the first one. Whether or not they liked it would not change my opinion, I just wanted this movie to be a critical success as well as a financial one. As I held my breath and crossed my fingers, I saw two yes votes for *Wrath of Khan*. I quickly turned up the sound and heard Gene Siskel say, "And two strong yes votes for *Star Trek II*." I was beside myself. I then proceeded to watch the entire review, which was very positive, and which made me feel very good. I was on a Trek high in Trek heaven.

I have been on this Trek high for several weeks now. There has been a lot of publicity on the movie, especially on the talk-show circuit. It was fantastic to see all the cast together on a show besides Star Trek. I must admit, however, if I see that scene where they are leaving space dock one more time, I might have to kick the television in!

Again I have to ask: Why do I let Star Trek affect me this way? Why am I so concerned about how this movie is doing? And why did I promptly throw *US* and *People* magazines into the trash after reading their less than supportive reviews of the movie? Obviously both critics were negative on Star Trek before they even saw the movie. It is so easy to spot a true Star Trek cynic. The thing that really bothers me about these publications is that both ran articles, before and after the reviews, on *Wrath of Khan* saying what a hit it was and so forth. I was pleased to see the *People* critic put in his place, however. Thanks to two loyal Trekkies who wrote in and told him the error of his ways. I knew someone would. Those reviews upset me a little, but I know all the rest were good. At least all I have been able to get my hands on.

I guess the main reason I am writing this letter is to find out if anybody else feels the same way I do about Star Trek. I know that is a strange question to be asking *Trek* readers; the very fact they read *Trek* is because they love Star Trek. Sometimes, though, I feel I go just a bit overboard. Every time I go into a bookstore I have to see how the *Star Trek II* novel is doing, where it is in the top ten. I also have a strange habit of making sure that the soundtrack album is placed in front of the stack so that people will see it. This seems like odd behavior to me. I have never really known a true Trekkie like myself. Is this normal Trekkie behavior?

You can plainly see my need for my fellow Trekkies or Trekkers. People who understand the Star Trek myth and the sometimes neurotic behavior that stems from that myth.

I was so moved by Spock's death that I wrote to *Starlog* expressing my thoughts about it, along with my views of the movie. I also expressed my disapproval of their handling of *Star Trek: The Motion Picture*, especially the critique by Harlan Ellison. I have nothing against Mr. Ellison; he was only expressing his opinion. My gripe was that *Starlog* had a critique in the first place. Why pick just on Star Trek? *Starlog* promotes a lot of what many people would consider "dog of the week" movies. Do they critique them as well? I rest my case. I realize that I am somewhat late with my criticism, but that was the first time I had ever written to a magazine and felt I had to express my feelings on the matter.

. . . On the death of Spock, it all started with those vicious rumors that Leonard Nimoy wanted the character killed off. I was appalled! I could not believe that he really wanted to do that. Needless to say, I was very relieved to find out it was all an elaborate scheme of Paramount's to drum up more box office. But the question still remained: Would Spock die?

I had, of course, watched all the interviews with Leonard Nimoy talking about the fate of Mr. Spock. And in every interview he would cleverly sidestep the question, but quickly add that he had been approached to do *Star Trek III*. That was enough for me. I could not and cannot imagine a successful Star Trek without Mr. Spock. So I was completely prepared to watch my favorite character of all time die right before my eyes. Or so I thought.

There are many circumstances and events that happen in life that are beyond our control. An unexpected death is the hardest to deal with. I know because I have been through it.

It was early December and my dad had just gotten home from work. He was in an unusually good mood, which was always nice. He had brought home a pair of red overalls as a Christmas present for my little niece Imalyn, and was writing her name on the tag. My mom and I were getting ready for work. Everything was as it should be. We both went to work that night, put in our time, and came home. Everything was still as it should have been—Dad getting up at 6:05, making his coffee in the microwave, and telling us it was time to go to bed. My mom and I always like to record something on the video so we have something to watch when we get home from work. So to get out of Dad's way to let him relax before he went to work, we both went into Mom and Dad's room to watch the rest of *The Patricia Neal Story*.

My dad came in a little while later to put on his boots. He sat on the edge of his bed, which I was lying on, and was almost sitting on my legs. Jokingly, he asked me if I had enough room. I replied that I did, smiled, and moved over to give him more room. My mom had fallen asleep, but I was still awake to hear my dad call my name. I listened a moment, then heard him begin to swear; he was in pain. I went into the living room and saw him lying on the couch. From that moment on my whole life changed. I lost my dad an hour later in a hospital emergency room. He had suffered a major heart attack. A few months later my grandmother suffered a stroke and died a few days later.

Consequently, the death scene in *Star Trek II: The Wrath of*

Khan really hit me hard. It just seemed to me everything and everyone I loved was dying off. It really depressed me for a while. No matter how you look at it, Spock is dead until *Star Trek III* is released. What really bothered me most, I think, was that the people involved had control of Spock's destiny and they chose to let him die. It is tragic enough that real people have to die, but when we start killing off our fictional heroes just to make a buck, that really hurts. What is really odd, though, is that it was my favorite part of the movie. It was done so beautifully by both actors. The relationship between Kirk and Spock has never been so fully developed as it was in that one scene. I loved it, but it still hurt.

Finally, I would like to share with you my little niece Imalyn's reaction to the movie. She will be five in August and is a very bright little girl. She has watched Star Trek reruns off and on since she was one. I had taken her to the first movie when she was barely three years old. Now she has to watch it every time it is on *HBO* or *Showtime*, which drives her father up the wall because he cannot stand it. To each his own. I wanted her to see this one too because I knew she would enjoy it more. Before we left I told her I would probably cry at the end because it was sad. She looked at me and said, "I won't." I knew she wouldn't. She had never cried watching anything sad. Even when her grandpa died she didn't cry. It is hard for a four-year-old to comprehend what death is. You try to explain it as best you can but that is all you can do. It was no surprise to me when she said she would not cry.

As we watched the movie and the final scenes were upon us, I quietly got out my Kleenex and watched my favorite Vulcan die once again before my eyes, declaring his undying friendship to Kirk. Did I hear Ima sniffling? I turned to her and asked, "Are you crying?" She nodded, but I did not think anything of it. I thought she was just tired. Well, the movie ended and I quickly dried my eyes before the lights came on. "That's it, Ima, are. . . ?" I was stunned. Ima had tears rolling down her face. I looked at her a few seconds. "Ima, why are you crying?" And with a voice that would break any heart she said, "Because Spock died." She then burst into tears and I had to console her right there in the theater with everybody watching us. I was so touched by her reaction that I started crying again too. How embarrassing! I tried to explain to her that he was just a character and that he really did not die. I told her that everything would be all right, that Spock was going to come back in *Star Trek III*.

But that did not help. "I want him to come back now," she bawled. Finally I calmed her down and we left the theater. Even in the car we were both still crying.

I was shocked by her reaction. She had never done anything like this before. I truly feel that Spock's death scene and the funeral scene thereafter triggered something inside her. She had been to both her grandpa's and great-grandmother's funerals. Perhaps seeing this happen all at once and seeing how Kirk and the others reacted toward their loss helped her to understand her loss. I know that sounds a bit complex for a four-year-old, but I cannot think of any other explanation. She told me it reminded her of when her grandpa died.

For a long time after I had quite a little Trekkie on my hands. I would be watching a rerun of Star Trek and she would come in and say, "Oh, there's Spockie." And, "I really do like Star Trek now, don't I, Auntie?" She can do the Vulcan salute now, too. She even wanted to be Spock on Halloween. But alas, I took her to see *E.T.* . . . and now she wants to be *E.T.* for Halloween. Why does that bother me?

Sandra Colson
Phoenix, Ariz.

I grew up with Star Trek, since I was about ten years old when it first appeared on television. I have never become bored with its reruns, and I doubt I ever will. I watched it at first because I developed a crush on the character of James T. Kirk! As I grew older I realized that there was more to Star Trek than mere entertainment. There had always been a "message" to the shows . . . something about dignity, or caring, or love, and there was always the underlying hope for the future.

I never considered myself to be one of the "fans" of the show until now. . . . I hoped quietly that the rumors of the return of Star Trek would come true. I was thrilled with the release of *Star Trek: The Motion Picture*, and saw it several times just to feast my eyes once again on the beautiful Starship *Enterprise*. Like many others, though, I was somewhat disappointed . . . there *was* something missing, but I just couldn't put my finger on it.

Then I heard that a new Star Trek movie was going to be released. Once again, my pulse quickened and my heart fluttered . . . but I also heard the conflicting rumors about Spock's death, and I knew I had to see the movie to find out. I went to the first night's showing and I came away totally dedicated to the magic that has been returned to Star Trek! As a crowd the audience sat in awe of Khan, we screamed with Chekov, we shuddered when the *Enterprise* was attacked, we cheered with glee when the *Reliant's* shields went down, and we stared transfixed when the smaller ship barely passed above the *Enterprise*! And at the end, we cried for the loss of Spock . . . but we all know that "there are always possibilities," so we will wait for *Star Trek III*!

I have seen the movie five times so far, and each time I come out happy. That's *it*, they've done it, they've brought it back! Suddenly I've found myself compelled to find out more about the "phenomenon." I would like to imagine that someday the "science fiction" that is Star Trek will become a reality. I believe that there can be hope for the future, as opposed to our constant fears of annihilation in the present, and I think that glimmer of *hope* is the magic of Star Trek. That hope, beyond all else, should be maintained, and maybe someday man will turn his gaze toward the heavens and dream of "boldly going where no man has gone before" instead of trying to create a new weapon of destruction.

I am hoping, for now, to learn more about Star Trek through *Trek*. It's good to know that the magic of Star Trek has touched so many intelligent people that, maybe, someone will become curious enough to solve the mysteries of technology from the show, and that they might become working reality. I have been interested to read about the "inconsistency" of the transporter within Star Trek's world. Isn't it fascinating that the Walt Disney movie *Tron* seems to have offered something of a solution . . . matter being broken down into its component parts by a laser, which then stores the information in a computer which can then reassemble the object! I wonder if that idea came from someone who watches Star Trek?

Barbara Corrigan
East Derry, N.H.

I'm not usually much of a letter writer, but I'd like to take this opportunity to put down some of my ideas and feelings about the new movie, *The Best of Trek #5*, and my interest in Star Trek in general. I have a feeling this may be the longest letter I've ever written!

First, I'm twenty-six, single, and working for a local company that manufactures printed circuit boards. I love to read everything, and I've developed a special interest in science fiction in general.

I love Harlan Ellison and Stephen King. My other interests include doing crafts like crocheting, latch-hook rugs, and making model kits. (I've made a model of the *Enterprise*, Spock, and the space shuttle *Columbia*.) Also, animals and wildlife, listening to music (the sound track from *Wrath of Khan* is just beautiful), collecting unicorns, and working out (weightlifting) in a gym.

I've been a diehard fan of Star Trek since the first episode aired in 1966, and I was only eleven years old. But even at that young age, I realized that Star Trek was something special, something above and beyond the usual garbage television had, and still does have, to offer. After the show ended, I continued to follow the careers of most of the stars, even seeing Leonard Nimoy in a theater production of *Fiddler on the Roof* in Massachusetts in 1972. One of the highlights of my life! But my interest in Star Trek itself waned a bit for a while, limited to just watching an occasional rerun. Then when I heard there was going to be a movie, my interest became stronger than ever, and I started collecting books, articles, anything I could find. My books alone number over fifty, and the collection is still growing!

I really can't add much to what has already been said about the first ST movie, so I think I'll just comment on *The Wrath of Khan*. To put it simply, I loved it, absolutely loved it! As DeForest Kelley said, "This is Star Trek I." What he meant, of course, was this is the movie that should have been made in the first place. Although I have a *few* criticisms that I'd like to mention ('I'm sorry, I can't help it, I'm a Virgo), my overall reaction is, to quote Khan, excellent, excellent.

This movie had everything—exciting plot and subplot, realistic and interesting characters, warmth, humor, love, danger, tragedy, and edge-of-your-seat thrills. I'm disappointed by a few of the reviews by newspaper and TV critics. They obviously totally misunderstood it, didn't try to, or didn't care. Some described Ricardo Montalban's Khan as "silly," "overplayed," and "hilariously miscast." They totally missed the point of who he was and why he acted as he did. And he couldn't be miscast, as he originated the role fifteen years ago. No matter, really, since the good reviews greatly outnumbered the bad.

There were fine performances by everyone in the movie. William Shatner's Kirk was more mellow as he struggled with middle age and failing eyesight (Jim Kirk, of all people, forced to depend on glasses—a nice, funny touch, making him appear quite vulnerable), the admiralcy he doesn't really want, the irony of *his* ship now in the command of his dearest friend, fatherhood (talk about your past catching up with you!), and finally the death of the aforementioned dearest friend.

Leonard Nimoy as Spock was, as always, terrific. Spock seems to have finally integrated both sides of himself to become a more complete person, more relaxed, more at home with himself, unself-consciously letting emotions come to the surface when appropriate, while retaining that lovely Vulcan dignity.

There is a lot of controversy among the fans over Spock's death. There was a rumor that it was Leonard Nimoy who had Spock "killed off," but that's not true. It appears that the people who made the movie were looking for dramatic effect. What could be more heart-wrenching to the fans than to have their beloved Mr. Spock die?

Personally, at first I felt very upset about the whole thing, and wished they could have found a better way to achieve that drama. But the story was written, is very good, and in the course of events as they were, there was really no other choice. Spock had to do what he did, and it was a noble sacrifice indeed. "The needs of the many outweigh the needs of the few or the one," he said, a quote that will go down in Star Trek history along with one of my favorites, "There are always possibilities."

I have heard that the third Star Trek movie's working title is *In Search of Spock*, and Leonard Nimoy has signed to star in it. The fans have just barely gotten over the shock of Spock's death, when it now appears that he will be revived in some way! My first reaction was: Unfair! Wrong! I did not want, as David Gerrold described it, my "grief jerked out from under me." It's not right to play with our emotions that way. It would also make meaningless the lesson that Kirk was supposed to learn at the end of the movie, that you can't cheat death.

Perhaps this would be a good topic for one of you to write an article on, including the theories on how they plan to revive Spock. For instance, will the Genesis Planet have anything to do with it?

The rest of the crew was wonderful, also. McCoy (whom I adore as much as Spock), Scotty, Uhura, and Sulu (none of whom had much to do, unfortunately), Chekov (how come he's the only one who seems to have gotten somewhere in his career in Starfleet?)—all terrific. I especially liked Kirstie Alley in her role as Lieutenant Saavik. A very welcome addition to the *Enterprise* family. One question, though: If she's a cadet, why does she have the rank of lieutenant?

I imagine we will be seeing much more of David Marcus in

future movies, as he and Jim Kirk establish their new father-son relationship. But probably Jim and Carol Marcus will remain just friends, as there is too much time and distance and there are too many painful memories for them to start over again.

Right after I saw the movie, I read the novelization by Vonda McIntyre. She was an excellent choice to adapt the script to novel form. Her original novel *The Entropy Effect* was one of the best. She obviously loves and understands the characters, and she was able to add much detail and a lot of her own ideas to the story without taking anything away from the original script. Although there were some small differences between the novel and the movie, they're probably just last-minute changes made during the filming of the movie.

On the subject of novels, there have been quite a few good ones published in the past few years. Unfortunately, there have been a few bad ones, too. My personal favorites (besides *The Entropy Effect*) are the two books by Kathleen Sky, *Vulcan* and *Death's Angel*; *The Price of the Phoenix* and its sequel, *The Fate of the Phoenix*, by Sondra Marshak and Myrna Culbreath; *The Covenant of the Crown* by Howard Weinstein; *The Klingon Gambit* by Robert E. Vardeman; *Planet of Judgment* by Joe Haldeman; and *The New Voyages 1 & 2* by Marshak and Culbreath. All of these were well-written and enjoyable stories.

In your *Best of Trek #5* article "The Myth and Journey of Dr. McCoy," Joyce Tullock mentions at the end that McCoy had been bragging about a grandchild in, the way I read it, the first ST movie. I don't remember that, or am I mistaken—does he have a grandchild, and where and when was this fact established?

I think I've finally "written myself out" and I will close this letter saying, Live long and prosper, and keep up the good work!

Ann Ice
Crystal River, FL

When I bought *The Best of Trek #4* I was absolutely delighted with it. That was only about three months ago. I immediately wanted to subscribe to *Trek*. Now, before I begin to tell you why I didn't, let me give you a little background.

I am fifty-two years old. In 1966 my children were twelve, ten, and three. We all watched Star Trek from the very first show (my husband, too). My husband missed the third season because he was in Vietnam, but the rest of us watched it faithfully. It was because of Star Trek that my older son (twelve) became an avid science fiction reader. Though I loved Star Trek, I never got into SF, in spite of the fact that I am always reading *something*. We watched the reruns until 1973, when we were sent to Germany for four years. By 1979 when we returned I thought Star Trek was all but dead, although the kids and I were delighted to find a station in Washington, D.C., that was still showing the series. Then my husband retired and we moved to Florida and I went to work full-time. When *Star Trek: The Motion Picture* was released we all flooded into the theater to see it. Wonderful! I loved it! Between videotape and videodiscs, I guess I've seen it about a dozen times now. (I don't own a machine, but my son does.) After *STTMP* there was nothing until *Star Trek II*. Again we all trooped to the theater. Super! I loved every moment and wept when Spock died (but I don't believe for a moment that he's gone forever, since he "landed" on the Genesis Planet!).

Now I come back to the beginning of this epistle. By this time I had become a co-owner of a small bookstore. All of a sudden we began receiving Star Trek books *and* I had finally succumbed to the urgings of my kids and begun reading science fiction. ("Mom, *try* it! I know you'd like it, if you'd just read a few of them!") My word! All of a sudden I discovered a whole new universe and couldn't get enough of it! I bought every piece of Star Trek lore I could find and "discovered" Isaac Asimov, Piers Anthony, Frank Herbert, Arthur Clarke, Jerry Pournelle, and Carl Sagan. Star Trek was/is my favorite, though.

As I began to collect the books about Star Trek, I suddenly found that there were still fans out there like me (I thought) who couldn't get enough of it. My husband began to tease me about being a "Trekkie." (My daughter: "Dad, she always was a 'closet' Trekkie! She's just come out of the closet, that's all!") I guess I was a "closet" Trekkie, because I didn't know until 1982 (!) that there were such things as conventions, clubs, fanzines, etc. I found I'm not alone in finding this out so late. Why, I wonder? I didn't live in a vacuum.

I agree with Mr. Irwin that *Star Trek: The Motion Picture* improves the more you see it, and with others who say that the book enhances the viewing, too.

At the end of *Best of Trek #5* there was a footnote to Mr. Irwin's article ("Love in Star Trek") that future issues of *Trek* would include articles on such things as ST fiction, animated series, fan fiction, etc. I hope so. My feeling is that recent ST fiction is superior stuff. My favorites are *The Abode of Life. The*

Galactic Whirlpool, *The Entropy Effect*, and *Trek to Madworld*. Among the nonfiction I am most fond of *Chekov's Enterprise*, *I Am Not Spock*, and *The Making of Star Trek*. I know there are Star Trek books I've not been able to get (or don't even know about!), and like one of your contributors I too would like to see a complete listing of Star Trek literature—fiction, nonfiction, and magazines. I study publisher's backlists but it doesn't always help.

I agree with your contributors that *no one* else could ever be Kirk, Spock, McCoy, or any of the other regulars. Like them, however, I can see Star Trek continuing with new characters on a new ship as long as the Star Trek fundamentals are followed. I too would like to see Star Trek as a three-or-four-times-a- year TV movie special, *or* a once-a-year theatrical movie. My only request is, please don't let it die! I hope the books keep coming from SF writers, too. There is one advantage for them—they don't have to spend time developing characters, but can get right into the story.

Kim Webb
Columbia, Mo.

I've been a devoted follower of Star Trek for as long as I can remember (I was only five in 1966). Naturally I have all the books I've been able to get my hands on. I especially appreciate the *Concordance*. It's very useful for settling arguments (I usually win).

What has really triggered my enthusiasm is the new movie, *The Wrath of Khan*. It is a masterpiece, everything a good Star Trek show should be, only bigger and better. That's really the crew of the *Enterprise* up there, not just caricatures of them, this time. There's also a feeling of continuity involved with Khan. I *know* what happened before and it's like seeing an old acquaintance again. The uniforms were great, also. The last time it looked as though they were wearing pajamas. These had a much trimmer, "military" look.

I loved Khan. He's definitely one of the all-time great villains. Strangely enough, I never really hated him, despite the destruction he caused. Instead, I understood his motives and I sympathized. I do think there should have been more direct reference to Marla McGivers.

I didn't think it fair that all of Khan's people were dragged down with him (so much for oaths of loyalty). What if, for instance, someone had been left behind on Ceti Alpha V? I've actually started writing a story based on this premise, a "historic occasion" for me. Once I was assigned to write a short story in junior high. I did so, but there was a good deal of kicking and screaming involved. I did get an A, but I didn't enjoy the experience. Lately, however, I've been coming up with so many ideas that I've just had to start writing. New characters keep appearing and I follow along to see what happens. I have no idea how the story will end; I won't know until it's finished.

Wasn't the music in *Wrath of Khan* perfect? It was a refreshing change from John Williams. Now, I happen to like Williams's music very much, but I also like a little variation in style, and James Horner did a great job. He even got some of the original theme in there. I missed that very much in the first movie. The music on the TV series was an intergral part of the show, and when I heard the intro music, I sat back and said, "This *is* Star Trek!" (And everyone told me to shut up and watch the show.)

Kathy Coleman
Tucson, Ariz.

I must be one of the newest Trekkers around, but I'm off to a good start. I really started when our local station ran a Trek festival, and I watched all twenty-two hours. Then I saw *The Wrath of Khan*, and I was hooked! (I've now seen it fourteen times.)

But the syndicated ST went off the air for the summer and I've had to rely on all the books I've managed to find, including yours. Mostly I enjoy Leslie Thompson's articles, especially "The Klingons" and "Star Trek Mysteries—Solved!" I'd also like to answer some of the questions in the Fan Poll. (By the way—there is a typo in the headline of this article in *The Best of Trek #1*—it reads "TREK FAN POLL RESUTS." The "L" is missing.)

1. My top ten favorite episodes: (1) "Mirror, Mirror," (2) "Charlie X," (3) "City on the Edge of Forever," (4) "Space Seed," (5) "The Trouble with Tribbles," (6) "The Devil in the Dark," (7) "Where No Man Has Gone Before," (8) "Journey to Babel," (9) "The Corbomite Maneuver," and (10) "Plato's Stepchildren."

2. Favorite character: No, not Spock—Dr. Leonard McCoy (by the way, I really liked the article on him by Walter Irwin).

3. Hard to answer number three. Every character contributed

equally, I'd have to say. I'm an actress myself and I know from experience that a show is nothing without everyone contributing equally. This goes for leads, supporting, extras.

4. My answer to this one is greatly influenced by the recent movie. My favorite villain is, of course, Khan Noonian Singh; then the Romulan commander in "The Enterprise Incident." A comment on this, though: Why was the Horta listed as a villain?

5. Male guest star: Here's another showing of a little influence. My favorite was—you guessed it—Ricardo Montalban.

6. Favorite female star; Jane Wyatt as Amanda.

The rest of the questions seem to have a great deal to do with the ST movie, not then released. By the way, *Star Trek: The Motion Picture* left a lot to be desired. The only thing I really liked was the closing sequence, when everything seemed to get back on track and Jim said, "Out there—thataway." It was a very fitting ending. My major complaint about *STTMP* is in comparing it to *Wrath of Khan*, and even in the episode "Space Seed," Khan said that the *Botany Bay* was lost in space two hundred years before, in the year 1996. So on that basis, I'd place *STTMP* in about 2215 or so, or the beginning of the twenty-third century. Yet when they found V'Ger, they discovered that it was Voyager 6, and Decker announces, "That was launched over three hundred years ago!" This would put the launch of Voyager 6 at about 1915 or earlier. *1915*?

Mr. Irwin, last night I read your review of *STTMP* in *The Best of Trek #3*, and then I heartily disagreed on all counts, except that each time I had seen it, I liked it better. Well, today I saw it again (it's running this month on *HBO*) and I realized that most of what you said was true. But some of it . . . Well, can you actually say it was on a par with *Casablanca* and *Gone with the Wind*? *STTMP* could have been whittled down to an hour and a half without any serious harm to the story.

For instance, you commented on "the long, lingering look" Kirk and Scotty gave the *Enterprise* from the shuttle. That long, lingering look lasted a full four minutes and forty-eight seconds! And without any dialogue! I started timing after Kirk's line "You're right" and stopped when the shuttle docked. Four minutes of nothing! Then at least ten minutes were wasted while the *Enterprise* crawled into V'Ger. During this period of no dialogue, we were treated to a look at V'Ger, Uhura looking shocked, V'Ger, then Ilia looking shocked, V'Ger, Kirk, V'Ger, Spock, V'Ger, Sulu, V'Ger, Uhura, V'Ger, Illia, V'Ger, Decker, V'Ger, Kirk, V'Ger, the bridge crew. More V'Ger, more close closeups of familiar shocked faces. The only really spectacular shots were the shots of the tiny *Enterprise* against the vastness of V'Ger.

And I didn't think much of the characterizations. The only one with any real resemblance to the original was Dr. McCoy. He had the best lines, as well.

But after seeing the movie seven times, I must say that I finally, really, honestly liked it. After several more times, maybe I'll find it as *great* as you said it was. Now, compare *STTMP* to *The Wrath of Khan*. I tend to agree with De Forest Kelley when he said, "*The Wrath of Khan* should be Star Trek I."

I've read more of *BOT #3* and every time I hit the Roundtable, I am struck with an overpowering desire to write. Karen Ellis's comments on "Amok Time" were extremely logical, even though she never saw the show itself. (Actually, I only saw *most* of the episode—I saw it during the aforementioned Trek festival, and "Amok Time" was my seventeenth episode in a row. I fell asleep during the commercial and missed the end—i.e., the fight with Jim, and the ending—and my best Trek fan/friend wouldn't tell me about it. I had to get hints about it from *Meaning in Star Trek* and the *Star Trek Catalog*.) I also enjoyed Dorothy Bradley's letter. She is very up on "Space Seed," and I heartily agree with her comment about Houston's "Rise of the Federation" and his handling of Khan's exile.

Michael Kolecke
South Elgin, Ill.

I would like to discuss how Spock will be able to return to Star Trek since he supposedly dies in *The Wrath of Khan* (which I have appropriately retitled "The Wrath of NBC"). The obvious answer to this question is that somehow the Genesis Wave will "rebirth" him (perhaps this is a bad word to use, as I really don't want him to be reborn, but to come back as he was). But how will this happen?

Well, according to Vonda McIntyre's adaptation, the Genesis scientists are apparently also computer programmers (as defined in our twentieth-century terms), or at least Vance and Del are. Also, I take it that Vonda is either a programmer herself or has learned the buzz words to be able to talk technically and know what she is saying. From what I get out of this, being a software programmer myself, Genesis is nothing more than a computer program (although a very, very large one), and like all programs it can only do what the programmers tell it to do.

(This is assuming that they still program like this in the twenty-third century, and since the only computer that I can recall in Star Trek that had independent thought processing was the M5 Unit—and that one failed—I have to assume that computers are still "dumb".)

Evidently, since Genesis can only do what it was programmed to do, nothing can exist on the newly created system unless Genesis has the information. This is partly supported by the scene when Saavik looks at a water-worn stone and marvels at the complexity of the Genesis Wave. It was this way because the Genesis Program had the information to do it.

This being the case, how can we expect Spock to be reborn if he was not in the original Genesis Program? Well, one possibility could be that he was introduced after the original world was formed, but before the life forms were created (Carol tells Jim that the life forms took a little longer). Now a computer program can only do what it's told to do, and if any foreign element enters the system that the program can't handle, then the program usually no longer operates the way it is expected to. It can produce unpredictable results, and can also "abend" (this is a technical term used lovingly by us people to indicate that the programmer failed to cover all the bases in writing the program). So one of the possibilities in the Genesis Program was the failure to account for this after the Genesis system was formed, and somehow Spock would be reborn because of the lack of programming.

But is this unlikely event possible? Because the Genesis Program was so large ("Boojum Hunt" was 50meg, which is about ten times larger than the current IBM MVS nucleus, which is supposed to be state-of-the-art, and "Boojum Hunt" seemed to be a mere speck in all the bubble memory that Carol had in spacelab), and there were relatively few scientists/programmers compared to the size of the Genesis Program, then it is extremely possible for Genesis to have subtle programming errors.

So one would think that it is possible for Spock to be reborn. However, there should be other pieces of matter that could fall into the newly formed system, such as meteors, asteroids, and maybe even a starship, so I would think that this possibility should be accounted for in the Genesis Program. And if it was, it would be likely that the program would just leave them as they are, that it would just ignore them. So why should it treat a dead body in any special way? So I don't think that Spock's falling into the Genesis World would make any difference to the Genesis Program and Spock would still be dead!

Can there be any other possibilities relating to the Genesis Wave? Probably—"There are always possibilities." I've been thinking, but of course, there is the answer that is so simple that I am too blinded to see it, and if that is so, well, I just hope that it is an acceptable explanation that makes sense scientifically and is sensible.

I do have another question, though. What will this do to the new novels that are bound to be published between this and the next movie? How will the authors handle Spock's demise? To me, there are three possibilities: They can leave Spock out of the book (no good); they can ignore the movie (Trek fans don't want to do that); or the novel can be star-dated before the movie. The last might be the best, although this could cause problems also. There are other possibilities, I'm sure.

I hope that I don't sound as if I am putting down the movie, because I thought that it was excellent! Ricardo Montalban is a superb actor, and I am very pleased that he was chosen again to play Khan and that he wanted to do it. It just goes to show what Star Trek has in the magic of all its actors! It was not "just another TV show"!

Well, I hope I didn't get too boring in this letter. I have ended up with a lot of questions, and Sarek has said if you have questions, but no answers, then that is a start in the right direction. So I've started. Does anybody else have answers that I can't see?

Susan Biedron
Chicago, Ill.

I was really bowled over by the new movie *Star Trek II: The Wrath of Khan* and would like to offer my comments and observations. First of all, in comparison with the first movie, this one had a much more understandable plot as well as a lot more depth and warmth. What particularly made it enjoyable for me were the touches of humor—the one-liners, so to speak, throughout the film. I was particularly impressed with the new character of Lieutenant Saavik. Perhaps I am imagining things, but I detected a spark of something between her and Kirk. The special effects were superb—especially the battle scenes between the two starships. Also, the new theme is really beautiful!

Needless to say, I was deeply saddened by Spock's death—but felt it was tastefully done, as well as beautifully acted. The part after Spock has incapacitated McCoy with the neck pinch (I *knew* he would do that!) and established the Vulcan mind meld really moved me. I didn't have a dry eye throughout that scene.

I can't wait to see how Spock is going to be written back in for the third movie. They'll have to find a genius to write that script!

In closing, I would like to add a personal observation. It involves the scene at the end in which Kirk goes to reach for his glasses and finds the one lens shattered. I interpret that the glasses might represent Kirk and Spock's relationship (two halves forming to make a whole) and the broken lens might symbolize the break (Spock's dying) in that relationship. It may be of no significance whatsoever, but it is just a thought which occurred to me.

Peter Davidson
Calgary, Alberta, Canada

As a lover of Star Trek and all it stands for, I felt that I simply could not let the opening of *Wrath of Khan* go by without expressing my feelings concerning the movie.

Just as with many a Trekker, I'm sure, I awaited the arrival of the second movie in the series with anxious anticipation. The month of May was more of a countdown toward June 4 than anything else. The last few days before the opening were spent in a sort of daze, waiting for one of the most important events of the year. This feeling of anticipation stayed with me right up until *the day*, and when it finally arrived and I was sitting in the theater, it seemed just too good to be true.

Unfortunately, it did turn out to be too good to be true. The first few scenes of the movie showed great promise. Seeing the inside of Starfleet was quite a bonus, and despite the poor quality of the soundtrack, the dialogue between Kirk and his friends on his birthday showed a surprising amount of humanity.

However, it was from this point on that the movie failed for me. From the rather violent episode on Khan's planet, the movie continued to sink deeper and deeper into a mood of depression rather than optimism. The pleasant exchanges between our favorite characters were all but drowned out by the excessive preoccupation with fighting and death. What, for example, was the need to have Mr. Chekov's brain eaten out? Or to have the young cadet in engineering killed? Or to show us the slaughtered people at the space outpost? By the time the hopefulness of Genesis was introduced, it was too late to salvage a film based predominantly on sensationalism.

Perhaps, it could be argued, the battle scenes were just more realistic than usual (although having Scotty cart the nearly dead cadet Preston up to the bridge instead of to sick bay hardly seems realistic to me!), my point is that they did not need to be. The philosophy of Star Trek as I understand it is one of peace and hopefulness for the future, one in which the human adventure is just beginning. Well, if this is the type of adventure humans have to look forward to, I'm certainly glad I'm not a part of it. *Wrath of Khan* ran more like a *Space: 1999* episode than a Star Trek one. The humanity and meaningfulness of the movie hinted at from the start were sacrificed in the name of gore and special effects.

My only hope is that by the time *Star Trek III* rolls around, Mr. Roddenberry will have realized that if the basic, meaningful ideals of Star Trek are to be preserved, he must take a more active role in the creation stages of the movie. Otherwise, Star Trek will have lost forever that special quality which has endeared it to so many over the past fifteen years.

Lisa Siege
Kingwood, Texas

My first encounter with Star Trek was in the summer of 1982 when I saw the second motion picture. Intrigued by the remarkable characterization as well as by the characters themselves, I worked backwards, watching all the reruns I could, plus the first motion picture (on cable TV).

By now I've realized what it is about Star Trek that fascinates me so—the entire phenomenon surrounding the life and hard times of Star Trek's main idea: a starship and its crew with "an ongoing mission to explore strange new worlds," etc. The fact that a TV series' reruns are more popular than the series was itself, along with the cultlike following that enables conventions to be held with attendance consistently numbering several thousand, shows the immense power of a good idea to survive and succeed—a power available only to a production willing to work together to keep such an idea alive.

I would very much like this phenomenon to continue and grow—but as a more or less outsider looking in, I can see something leading to the destruction of this saga. The members of the crew of *anything* have to work as a team to be successful. If one tries to outshine another, they are no longer a team, so they will fall apart and be destroyed.

This concept is an old one, but the actors and actresses who play the members of the crew/team should learn to live by it. So many times I've heard the supporting-cast role players complain about not having enough to do on the series or in the movies. Being in Walter Koenig's, George Takei's, Nichelle Nichols', or James Doohan's situation, where they are best known for supporting roles, can, I'm sure, be frustrating for a performer. What these people should realize is that a work of art such as this cannot have several starring roles. Some *must* be costars; otherwise the adventures of the starship *Enterprise* would become *The Love Boat* in space.

It would be tragic if a future production had to be canceled because actor X refused to perform because actor Y had Z more lines of a dialogue. Such a creation should be above and beyond that. Keep the teamwork of Star Trek and keep the idea alive.

Doris Skiba
Shawboro, N.C.

I have seen *Wrath of Khan* twice (so far) and read Vonda McIntyre's novelization. If I could narrow it down to a few words, I think my frame of mind at the moment can be summed up in one glorious statement: *Star Trek Lives!*

Oh yes, you say, Star Trek has been alive (and well and thriving, no less) for years now. I agree wholeheartedly, but for me, to *see* and *experience* this living, breathing manifestation of the Star Trek idea is an occasion for celebration! The great charm of the ST television series has been endlessly discussed by fans, and I think most everyone would agree that its unique spirit came from the interaction of beloved characters inside just-plain-good stories. Those stories sometimes had profound things to say. Sometimes they were a romp and other times the story was flawed but was saved in the end by the intricate interaction of our good friends on the *Enterprise*. I liked *STTMP* and was overjoyed to see *something* (anything) visual after so many years, but the dynamic action/reaction of characters is not the focal point of this film. I am reminded of the man dying of thirst, who, upon being offered water, complained bitterly that it wasn't Perrier. I won't tear apart *STTMP* . . . we were lucky to get it, no matter how many weak points it may have had. If it had not been for the financial success of *STTMP*, *Wrath of Khan* would never have been made. . . .

But it *was* made, and in it, I think, there is a return to the integrity of the series. ST has remained alive *all these years* because its very core—its spirit—speaks so clearly to so many people. If that spirit is not faithfully followed in the making of any ST material, book or film, the end product is handicapped or even unrecognizable. Imagine someone producing a Sherlock Holmes film with a short, stout, accordion-playing Holmes . . . I suppose it's possible, but one wonders: Is there any point in the exercise? The group of people who brought us *Wrath of Khan* came together in an effort that *understands* the ST ideal and operates therefrom with much success. Whoever is behind the return to the real essence of ST should be heartily congratulated for outwitting "the powers that be" . . . the people with the purse strings have demonstrated repeatedly that they do not and don't care to understand what it is they have. Perhaps the fact that the grosses from *Wrath of Khan* (which was modestly produced, I might add) are breaking box-office records right and left will *finally* bring home to them what we fans have been patiently telling them all along: Allow ST to be what it is and the profits will take care of themselves. I hold few illusions about the corporate mentality . . . I won't hold my breath, but it's a thought!

This new film does a lot of things that we have been hoping for . . . like using snatches of the Alexander Courage TV theme. ST will always be associated with that music, and it was like coming home to hear it again. There is a joyful return of that old ST humor, too. One of the funniest moments in the film is when Kirk, after getting one of McCoy's famous lectures, says, "Don't mince words, Bones, tell me what you *really* think." There are some delightful moments in the book as well. Spock instructs Saavik to set the course for "out there," the technical term for which is "thataway." Now, this is *vintage* ST! I was pleased to see some of the old ST characters in more than virtual stand-in roles. I think ST fans are interested in the fortunes of the old crew . . . like Scotty's precocious nephew, and Sulu's upcoming first command. Mr. Kyle is even there with a very dashing goatee. I missed Christine Chapel . . . maybe next time?

I really enjoyed the exploration of the age of the principals in *Wrath of Khan*. After all, its been fifteen years since the series and we haven't yet developed a stasis field to keep actors from aging. *The Wrath of Khan* has a very human Kirk expressing human distress about the process of aging. . . . it reminds us of how young the *Enterprise* crew was on her five-year mission and we are asked to consider whether the cadets on this training cruise are made of the same fine stuff. Young Peter Preston's (Scotty's nephew, as revealed in the book) heroic sacrifice to stay at his station says that the *Enterprise* does indeed have an honorable crew! (Peter is *fourteen*! When I was fourteen I dreamed of being an explorer in space . . . at age fourteen Peter *is* one! Amazing!) In discussing age in *Wrath of Khan*, there is also the strong feeling that young is not necessarily better. Our society tends to discard its old people. In this film Kirk (who must be in his fifties) and McCoy (who is in his sixties) are still valuable, functioning people and probably will be until they drop. If we can accept aging (and certainly death, in the context of the movie) as a natural progression, then we have found yet another boundless avenue of freedom to explore . . . freedom from fear.

I must return to my great pleasure in seeing the characters I love so well in logical continuations of their personalities from the series. Whatever turmoil Spock was going through in giving up *Kolinahr* in STTMP seems to have given way to his finding and accepting his own special place in the galaxy. It has always seemed a shame to me that Spock, whom so many rightly admire and love, cannot even *like* himself. In *Wrath of Khan*, Spock gives every indication that he is "easy in his skin"; he has at last embraced his unique self. He appears at peace or even (dare I say it) happy. There is something so right about Spock riding herd over a bunch of children. Here is a place for him to pass on those things he learned at the cost of much inner pain . . . particularly to Saavik. Since he seems more at one with himself, who better to advise her to be true to herself, rather than strait-jacket herself into someone else's idea of perfection? He has certainly been down that road!

Kirk is still going through the same inner battle to meet the impossible standards he sets for himself. He learns a valuable lesson in *Wrath of Khan* about living the life he is best suited for. McCoy is his old lovable self too. In STTMP all the major characters were tied in such knots inside themselves that the old feelings never came through. They're okay now, and this film is that much better for it.

I want to say a few words about the death of Spock in *Wrath of Khan*. All during the TV series, the very best moments were

those times of *pathos*, when one or a combination of the characters lost something (or thought they lost something) in order to
achieve the greater good. Those times of audience interaction,
identifying with our beloved friends' pain and loss, allows us to
get in touch with similar feelings in our own lives. ST takes
fictional characters (and it is difficult for me to concede this, as I
come more and more to believe that the ST people are actually
living beings in some fashion and not just fictional, but that is
another story) in a world alien to our own and makes us *love*
them, and further, *cry* for them! The death of Spock is a *tremendous
cathartic experience* for the audience. Here we are, emotionally
overstimulated by intensely desiring a physical manifestation of
ST that proceeds faithfully from the ST we loved on TV. We
have been, seemingly, thwarted at every turn by "them" and by
fate. There is also the extremely strong unspoken desire for
Spock to come to terms with himself and his feelings for Kirk so
that their friendship will have actual spoken expression without
shame or embarrassment from either. Add to this the suspense of
the plot in *Wrath of Khan* at that moment.

So off Spock goes, only to be stopped by McCoy . . . McCoy,
who does love and admire Spock. He can't let Spock commit
suicide, no matter how much good would come of the action.
McCoy succumbs to the infamous Spock pinch. Spock lets Bones
gently down to the deck, giving him the mind touch with the
message "*Remember.*" (Remember what? Spock himself? Is he
leaving a message for Kirk? Is he perhaps telling McCoy to
arrange to have the coffin deposited on the new Genesis world
after it's all over? Is he telling McCoy that he's not really
committing suicide?) When Kirk sees Spock, in extreme pain
and dying before his eyes, we *know* what he is feeling . . .
intense grief, guilt, helplessness, rage. . . . Spock, with super-
Vulcan effort, struggles to his feet, *straightens his uniform* (how
true to form this is), and manages to walk to the side of the
booth outside of which Kirk is standing. He bumps into the wall
because he is blind and we grieve that this tower of dignity is
fighting so hard to maintain control. "Do not grieve for me," he
says to Kirk, telling him he is at peace with his decision. "I am
and always have been your friend." Kirk and Spock try to touch
in the Vulcan salute, but the glass prevents their touching. How
cruel this is. God, what a *scene!* I defy anyone who has the least
feeling for ST to remain tearless through this scene. All that is
truest and best of all the characters comes through . . . with the

irony that Spock finally makes his verbal affirmation of friendship to Kirk seconds before he dies.

The funeral scene has impact, too. We as a society place a great deal of value on self-control. We don't cry very often. As a matter of fact, unless some tragedy is extremely personal, we don't feel anything much anymore. This absolutely touching, gut-wrenching scene is a gift to us, to let us get in touch with feelings of grief, loss, and hopelessness that we have buried deep inside. We cry for Kirk and Spock and we cry for ourselves. To really experience joy, you must descend to the depths of sorrow. It is a test of character . . . how we deal with death is at least as important as how we deal with life. Sounds familiar. Then, as if this were not gift enough, after this enormous catharsis, *Wrath of Khan* gives us *hope* as well. Quite an accomplishment for a movie. I'm not surprised at all. *This is Star Trek*.

I do not believe that Spock is dead. Whatever new and life-generating force is happening on the Genesis Planet will regenerate his lifeless body. Kirk believes it himself, or wants to. He says that if Genesis really is life out of death, he must return to this planet. He will return to find Spock reborn out of the raging fire of radiation that took his life, ready to take his place at Kirk's side. In the continuing voyages of the Starship *Enterprise*, can there be *any* doubt that our beloved friends will be at the helm, taking us with them where no man has gone before? When Carol Marcus speaks of carrying Genesis to its logical conclusion, what is the conclusion? Life from death. Edith Keeler says in "City" that Spock looks as though he belongs at Kirk's side, has always been there and always will be there. Spock says in *Wrath of Khan*, "I am yours." Their relationship stops just short of symbiosis. I'm sure that Spock will find the experience of renewal fascinating! With Spock physically reborn, and Kirk at last spiritually renewed, feeling young again, we are truly ready for those continuing voyages. I for one am dying for the next one to begin!

Sherin Vang
San Francisco, Calif.

I came to Star Trek a little late, never having seen a single episode until they were well into syndication. But once I found it, I treasured it, watching every single one over and over. Now I've grown a little more discriminating (incidentally, I was gratified to see that most of my favorite and least-favorite episodes agree pretty much with the choices of your readers). But except for the Blish novelizations of the TV series, and the earliest nonfiction books, those episodes were my only contact with the world of Star Trek. I did try going to a convention several years ago, but I guess I'm just not the crowd type. I've never repeated the experiment, and for years now, I've felt cut off from the mainstream of Star Trek fandom. I'm not even sure what to call myself. I *know* I'm not a Trekkie, but as I understand the definition of a Trekker, I know I'm not enough involved to be one. Is there some sort of middle ground for us middle-aged, single women who just don't fit in anywhere else?

Anyway, a little over a month ago, I saw *Star Trek II: The Wrath of Khan*, and it rekindled my enthusiasm. *This* is the movie I wish Paramount had made the first time around. The first one was okay, I guess, but this one . . . well, all I can say is, I've seen it six times already, and certainly plan to go back a few more times. And your books have really helped in my added enjoyment of the film, giving me a depth of understanding I just didn't have before.

Let me be a little more specific. I can't pretend to understand the heavily technical articles, but I read them anyway, hoping a little of the knowledge will rub off on me. But then, I never really *cared* how the transporter or the warp-drive engines worked. They were things I accepted on faith, the same way I accept television. What I really love about *Trek* is the simply marvelous in-depth analyses of characters, cultures, etc., truly inspiring feats of informed speculation, always carefully rooted in what we really *know* about these things. A year or so ago, I would have thought this sort of accomplishment was relatively easy, but lately, I've been trying my hand at writing fiction, and now I know just how difficult it is. So my hat's off to your wonderful contributors, especially Leslie Thompson. What an intricate mind she must have, and how well she expresses herself!

I guess I've come to the point where I should say something about "what Star Trek means to me." You know, in all the years I've been devoted to the program, I never really tried to put my feelings into words. Now that I sit in front of the typewriter, it's not easy. First of all, I agree totally with countless others that part of its appeal is the feeling of optimism, that we *will* have a future we can look forward to. But it's more than that, at least for me. Most of all, I'm drawn to the sense of reality. Unlike films like *Star Wars*, *Superman*, *E.T.*, etc., in which I, at least, never forget for a moment that what I am watching is fantasy, Star Trek always seems so *possible*. I feel I'm watching the activities and adventures of people I know really well (perhaps that was what I didn't like about *Star Trek: The Motion Picture*—I felt that I suddenly *didn't* know the characters), and because of this sense of reality and intimacy, when something terrible happens, it is *personally* painful, because it's happening to someone I know and care about.

Well, it's just struck me that I've been babbling, but I have literally no one else I can talk to about Star Trek. Friends and family look upon my devotion to a show canceled thirteen years ago as a sort of affliction which they choose to overlook. So I've inflicted myself on you. I hope whoever gets the task of reading this isn't bored to tears. I'm sure you've heard all of this before, many times.

SPOCK RESURRECTUS—OR, NOW THAT *THEY'VE* KILLED HIM, HOW DO *WE* GET HIM BACK?

by Pat Mooney

Pat Mooney (better known as "Wheelchair") has been a devout Star Trek fan from Day One—yet he had never written a word about the series until a series of discussions with Walter and G.B. bestirred him to do so. The result is the article you are about to read, and we think it's one of the finest first efforts we've ever seen. And we say that even though Pat has craftily taken all of our logical, rational and carefully wrought arguments and ripped them to shreds. Oh, well. . . .

To paraphrase the ancient dirge, "The Vulcan is dead! Long live the Vulcan!" For those of us who hold the Star Trek mythos just a little bit closer to our hearts than we would like to admit, the death of Mr. Spock is hard to accept. And if the sun shone a little bit dimmer as we left the theaters, well, we have put that behind us and are eagerly looking forward to *Star Trek III*, with its working title of *In Search of Spock*. For apparently Spock *will* return, the only questions being "How?" and "When?" Almost as if in answer to these questions, Kirk quotes Spock in *Wrath of Khan*: "There are always . . . possibilities." Naturally, the most likely possibility involves the use of the Genesis Effect (the script made that more obvious than necessary at the end of *Wrath of Khan*), but there are several other methods by which Mr. Spock might be revived, each consistent with previous episodes and the Star Trek universe. But each of these methods (including Genesis) also has problems.

First, we must uncategorically reject the idea of Spock's existing on a higher plane of consciousness. Fans will not stand for the illogic of Mr. Spock shimmering into view during a crisis situation and telling Captain Kirk to trust the Force and let his feelings go. That's fine and quite effective within the universe for which it was created, but it won't hold up in Star Trek's "reality." The less said about this "possibility" the better.

Having gotten that out of the way, let's consider the possibility of utilizing time travel as a means of preventing Spock from ever dying and thus neatly avoiding the question of how to bring him back.

The *Enterprise* crew have time-hopped several times, the most famous instance being the events in "City on the Edge of Forever." So we can have dreams of Captain Kirk determinedly leading a party of volunteers through the Guardian of Forever to arrive, say, on the bridge of the *Reliant* with phasers blasting.

This won't do, however. Not only is it out of character for Kirk, but there is no guarantee that such a commando raid would ever reach its target. Getting to the Time Portal itself is no problem, but the Guardian was made to offer its destinations at a given rate, which, in terms of the original episode, was "Perhaps a month, a week if we are fortunate." That's just not precise enough for the purpose at hand: A week too soon and Captain Terrell is still in command of a calm ship; a week too late, and there's no *Reliant* to land on. And all of those calculations assume the bridge of the *Reliant* is even offered as a potential destination by the Guardian!

In an earlier episode, "Tomorrow Is Yesterday," the *Enterprise* inadvertently went back in time because of a "slingshot effect." Even if Kirk and Scotty decided to utilize a handy star and duplicate this effect (as they did on Starfleet orders in "Assignment: Earth"), the *Enterprise* would then find itself in a time where it existed in two places at once. This is theoretically impossible, although the paradox was ignored in the animated episode "Yesteryear," in which Spock goes back into Vulcan's recent past to save his own life when a boy. (One rationale for this is that the adult Spock could coexist with his younger self only because he was trying to correct a flaw in time lines which he and the other members of the landing party knew to have occurred *since* their arrival on the Guardian's planet—perhaps even *because* of that arrival.)

Of course, the *Enterprise* could avoid the problem of being in two places at one time by simply returning to the time of the Eugenics Wars, where a couple of well-placed photon torpedos would remove the threat of the *Botany Bay* before she even reached deep space.

The main problem with such a long-range jaunt is that old bugaboo about the effects of time travel increasing geometrically the farther back one goes. Beyond saving Spock's life, what effects would destroying the *Botany Bay* in the past have on the present as the crew of the *Enterprise* knows it? In fact, the ripple effect of Spock's death begins with that death, and any attempt to alter the time line created by it will have some effect—perhaps minor, perhaps major.

Also, what if the past cannot actually be changed? An action that saves Spock from death in the reactor room might set in motion a chain of events that would lead to his death on the bridge. Whether or not the past can actually be changed is a question which has never been satisfactorily answered on Star Trek: Do the actions of Gary Seven and the personnel of the *Enterprise* in "Assignment: Earth" fulfill history or change it? Could Dr. McCoy have affected the past in "City" if Spock and Kirk had not been present to set things right?

In any case, we can assume that Kirk would reject all time-travel options to save Spock as being too risky (although not without much soul-searching). Neither would the Federation order or authorize such a gamble; Spock was a valuable asset, but not an irreplaceable one. Besides, the two instances we can draw on as authorized time missions ("Assignment: Earth" and "Yesteryear") were for observation purposes only, and even then both almost led to disruption of the time flow known to the men and women of the *Enterprise*.

The second possibility to resurrect Spock is cloning. Cloning, though in reality little more than a primitive form of Genesis, has the added dramatic bonus of irony: The same forbidden science that gave us Khan would return Spock to us.

To clone, all one needs is the method and a tissue sample with which to begin the cloning process. Presumably, the procedural information would be an almost everyday facet of Federation science (any science which can construct Genesis has probably long since perfected cloning; it is likely that most of the Federation's food animals are cloned, for example), but obtaining permission from the Federation to clone a living being might prove difficult, as the horrors of the Eugenics Wars would have

instilled stringent taboos. Tissue samples of Spock would probably be available in a number of places; if nothing else, McCoy
would have taken them when he had to operate on Sarek and
cross-matched Spock's blood in "Journey to Babel." If no one
at the Federation can or will oversee the process, Kirk and
company could return to Phylos to seek the expertise of Dr.
Keniclius 5 and his giant Spock clone, "The Infinite Vulcan."
These two had solved the thorniest problem of cloning—duplication
of the subject's memory.

For without this methodology, a Spock clone—any clone—
would not be unlike the Spock body in "Spock's Brain," the
difference being that instead of a body with no brain, a cloned
Spock would have a body possessing a brain with nothing in it.
Were Spock regenerated in this way, he would have to be
reeducated à la Uhura in "The Changeling." This is certainly
feasible, and would doubtless delight Dr. McCoy, but the cloned
Spock, no matter how skillfully retaught, would miss out on the
millions of nuances a sentient being picks up just by living day
to day. (Unlike Uhura, whose original personality remained
beneath Nomad's overlaid "erasure"; as she regained factual
knowledge, her prelearned experience and nuances returned,
restoring her to normalcy.)

A Spock clone, however, would have no prelearned anything
on which to draw. For example, McCoy could and would tell the
new Spock that Kirk and McCoy are his best friends. Spock
would accept this—he'd have no reason to doubt it—but he
would have no memory of the friendship, no depth of shared
experiences, the kind of thing that develops only with the passage of time. Even the knowledge the clone received might be
colored by the memory of the teacher.

Because of the unique hybrid nature of Mr. Spock, another
problem comes to mind. Let's assume that Dr. McCoy tried to
train the Spock clone. Ultimately, McCoy would come to a
point—probably rather quickly—where he would realize that for
this new Spock to have any chance to resemble the original, he
must be trained on Vulcan to have full exposure to the Vulcan
Way. As the clone received this Vulcan training, however, he
would assimilate it as an adult rather than in the ongoing,
maturing way a growing child receives his education. Thus, the
Spock who would eventually return to Starfleet would in effect
have been raised in an environment "different" from the original
and would necessarily be a different person.

In fact, the entire cloning procedure might backfire because of this reeducation. Remember, the original Mr. Spock did indeed have emotions. His lifelong struggle was to control them, to suppress them in favor of the logical intellect. Spock's clone would have been told of these emotions, but deprived of the influence of a human mother through years of normal growth, he would feel them in only the most clinical sense, if at all. As he trained on Vulcan, it might thus be easier for the Spock clone to attain *Kolinahr*, in which case he would logically not wish to return to the *Enterprise*.

Obviously, then, cloning is unacceptable because it gives us the form but not the substance of Mr. Spock. An individual is the sum of his entire life—his knowledge, experiences, environment—and, more important, the simple action of day-to-day living. Such cannot be duplicated, even in the abstract. Even the loss of childhood would profoundly alter a clone's personality from that of the original; to lose an entire lifetime would produce a vastly different being. It is *Spock* we care about—the proverbial reasonable facsimile will not do.

However, there *is* just such a reasonable facsimile available; he exists in the universe of "Mirror, Mirror." Spock-M, we'll call him, is a true Mr. Spock. He is half human, half Vulcan, and as such would have been subject to the normal span of growing up in two cultures where neither really accepted him. In short, all of the developmental deficiencies of a Spock clone would not exist because Spock-M would have grown into what he is—nurtured rather than hatched, as it were.

Spock-M would still miss the brass ring in a crucial sense if he were tapped as a replacement for our Spock: There would be no relationship between him and his new captain, despite the fact that at least some of the fireworks between him and McCoy would soon develop. Spock-M might even be incapable of developing the ties of friendship, since the culture from which he came did not encourage friendship and trust. In any case, because of the vast differences in the societies of the two universes, Spock-M would be quite unlike our Mr. Spock, however similar their childhood struggles might have been. For example, you'll recall Spock-M didn't seem to have any moral objections to the Empire, he just felt it illogical to preserve a system doomed to self-destruct. It is very doubtful that Spock-M could fit into our scheme of things.

But the most important reason Spock-M could not be considered as a replacement for our Mr. Spock is also the simplest: Why would he want to be a replacement? This is, after all, not his universe. Between the time we last saw him and the proposed visit by the *Enterprise* to sign him up as Spock's replacement, he may have effected enough change to make his universe a better place for his purposes. Even if he hasn't, why would he want to change universes to become a surrogate friend to a man he has met only briefly? Logically, he would not, and therefore is unavailable to replace Spock.

We cannot believe that Jim Kirk would accept—or even want—such a surrogate, be it Spock-M, clone, or something else. To Kirk and McCoy, Spock was a friend, a very special individual, so why should they wish to replace him? But they might, however, try very hard to *revive* him. . . .

Which finally brings us to Genesis—which is probably where those who are behind Star Trek wanted us in the first place.

Sherlock Holmes, another beloved fictional character who would not die, might well have been speaking of Genesis when he said, "When you have eliminated the impossible, whatever remains, however improbable, must be the truth." That truth is "improbable" because, in terms of the film itself and in Vonda McIntyre's excellent novelization of *Wrath of Khan*, the detonation of the Genesis Device by Khan *cannot* result in the rebirth of Mr. Spock. That isn't to say we cannot use Genesis, but we aren't that far along yet.

When we last saw Mr. Spock, he had just saved the *Enterprise* from the effects of the expanding Genesis Wave. In doing this, however, he absorbed lethal doses of radiation from the ship's warp engines and died following one of the most moving farewells possible. Presumably, he was placed in the photon torpedo casing—as effective a coffin as any—and launched into space, finally coming to rest on the newly created Genesis World.

Here's where the problems arise. At this point, his body *must* be lifeless—even on a cellular level. If it is not—if, say, Mr. Spock had slowed his bodily processes to their absolute minimum—the Genesis Wave will destroy that living matter in favor of its preprogrammed matrix. At the beginning of the film, Dr. Carol Marcus is insistent that not even proto-life can exist on the test world, so all-consuming is the effect of Genesis. And even if the body is lifeless, the Genesis Wave will touch the casing and convert the inanimate matter both inside and out into fuel for its matrix. There might thus be a tree or a rock with pointed ears somewhere on the planet (!), but no trace of Spock's body should remain.

It is marginally possible that the Genesis effect had spent itself by the time the burial capsule made planetfall. Carol Marcus says that the Phase II (the Genesis Cave) matrix took a day to develop, but that vegetation and other life forms took longer, though still at an accelerated rate. This indicates that Genesis is an ongoing effect which continues at least until its program is fulfilled. One must assume that the larger the device, the longer the effect will continue, and the device set off by Khan was designed to terraform a world. Such an extensive program might take weeks, or even longer, to execute.

Nor is there any basis to assume that Mr. Spock will be reborn on the planet's surface as part of the Genesis process. There would have been no reason for any genetic information relevant to Spock to have been programmed into the test, nor any need to do so. Spock was, after all, completely healthy until three minutes before detonation, let alone matrix programming.

In fact, we don't have any idea what the programming was—or, ominously, what it might have become. Suppose Khan cracked the code for the matrix—considering his origin, he must have had more than a passing interest in eugenics—and reprogrammed it to suit his own ends? Presumably those ends would not have included Mr. Spock. Until we have evidence to the contrary, however, we must assume that Khan did not have either the time or the opportunity to reprogram the Genesis Device.

Since we were shown the torpedo casing resting undisturbed on the planet's surface, we must accept that there is a body inside, albeit one ravaged by radiation poisoning. Once presented with that coffin, we can grant an exception to the cold logic of Genesis and postulate that the interaction of the radiation in Spock's body with the brand-new kind of radiation created by and for Genesis caused the body to be preserved intact and with all damage repaired, but still inert and lifeless.

But Genesis provides an even simpler way of restoring Spock that does not require any stretch of logic. Nothing could be simpler than for Dr. Marcus to study Spock's genetic code and devise a small, completely insulated matrix dedicated solely to restoring the Vulcan. Spock's genetic code is probably on file in any number of places; as captain of a starship, he would have need of certain kinds of information, access to which could only be obtained through use of a retinal scan (like the one Kirk used early in *Wrath of Khan* to view the Genesis Tape). Retinas have cells and cells have genetic codes; once the Genesis scientists have that, the result is preordained.

As we have seen, however, a physical duplicate which is little more than an animated mannequin is insufficent for our—or Kirk's—purpose. We need the essence of a man—or, in this case, a Vulcan—and that usually perishes with death.

Usually, yes, but perhaps not in the case of one who is the acknowledged master of both the Vulcan nerve pinch and the Vulcan mind meld. It should be relatively simple for such a one to transfer "himself" into the body of another, all the while maintaining mental control of his own body in order to direct it to the task at hand. There is plenty of precedent for this within the series. "Return to Tomorrow" features Spock's essence residing in the body of Christine Chapel until his body is safeguarded and ready for his return. In "Requiem for Methuselah," Spock uses his linking ability to rob his great friend Kirk of the unbearable memory of his impossible love for Reena. And now, in *Wrath of Khan*, he has obviously arranged for McCoy to remember something, although we can only guess what that "something" is.

One thing for sure is that McCoy does not remember it *now*. We will, however, for if Spock has set up the means for his own revival, he would also specify a set of conditions which would trigger the memory in McCoy whenever it was needful for him to produce this information. Since Spock would realize that the scientific community would never tire of studying the Genesis World, he might couple this knowledge with an evaluation of human character to surmise that Kirk would one day be drawn to the scene of his friend's death, probably with McCoy in tow. At that point, the trigger for McCoy's heretofore suppressed memories would be pulled, and Spock's essence would be available for introduction into a newly available Spock body. (This scenario is particularly attractive if we adhere to the lenient exemption of allowing Spock's body to remain intact on the Genesis World.)

There are variations possible on this—for instance, McCoy might suddenly develop distinctly Vulcan mannerisms, causing Kirk to suspect enough to return to the Genesis World—but all in all, the "Spock body restored by Genesis and his consciousness in McCoy's body" scenario is probably what the people behind Star Trek are aiming for.

We should also speculate briefly on what role Saavik might play in all of this. Much of our information about and insight into Saavik comes from Vonda McIntyre's novelization of *Wrath of Khan*, and although there are some inconsistencies between the novel and the film, enough threads remain in the film to weave an intriguing fabric of speculation. In the novel, Saavik's protége-mentor relationship with Spock is richer, and it is she who has the first glimmer that all is not as it seems in regard to his death. She is also probably most responsible for the body of Spock being on the Genesis World at all, for in the novel, Kirk orders that the casket be sent into a decaying orbit to burn up when it enters the newly formed atmosphere. Saavik, however, programs a course into the launching system that results in landing the torpedo casing on the planet's surface.

One could easily argue that the Spock-consciousness residing in McCoy's body made mental contact with Saavik's subconscious and ordered her to reprogram the guidance system in order that his body might survive for future occupancy. In any case, the mind link with McCoy must become an integral part of any revival of Spock—else the use of Genesis opens a Pandora's Box that would soon destroy Star Trek's illusion of reality.

Consider: If Genesis alone can be used to recreate Spock, what limits has it? Why not reanimate Mirimanee? Or Edith Keeler? Or even Kirk's boyhood idol Abraham Lincoln?

Theoretically, once word of Genesis reaches the Federation at large, whoever has access to Genesis could live forever, continually recreating new, healthy bodies after the old one has aged or died. In fact, every defect in the human condition—or in creation, for that matter—could conceivably be corrected by Genesis . . . probably altruistically (with Federation approval), but at least potentially "for a price" in unscrupulous hands. And let us never forget its horrifying potential for destruction; were it to be used on a wide scale to solve problems, sooner or later it would be used to *eliminate* other problems. Certainly, stringent controls and orders would be passed regulating its use, but rules are made to be broken, and someone who felt strongly enough that his use of Genesis was justified would not hesitate.

Clearly, a limit is called for, and it would be logical to establish at the earliest opportunity that observation has determined that Genesis cannot reproduce sentient forms. Since the original intent of Genesis was stated as being to reform worlds with a view to accepting and nurturing life forms the Federation *might later choose to introduce*, this limit would be right in line. Arguably, of course, the film has already gone slightly beyond this limit by showing a fawn in the Genesis Cave, but unless one considers Bambi, deer are not known for their sentience. Anyway, the fawn and any other life form in the cave could have been placed there after Genesis.

But the importance of this limit on Genesis cannot be overstated, for in addition to tying up some monstrously loose plot ends, it also demonstrates the relevance—make that *necessity*—of the McCoy/Spock mind link. If McCoy does indeed have Mr. Spock's essense safely tucked away in what Spock would not hesitate to point out are vast unused areas of his brain, then the reversal of the mind link at the appropriate time would provide the unique spark which would allow the Genesis Effect to succeed in creating this one particular instance of sentient life.

Nor could the process be successfully repeated unless one party to the effect knew the mind-melding technique, but there are several races, such as Vulcans and Medusans, who can mind-meld. They do not do it casually (remember Spock's ethical and cultural bias against melding mentioned in "Dagger of the Mind"?), but the revival of a deceased loved one or very important person might be enough incentive to overcome any reluctance. So the potential for abuse (or altruism) is still there, with the selective stirring of consciousness becoming a powerful weapon in the hands of anyone with knowledge of how to duplicate Genesis, the mind-melding and shifting process, and the means to place particular "essences" in selected life forms.

The implications are frightening, so frightening in fact that Dr. Marcus (or the Federation) might even refuse to employ Genesis to restructure Spock (should we go that route) without a much more compelling reason than we have produced so far. Even Spock himself realized there were a plethora of ethical considerations surrounding the use of Genesis, although he would not debate the issue with McCoy.

In fact, in any of the scenarios we have postulated so far, McCoy would probably be constantly at Kirk's elbow to remind him of the ethical impropriety of what they were trying to do. For all of his friendship with Spock, he would definitely not approve, and like Dr. Marcus, might not participate—consciously, that is. Remember, he appears to have forces at work within him that he is unaware of, forces that may override every veto and lead to the return of Mr. Spock.

Even with all the problems inherent in every means described for the return of Spock, we can certainly accomplish it. That we want him back is without question—but should we bring him back? Maybe not.

Of all the "possibilities" raised by Mr. Spock's death, the possibility that he should remain dead is the most distasteful. And perhaps the most important. Viewed on one level, *The Wrath of Khan* is a grand action piece, arising out of one of the most popular episodes of the series, and proceeding beyond the limits of the small screen of television to take movie technology with all its scope into the Star Trek universe. But if it were *just* that, we might as well watch *Forbidden Planet* or *Destination: Moon* or any of hundreds of science fiction movies.

But *Wrath of Khan* is a Star Trek movie. Those of us who loved the series come to the film to see the characters we care for face whatever situation is dreamed up for them. In this case, the entire film is about change and how the characters react to it. Saavik has trouble understanding *Kobayashi Maru*; Kirk understands it, but avoids it by changing the rules of the game—"I don't like to lose." He cheats death at every turn and, as the hero of countless battles on behalf of the Federation, he should do no less. Finally, however, he faces a no-win situation which is beyond his ability to fix and survives only through the self-sacrifice of his dearest friend. The *Enterprise* is saved—but at a price. "The needs of the many outweigh the needs of the few. Or the one."

The characters in Star Trek have always, for the most part, been treated with intelligence and so drawn as to react realistically to a given situation (dramatic license aside, of course). William Shatner recently reinforced this in an interview. He said that he believes the enduring popularity of Kirk is due in part to the fact that Shatner the actor has Kirk the character react in a way that Shatner the person would like to think he would react in an idealized situation. And, with the passing of the years, as Shatner's reactions to a given situation have changed, so too have Kirk's. Realism is the key, and Kirk must react realistically to the death of Mr. Spock. In *Wrath of Khan*, Kirk is finally forced to acknowledge that "the way one faces death is at least as important as how one faces life." Having accepted that, what will be the effect on Kirk if and when his friend returns? Perhaps a tiny speck of his character will be weakened as he says, probably on a level which he doesn't even consciously recognize, "Well, I won again."

Granted, the milieu of Star Trek is fictional; nevertheless, the reactions of the characters should be, and always have been, *real*. In our "real" world, the first reaction to the death of a loved one—and there's no sense in saying that Mr. Spock is anything but that to thousands upon thousands of fans—is one of rejection. There is a feeling of "this can't be happening," a period of worrying over what might have been, what should have been, and "if only . . ." But ultimately, the living get on with the business of living. Ought we to expect any less or respond any differently when the death involves one who we have insisted for fifteen years should react realistically, and who has been treated, in a sense, like a living being?

No, for the bitter lesson which Kirk learns with the death of his friend really applies to all of us who see the movie. After all, Star Trek may sail the galaxies for years to come, but the people who are in it will change and will be replaced by others who, if the transitions are handled with taste and skill, will come to merit out admiration, respect, and maybe even love as the films roll on. Who would have thought in 1965 that these particular characters would so capture the hearts of fans?

Although these questions are posed in all sincerity, we *know* in all certainty that Mr. Spock, "dead" though he is, has joined a very select company. He sits at the left hand of Sherlock Holmes in that fine limbo where beloved characters never die, but merely wait for the next adventure. And, again to paraphrase, "There are always . . . adventures."

THE ALIEN QUESTION

by Joyce Tullock

Joyce Tullock should be no stranger to Best of Trek *readers—her articles have elicited more comment and controversy than perhaps any other fan writer's. If you've enjoyed Joyce's thought-provoking articles before, you'll find more of the same in this one. And if you're experiencing Joyce Tullock for the first time, well, all we can say is . . . you're in for an experience like none you've ever had!*

Once upon a time in a galaxy not so far away there were, are, and always will be creatures of strange and beautiful mind and form. They were not human, but they were loved by humans for the differences they portrayed with dignity and elegance. They were the aliens: Each of its own kind, living in a world of human conformity, challenging the Terrans to open their minds, hearts, and eyes to the beauty of individuality. Like Mr. Spock, who is admired for his private and unwavering respect for his own uniqueness, these strange individuals of the Star Trek universe have come to represent the beauty and courage involved in the simple act of *being*.

But the alien in Star Trek is not completely popular or completely safe. He has enjoyed what must be called a "mixed" success from the time of the first episode up until our most recent motion picture. Whether he be Mr. Spock the Vulcan or a being from a far-off galaxy or a creature whose physical differences are too much for the human eye, the Star Trek alien has been at once loved, hated, helped, abused, trusted, or rejected by virtue of his differences.

But we love the aliens, don't we? Especially Mr. Spock. Fans maintain over and over that they value Spock and many of the other fine Star Trek aliens because these beings allow them to see themselves more clearly; they come to recognize that the "alienation" is a reflection of "lonely" American society.

So in looking at Star Trek and examining it objectively from the overall view, a question comes to the fore: Do Star Trek fans and writers alike have a split personality when it comes to the alien question? Could it be, for example, that we tend to humanize alien personalities to the point of showing a kind of smug disrespect for their own alien life-styles and traditions? Has Star Trek, however subtly, taken the authoritarian standpoint that the only way to true happiness is the human way? (And the Western Human Way, at that.) Take Spock, for example: Could it be that deep down we are hoping that by discovering Spock's nature and—as we like to say—"watching it grow," we may eventually find him to be "one of the boys"? Good grief, if we humanize Spock, will he be Spock anymore? Will he any longer have value?

Tough questions, but ones deserving of discussion as we examine Star Trek's split-personality approach to alien life. And we may be a bit surprised to discover some of the things Star Trek has to say about the state of being truly different.

In most ordinary terms the word "alien" refers to someone who is from another culture, whose origins, upbringing, life-style, and perspective are noticeably different from those of his companions. In fact, every child goes through the experience of discovering that the set pattern of living to which he is accustomed in his own home is often extremely different from that of his playmates. As children we are presented by our parents with certain rules for living. For a time we believe in those rules as absolute and distrust anything which deviates from them. As we grow, however, we build from that parental groundwork, continually developing new rules of our own. If we are lucky, as we reach maturity, we come to that point in life where we can look around and note almost casually that each of us is in some way very, very unusual. This was one of Gene Roddenberry's major points in his early remarks about Star Trek. We are each a little alien, even in the conglomeration we call the Western World; we are sometimes proud, often ashamed of our individual "differences," which are labeled as anything from independent to eccentric to misfit. The Star Trek alien, at times, fits all of these definitions. He is certainly the outsider, the unusual one, the one who is most specifically "not like us." Most often the aliens, including Mr. Spock, appear to be misfits in one way or another.

Star Trek aliens, then, are very much outsiders, people/creatures who appear to be out of synch with the generally Western-oriented society of the *Enterprise*; they *react* to our world according to their perspectives. The salt creature, for example, is as alien to us as we are to it. In "The Man Trap" we see that this alien creature who requires salt to live has already psyched out its human victims/enemies. It turns the tables on the *Enterprise* crew; using its own knowledge of what it is to be different, it defends itself by taking the forms of trusted, familiar, attractive humans—and presenting crewmembers with the kind of people they *want* to see. It is a desperate alien, the last of its kind, and so, like many people in the real world, it throws up a mask and attempts to "fit in" in order to survive. Not so dumb, that salt creature. Not so alien, either, when you get down to it.

Mr. Spock, this precise, logical, unemotional Vulcan, certainly must have understood how the creature's fine talent for the use of "disguises" could have evolved. Spock, a Vulcan among humans, is constantly prodded to give up his stoic alien ways in favor of the more acceptable emotional behavior of humans. (And it is good friends Kirk and McCoy who keep after him the most. They want him to be happy—by the *human* definition of happiness.) At times Spock must have felt a lonely, threatened creature himself, for he makes it clear that he cherishes his Vulcan heritage.

Ahh . . . but there's a difference, right? The salt creature was ugly. Mean and ugly as hell. Well, it's a matter of our own alien perspective again. Who knows, maybe the salt creature felt like retching every time it had to disguise itself as one of *us*. We'll never know, though, because "The Man Trap," like *Star Trek II: The Wrath of Khan*, is basically an easily solvable good-versus-evil story. Our heroes never accomplish communication with the salt creature and, after busily chasing it around the screen for an hour, they kill it. But it's a safe bet that it was a satisfying ending to all who watched it, and that the mass audience on the other side of the tube went to sleep that evening knowing that (at least in the world of make-believe) those hideously different ones could be dealt with easily.

Star Trek is full of ugly aliens: ugly ones who are ugly to the bone, like the rock creature of "The Savage Curtain," who is evidently some kind of self-styled philosopher. His depth of logic is open to debate, however, as he seems to think that good versus evil is a question which can be settled by a show of strength. This alien, too, is representative of what can happen to one who is an outcast, for though he is in some ways quite advanced, he has quite obviously not had much of a social life (by anyone's standards!), and that probably explains his shortsighted theory of personality.

The Vians of "The Empath," too, are as ugly inside as out. Almost more ugly, for they nearly have us believing that their atrocities of torturing Kirk, McCoy, and others are for the "greater good"—one of the most successful and chillingly deceptive excuses for barbarism employed by sadistic monsters, human or otherwise, to this very day.

While it is true that there are some creatures in Star Trek who are ugly to the core, there are others who are not. Star Trek, if it has given us nothing else, has provided a broader view of what it is to be different. While Star Trek aliens are seldom truly presented in an unbiased light, they are at least—for the most part—very believable personalities who have troubles like everyone else. Often the alien represents a dying species ("Devil in the Dark," "The Empath," "Wink of an Eye," "The Man Trap") or it may have trouble "adjusting" to the way of humankind (the "alien" human, Charlie X, the Companion, Lieutenant Saavik of *Wrath of Khan*, and, of course, Mr. Spock himself). Their troubles are almost always complex, and quite often remarkably human in nature.

The unfortunate mama horta of "Devil in the Dark" is a terrific conglomeration of all the elements of a Star Trek *troubled alien*. Not only is she unusual in appearance, but she has problems communicating with her human adversaries and is in desperate fear for the continuation of her species. Once more it is *Spock the Vulcan* who is able to use his outworlder abilities and perspective to communicate, understand, and pave the way to friendship. As with the salt creature, the alien Spock is able to at least glimpse the frustration and loneliness involved with the horta's difference. It is good to remember, however, that on the horta's planet, *man* is the alien, the intruder. He is busy destroying *her* planet and *her* kind. The horta even makes it clear that it is *we* who seem ugly to her. She appreciates Mr. Spock, not because he looks like her, but rather because he does not—and says so in as many words by making a kind remark about his ears.

But even the mama horta can't be left completely alien. We discover that once the miners come to think of her as a "mother," she becomes ever so slightly humanized. The next thing we know, the human miners are admitting almost apologetically that there is something kind of cute about the baby hortas. Their final reaction to the hortas is nice, and it certainly does go along with IDIC, but it also serves to illustrate Star Trek's tendency to humanize its aliens.

So alien isn't all that alien anymore. While it's true that certain "human" traits are necessary from the writer's standpoint—to allow the reader/viewer a point of reference—it does seem that many Star Trek episodes take that writer's rule of thumb a bit too far, and it causes one to wonder: If the alien becomes totally "acceptable" in his new world, is he really alien anymore? Is he a *true* outsider? If the conflict with his society ends, does his value as a character end with it?

With Mr. Spock this question becomes most poignant because Spock is generally believed to have a specific purpose in Star Trek. That is, he is usually considered to be the literal embodiment of the concept that difference can be a very good, positive thing. His isolation and apparent loneliness come into play here also, for as a character of fiction, it is his continuing *conflict* with his human/Vulcan personality that makes for Star Trek's better-than-average storyline. A contented Spock will not entertain for long, will not live for long as a gigantic fictional character. Take away the hidden torment and you take away the mystery, the mystique; take away Spock's mystique and you take away his life. The Spock of *Wrath of Khan* is a more contented one than we have ever seen. Perhaps that explains a lot.

Of course, some aliens in Star Trek will never "adjust" or become acceptable, The Tholians, those crystalline, nearly featureless creatures of precision, are too sure of themselves and their ways; like a first-generation immigrant who refuses to give up his ethnic ways, the Tholian could never (and would never want to) adapt. Apollo, the god-alien, gives up his humanoid physical existence when he discovers his incompatibility with his beloved mankind. If he cannot be worshiped, he cannot live—it is part of *his* heritage, his way. The dastardly rock creature of "The Savage Curtain" hasn't a chance in our society, for it clearly could never adjust to the ways of others. It is fitting that it is made of stone.

Pliability, it seems, is the answer. Change is the key. There is a painful irony here, too, for as the alien changes into the human, one cannot help but feel that something beautiful, even precious, is lost. But maybe it has something to do with a kind of Cosmic Law of evolution: Change or die. Whatever, the trend to become "humanlike" seems to be the rule of the majority of Star Trek episodes and gives one cause to wonder if the acceptance of differences and the concept of IDIC play the genuinely large roles in Star Trek that we like to believe. Is it possible that IDIC and the like were merely gimmicks cooked up to capitalize on the largely liberal, mid-sixties audience for which Star Trek was initially designed? Star Trek is a business commodity, a marketable product. Will its concepts change to fit a new market? A market to satisfy the more conservative audience of the eighties? Will Spock and his kind survive?

In the first season of Star Trek, as we discussed with "Man Trap," aliens were primarily just that: creatures/personalities of totally different worlds. Unique. Sometimes they were beautifully challenging in their newness. Admittedly, many were monsterlike (the salt creature, the horta, the Gorn), and were frequently maladjusted from the human perspective. "Charlie X," a fine episode, dealt with the human-as-alien concept—Charlie was a human who had never known humans and couldn't deal with life among his own kind—and so its symbolism touched keenly on the problems of the real-life, maladjusted, antisocial personality. Trelane, in "The Squire of Gothos," is an immature (and also somewhat maladjusted) young alien, but we can trust that his parents will straighten him out by the time he's grown. Like Charlie, he sees humans as a kind of curiosity, and sadly wants to fit in, to play their games, but like Charlie, his problems are too involved. Both episodes are resolved when superaliens simply remove the problem children from the scene.

Khan, of "Space Seed" and The Wrath of Khan, is, like Charlie, a human who is maladjusted—more so in the movie than in the episode. In the episode, Khan is a relatively sane deposed dictator; in the movie he is a lunatic (and understandably so, after fifteen years of bare survival on a ruined planet). In either case, Khan can be seen as maladjusted—he continually puts himself above all others. If we look at it optimistically, Khan is alien too, for with his outdated, egotistical dreams of grandeur, he is hopelessly out of touch with the thinking of Terran society in the age of our *Enterprise*.

Spock also has his maladjusted moments. In "The Naked Time," he admits tearfully to his confusion about his identity, regretting that he had failed to show his mother the kind of attention she deserved and craved as a human being. (And Nimoy once again gallantly carries off a scene that could have appeared trite in the hands of a lesser actor.) This scene is also important as the beginning of what may someday come to be recalled as the slow death of Spock the Vulcan. Call it the "Kill Spock Syndrome." Even early on, the Star Trek writers were obsessed with making Spock "human"—and they went about their work only a little less shamelessly than do the fan writers. (We'll talk about this self-destructive element in Star Trek in depth a bit later.)

But Spock wasn't the only alien to be humanized in Star Trek. As was mentioned earlier, those aliens who couldn't adjust were simply removed from the scene. Put out of *our* misery, one might say. The salt monster, Charlie X, even poor Trelane were all misfits who were finally taken from the scene of action in one way or another. It seems that their kind represent the sort of problems which can't be solved so easily, or at least they can't be neatly tied up in sixty minutes.

To be fair, it isn't that some of the aliens don't *try* to fit in. Sometimes an alien goes as far as to show human qualities that we can admire and *still* he has to pay the price of death. Korob, in "Catspaw," a very alien creature indeed, took on the kindest of human qualities; but after saving the lives of Kirk and friends, he was killed by his alien companion, Sylvia, who had taken on those qualities which are representative of the worst part of human nature. Oh well, it's very likely that the gentle Korob would not have been happy for long in the human universe, so perhaps his death was a mercy. Perhaps he was too kind, and might be thought "maladjusted" for that. (Or so McCoy might have said.)

In the episode "Metamorphosis," we have the dazzling and mystical Companion, who sacrifices her beautiful alienness to become "acceptable" in the eyes of her beloved Zefrem Cochrane. The gist of this story's ending seems once again to be pointing out that one can only find true happiness by conforming to the norm, by being traditionally, attractively "human." Acceptability is once again the key to happiness. Still, I suspect that even the most dull-witted of viewers must have sensed a vague loss when the Companion gave over her identity and birthright to please her frankly prejudiced and reactionary Mr. Cochrane.

Elaan, the fiery lady from "Elaan of Troyius," lost all of her gleam, mystery, and fun once she was civilized by the captain in this Star Trek remake of *The Taming of the Shrew*. The list of aliens who "came over" to the human point of view is a long one, so let's get down to the prime example (next to the humanization of Spock) of the *human is best* attitude in Star Trek.

In "By Any Other Name" the Kelvans learn what a great thing it is to be human. These creatures from another galaxy never appear to us in any but the human form, but we are given the rough impression that their true appearance is quite repulsive to the human mind. We know that they were originally large creatures with tentacles (of course) and that, most important, they are alien to human ways (i.e., physical sensations, emotions, sex). Well, it *was* the third season, after all. But that is important, too, as it illustrates the fact that the changing attitudes in Star Trek toward the alien idea have followed a kind of unconscious, haphazard progression since the series left Desilu. The trend seems to be moving away from the concept of alien as different but equal (and even superior) to one that uses the alien only as a monster, a pitiful curiosity, or a handy enemy. The overall message of "By Any Other Name" is that different is *not* good. In fact, Kirk points out to the Kelvans that they can survive only if they accept human form as their own. After learning about the superior intelligence of the Kelvans, this solution seems a bit mundane (I like to call it "jockish").

Surely the Kelvans, who had traveled so far and accomplished so much, could have made provision for their differences, could have found a way to preserve their physical heritage. Instead, the whole plot of the story is devoted to Kirk and crew's antics as they enlighten these emotionally impoverished beings from the galaxy Andromeda about the glories of being human. Never once did Kirk ask one of the aliens what it was like to be Kelvan.

One can't help but wonder if Mr. Spock was secretly appalled at the lengths Kirk, McCoy, and Scotty went to in order to arouse the conflicting emotions which stirred within these aliens with human forms. How much was it like his own alien experience in a human world? How many times had he been subjected to the pressure, however gentle and "well-meaning," to show and feel human emotions, to follow a way which was contrary to one he had accepted as his own?

Of course, from the human perspective the *Enterprise* crew is always doing the right thing in such matters. As with the Kelvans, they are showing that to be human is good, and that is a very nice, positive statement to make. In fact, the idea that the human creature is a progressive, positive creature is one of the main concepts of the original Star Trek. But the very stress on that progressiveness was placed *heavily* on the premise that man would one day learn to overcome prejudice, to understand, accept, and appreciate difference for its own worth. One wonders, then, about IDIC as it appears in episodes like "By Any Other Name." The value and reverence for difference is not always so clear. Hmmm . . . didn't I once read somewhere that Star Trek fans have a split personality when it comes to what they say they admire in Star Trek and what they *really* look for at the box office? Well, maybe not, but there certainly does seem to be a conflict of ideals here. It may be true that the Kelvans *needed* to become human for the purpose of the story, but on a symbolic level (and this entire article is based on the subtly symbolic, not the storyline obvious) the Kelvans were made to forsake their alien identities in favor of the Human Way. Saddest of all, it seemed there was no question in everyone's mind that nothing was lost and all was gained through this rather drastic transition.

All the aliens of Star Trek who play major, active parts in a story go through a metamorphosis of some kind. It may be a changing of body, as with the Kelvans, or of mind, as with the horta. Most commonly, however, it is a change of both body and spirit as with the Companion and the Kelvans.

As for those who cannot adjust to human patterns, they simply metamorphose themselves out of existence, as we have seen with Apollo. This ultimate metamorphosis is what happens to Thalassa and Sargon of "Return to Tomorrow" when they do indeed try to return to the human form after existing for centuries as disembodied spirits. Eventually these aliens (who had evolved from the humanoid form) discover that they can't go home again, and they return, somewhat like Apollo, to the cosmos. Like the Metrons of "Arena" and the Organians of "Errand of Mercy," Thalassa and Sargon have simply evolved beyond the human form (and the concepts involved with it) and so it is evident that the viewer is intended to feel that through this transformation these god-people have lost something very dear indeed. All this without anyone's asking or trying to get an objective understanding of what it is like to be the entities these beings have become.

So the alien who cannot become "humanized" in Star Trek

almost always comes up the loser. The closest they ever come to not losing is when they at least appear to be evolving into something (gasp!) *greater than man*. Like Decker and Ilia, these beings virtually evolve out of the scene. Whatever kind of existence they are experiencing, it seems that we are not to be told about it. It's as if there is some secret shame involved and we'd just rather not take a look.

In *Star Trek: The Motion Picture*, V'Ger is seeking those qualities which are human; it wants to touch the creator, man. And on that note, the superiority of humanness is given bolder underscoring. Here is where the danger comes in, too, for in this movie the beautiful and provocative concepts of the value of difference and the greatness of man reach a fork in the road. Spock goes one way, Decker the other. We will talk shortly about Mr. Spock's slow and probably unavoidable death into humanization, but before we do, it might be wise to discuss the Star Trek theme of man's alienness in his own human world. It all builds up to Spock, his place in Star Trek, his purpose for existence as an alien. He is, after all, the personification of the Misfit in our conformist human world.

On the symbolic level, Spock is the human misfit who can find true happiness only by discovering the joys of being human. He is always testing himself, discovering. Like his pretend foe, McCoy, Spock is a grand and poetic explorer of human self. It is his *continuing* inner conflict which makes him live in the minds of the viewers. The intrinsic nature of his character requires that he always feel a bit different, a bit out of place.

Of all the episodes of Star Trek, one in particular deals most realistically with the true meaning of what it is to *feel* alien. This episode is "The Return of the Archons," and although it is certainly not widely praised as one of Star Trek's best, it deals cleverly with a couple of humankind's most deeply rooted and stifling problems: the self-destructive nature of outmoded *organized* belief systems, and the stagnating pressure of mass conformity within a society which thrives on change. In this episode, which was written by Roddenberry, the people of Beta III enjoy a stagnant but stress-free life as part of the mass mind known as "the Body." All except for a few underground freedom fighters live mindless existences because of the conformity-inducing powers of the computer mind, Landru. The bottom line of this story is that those who do not comform are "not of the Body." They are considered to be enemies of the Whole, and drastic measures are taken to see that they give up their uniqueness to become one with Landru. In a very real way, those who are not "of the Body" are alien. On this planet, among people who appear to be traditionally human, Kirk and his crew find themselves to be very alien indeed. They learn some harsh lessons about group pressure and about what it is like to be different.

No doubt the situation is a little less foreign to Mr. Spock, because he has spent so much of his own life being different from those around him. Quite naturally, he is the one most able to help Kirk outsmart the conformists (with the help of a freedom fighter or two). Together they persuade the computer mind of its own (less than human) inadequacy. This story is a good one for its exploration of the idea of peer-pressure-turned-nightmare. The one scene in which McCoy comes forth processed and purged of all those nasty human qualities that make him real (and unique) is lesson enough about the dangers and pitfalls of conformity. McCoy is an alien-turned-native, and because the qualities he lost are *human* ones, we feel threatened. Kind of puts the shoe on the other foot for a change, and it makes one wonder how the Kelvans must have felt. Or the Companion.

But now it comes as no surprise that the only solution in "Return of the Archons" is for Kirk and friends to overpower the Body and swiftly go about the business of making everyone happily human again. It's only fair to remember, however, that though the people of Beta III were static and unproductive by our standards, they *were not* living by our standards, but by their own. Happiness does not have the same definition for everyone, but throughout Star Trek there is a recurring message that what is good for humans is good for the universe. It seems to be Kirk's rule of thumb.

So, with all the talk of IDIC and the Prime Directive, aliens as a whole do not fare all that well in Star Trek. A major exception to the rule is *Star Trek: The Motion Picture*, in which we see a starship manned with as healthy-looking a bunch of aliens as we've seen since "Journey to Babel." In fact, in the first movie we even see a new life form born of a human/Deltan/machine mixture. *STTMP* was most significantly a story about the *growth* of the human race and its use of difference to evolve into something better (we hope). The Decker/Ilia/V'Ger transformation is certainly the culmination of Star Trek's emphasis on the beauty of difference and the progressive nature of man. Ironically, it also seems to be a last bow for those ideas as we wave bye-bye to the aliens V'Ger and Ilia and say hello to good old familiar Kirk and crew. It's as though there is a mental sigh of relief when Decker, Kirk's supplanter, is finally out of the picture for good. We are safe again with our old, familiar captain. Maybe there *is* a bit of split personality at work here.

When all is said and done the general trend is to move away from glorying in difference in favor of that which is recognizably, traditionally, human. Cosmetics are in, superior intellects are out. On a galactic scale, it represents a rather genocidal belief that to improve is to humanize. (Which was also the theory with V'Ger, but only to the extent that Decker, as a human, was *contributing to the whole* of the new being. It cannot honestly be said that the new child V'Ger is human—far from it.) While Decker took the road to something more alien in *STTMP*, Spock did the reverse. His traumatic experience during the V'Ger meld shocks him into a grand self-discovery which sets him firmly on the inevitable road to humanization. This change in Spock poses an interesting, if unanswerable, question, and it seems only fair that we give it a good, close look.

It's fitting that Mr. Spock is a half-breed. After all, his creation was brought about by Gene Roddenberry and Leonard Nimoy through a process which might be best described as fifty percent genius and 50 percent trial and error. They kept at it until Spock's personality jelled, changing the color concept from red to green, adding the all-important stoic mannerisms and aloofness in greater proportions until the Spock we have come to know and honor became a complete imaginary being. In fact, Spock may well be Roddenberry's dearest creation, for he has been fighting for him since inception (demanding that the ears be kept, and later openly protesting his "death" in movie II). In articles, books, interviews, and speeches Roddenberry has maintained that as a child he had some painful lessons himself in what it means to be "different." It's possible that he has defended Spock's difference for that very reason. No matter; the important thing is that to millions of fans, Spock is a kind of assurance that difference can be good, even better, and that to be "the odd man out" does not necessarily mean something negative or abnormal. Yet there are those who point out quite correctly that from the human sociological and psychological standpoint Spock *is* abnormal—that he is emotionally retarded. After all, doesn't he have extreme difficulty showing his feelings to those he loves? Why is he afraid to laugh, to cry? And what of the Big Question: Does Spock have the normal, *human* appetite for sex?

"Tsk, tsk, tsk," say those of the latter school. "Spock is

missing so much. He's so underdeveloped. Let's help him come to terms with his emotions so he can grow.''

And so the "kill Spock syndrome" is born. Some have become so enamored of the personality of Spock that they have forgotten that he is not flesh and blood. He must laugh and cry, we are told, because real people do those things. He must die because real people die. They forget that the *real* Spock is not a living being, but a gathering of concepts and ideas, a creation of literature and film that is constructed, not to be happy, but to present an aesthetic, beautiful, almost melancholy vision of certain aspects of the human condition. His *conflict* is his life, his purpose is to show us bits of ourselves. And Spock, always the practical one, cannot continue without purpose.

But through a well-meaning desire to help the personality Spock discover his human self (and so, perhaps, to vicariously instead of realistically come to terms with their own human inadequacies) fans and professional writers alike have been busily at work trying to show everyone that Spock is, after all, just an old human softie beneath that icy Vulcan surface. As if we didn't know that all along. So it is that we see the crying Spock in "The Naked Time," the laughing, loving Spock of "This Side of Paradise" (where he is smitten by the harmony-producing spores—from the episode's viewpoint giving us an *abnormal* Spock), the angry, jealous Spock of "All Our Yesterdays," in which he threatens McCoy's life over the beautiful Zarabeth, and, of course, there is the laughing, hand-grasping Spock of *Star Trek: The Motion Picture*.

It's good to remember that always in the Star Trek television episodes Spock was allowed to finally come back to his normal, logical, Vulcan self. That's because his character was needed for the next episode. His slips to the human side were only temporary and usually due to some sinister force working within the story. These moments have *great* value, for they illustrate the conflicts at work within every human mind: logic versus emotion. When Spock's stoicism slips in those episodes we always find out very quickly just how important his aloofness is to this character and Star Trek in general. We are always glad to have the old Spock back by the end of the episode. With the events in *STTMP*, however, a change is set in motion. After the V'Ger meld, Spock acknowledges his human half in one of fandom's favorite (and most widely reproduced) scenes, the sick-bay scene, by grasping Kirk's hand, smiling, and telling us that what V'Ger lacks is "this simple human feeling." From this moment on we must accept it to be fact that Mr. Spock has changed. He has grown. He has reached the logical conclusion that his human heritage is as real to him as his Vulcan heritage. For Spock, the real personality (as many think of him), this change is an altogether good thing. But it is the beginning of the end of his conflict, and so for Spock the fictional figure it could possibly be seen as the beginning of the end, a kind of death.

If Spock does represent the "alien" in all of us, then his value to the triad of Kirk, Spock, and McCoy lies in his icy, logical, "untouchable" uniqueness. His mystique is due in part to his alien nature for its own sake, due in part to his being half alien, half human—an analog to the part in each of us that is afraid to feel. Once that conflict is taken away, his impact as a literary figure is diminished in almost mathematical proportions. Spock is mystery. Beautiful mystery and beautiful pain. If the conflict and the accompanying pain are gone, so is the mystery. He is an alien no more.

So the question stands: If Spock is no longer at odds with his human half, does he serve an active part in the Star Trek saga? What is his place in the triad? Has he outlived his purpose? Fair though these questions may be, they are ones which fans and pro writers alike will ignore in their desire to keep Spock as a character in future Star Treks. Nevertheless, even in *Star Trek II: The Wrath of Khan*, we see Spock fading into the background in a story which literally should have been his own. The story is, after all, about an endangered starship which is manned by children—Spock's children—and yet emphasis remains on Kirk and his now thirteen-year-old midlife crisis. A good, meaty story is overlooked for the more popular our-side-is-right thrill of the chase.

But the second movie, as fun-packed and genuinely entertaining as it is, is still a pat example of the trend in Star Trek to underplay IDIC and the celebration of difference. *Wrath of Khan's* Spock is a more human one, and so we are told that it should be expected that the characters of Star Trek "will grow." (For Spock, that evidently means that he will become more human—and grow right out of the picture.) Saavik, Spock's charming ultimate replacement, is half Romulan, half Vulcan— and an odd mixture at that, for she is allowed tears and some signs of emotion, yet is unable to appreciate human humor, labeling it "illogical." One wonders if that is supposed to mean that a chuckle is more illogical than a tear. To be fair, I suppose we'll have to wait for number three. . . .

It has always been the way of Star Trek writers and producers to try to employ the best of both worlds. They are fitting their product to the market. But compromise, especially in the arts, can be a dangerous thing. It can lead to conformity when taken too far. (This is evidenced in the several unimaginative, uninspired third-season episodes. Quite obviously, *someone* during that period was unwilling to take a chance.) Saavik and Spock appear merely as aliens by name in *Wrath of Khan* and we can only hope that the lack of other aliens in *Wrath of Khan* is a temporary lapse.

As for Spock, his time is clearly short, so it's only appropriate that he should choose to sacrifice himself for his human children, saying farewell to his beloved Kirk and McCoy in his own way, going out with a good Christian sendoff to the tune of ''Amazing Grace.'' He is declared human now, and so it is supposed that he is at peace. According to all that we have seen, his usefulness as an alien is done. It's time to move on, so like Decker/Ilia/V'Ger he gives himself over to the blue fire and the cloud and takes part in a new creation. For an alien who must grow, that's just the way it is. It wouldn't even be surprising to find in the next movie that Spock is given a new kind of life through the magical wonders of Genesis and becomes—dare I say it?—a *human* creation.

SPACE WEEDS

by Kiel Stuart

Of all the articles and features we include in these collections, Kiel Stuart's Star Trek parodies are among the most requested. With the success of Star Trek II: The Wrath of Khan, *we were deluged with demands that Kiel do a parody of the film. Kiel didn't feel quite up to that much work, but we prevailed upon her for something almost as good: a parody of the episode which gave birth to the movie:* "Space Seed." *If you liked Kiel's previous parodies, you're going to* love *this one!*

"It was too an Earth wessel!" Ensign Wackov tossed his hair for emphasis.

Captain Jerk was only half listening to his navigator argue with Science Officer Shmuck, doubting that a disagreement about the origins of the unknown vessel now floating before the *Enteritis* would lead to blows.

"Are you presuming to tell me my duties, ensign?" The Vulgarian's lengthy nose lifted a bit in annoyance. "Are you insinuating that I, as ship's first officer and science officer, would not have the knowledge and experience necessary to ascertain the origins of said ship in question, and that you, a mere ensign with a dreadful pseudo-Russian accent (who in reality hails from New York), can, in a mere five seconds, be sure as to this ship's make, model, and license number?" He made an elaborate show of turning his back on Wackov to begin fiddling with the ship's Pac-Man controls.

"There be Morse code coming from that ship," said Lieutenant Uhorta somewhat smugly.

Jerk grinned. "An Earth vessel, right?"

Shmuck silently ground his teeth as Uhorta nodded in the affirmative and Ensign Wackov danced a quick victory mazurka about the bridge.

"Hey, y'all," Dr. McCrotch broke in over the intercom, "Ah detect some heartbeats comin' from that there ship. Cain't be human, though. Too slow. Ah think. Oh th' othah hand, *could* be instrument trouble. Sorta. Or maybe it's . . ."

"Ah, well," yawned Jerk, "let's all barrel over there and see what we can see. A bunch of you guys come with me, eh?"

"There is no listing for this ship, the *Botany 500*, in any of our computer banks," said Shmuck, anxious to recover from his previous humiliation, "but records of that particular era, the late 1980s, seem to be fragmentary at best. If you will recall, that was the time of the Great Ratings Wars."

"Whew," breathed Jerk aa they entered the turbolift and headed for the transporter room. "Who could forget? It was a grim time in human history indeed: *Battle of the Network Stars, Monday Night Football, Real People* . . . and spinoffs. My God, Shmuck, spinoffs . . ." He closed his eyes, shuddering. "*E.T. Knows Best, Little E.T. on the Prairie, Leave It to E.T., E.T.T.V.* . . ."

"Enough," said Shmuck firmly.

Jerk caught hold of himself. "Too much for me. We need a specialist. Say, don't we have a historian floating around onboard somewhere? See if you can dig 'er up, that what's-her-name, McTavish, McDougal . . ."

"McAirhead," reminded Shmuck.

He sent for the historian, and when they arrived at the transporter room, Lieutenant Madeline McAirhead was waiting along with Dr. McCrotch and Engineer Snot. She had only reluctantly left her current project, but duty was duty; her lard-and-felt sculpture of *Return of the Son of Rocky Meets E.T.* would have to wait.

Jerk led them all onto the pad and they were quickly beamed over to the *Botany 500*

"Gee," said Jerk, "sure is big in here. I should've brought my badminton set." The others followed him to a large, open-fronted Kelvinator. Within it, covered by a thin layer of permafrost, lay a splendid specimen of muscular manhood.

"Ooooh," sighed McAirhead. "What a hunk."

"Hey, said McCrotch, "y'all are droolin' on mah salt shakers."

"There's a whole lot more of these guys around here, captain," said Snotty.

"Who are they?" said Jerk. "Who's this?"

With some difficulty, McAirhead answered, "This is obviously the leader. *Pant*. His unit was to be defrosted first. *Sigh*."

"Oh-oh," said Jerk as a small puddle began to form at his feet. "His unit *is* starting to defrost!"

McAirhead clung to the captain's arm. "Don't let him melt!" she cried.

'Better get him out of here," Jerk said sourly. "We wouldn't want to spoil the lady's plans, would we?"

McAirhead watched anxiously, wringing her hands, as Jerk and his crew laid to with icepicks. . . .

Back on the *Enteritis*, McCrotch labored over the newly defrosted man with Kool-Aid, mint juleps, and bourbon whiskey. The strange human revived, croaking, "What time is it?"

"Gosh, said Jerk, who had been assisting McCrotch in his medical treatments. "Speaks English and everything."

As McCrotch leaned over to examine him, the stranger grabbed him by the throat.

"Way to go," chuckled Jerk. He glanced over at Security Chief LaRue, who lay on his back, bottle in hand. Right on the job.

"I have many questions," said the stranger, shaking McCrotch violently, then releasing him.

"He has many questions," whined the doctor.

"Why do all these mongrel creatures we pick up always have many questions?" asked Jerk wearily. "Just hook your screen thingy up to our library and computer system and don't bother me, willya?"

"Revive my people," demanded the stranger.

"Fat chance," replied Jerk. "It's my turn to ask many questions. What's your name, anyway?"

"It's Khan," said Khan. "And your vindictive, harrowing cross-examination has left me tired. I am going to sleep."

"That was Lokai's line," reminded Jerk. "Need anything else? Want a Fizzer? Some dangerous drugs? A checking account?" He turned on his heel and left.

He ran right into Shmuck.

"I have been monitoring the actions of this Khan gentleman you picked up. He seems to already be making extensive inroads into our technical manuals. Does his curiosity not worry you, captain?"

"Nah," said Jerk. "He's just one guy, right? What can he do?"

"Also, I suspect that he may be a product of extensive inbreeding, which was a sinister factor back then. There were about seventy-five of these young and hulking creatures. They were known as the Superprogrammers, and they took over television programming at networks and stations all over Earth. Then, suddenly, they all disappeared."

Jerk laughed. "And you're saying that this guy might be one of those guys? Aw, c'mon, Shmuck, don't be paranoid."

The guy in question, meanwhile, having absorbed all he wished to about the inner workings of the *Enteritis*, wasted no time in thrusting himself into McAirhead's quarters.

She was painting. As she stood, blinking in surprise, he strode over and examined the works one by one.

"Ahhh, Conan the Barbarian. The Incredible Hulk. Tarzan. Woody Allen. All brave men from the past. And you . . . you've made your hair look stupid just for me. A hobby of yours, degrading yourself like this?"

McAirhead merely drooled in assent, trying unsuccessfully to cover up a painting of Khan in a centerfold pose.

"I am honored by this," Khan said, "but I warn you—such men as I *take* what we want!" His nostrils flared forcefully.

"Ooooh," she squealed. "Drag me by the hair into dinner!"

The formal dinner to which all the officers had been invited was a gala affair. Jerk noted with pleasure that the main course was braunschweiger, a particular favorite of his. Happily tucking his napkin under his chin, he turned to Khan. "So what brings you here?"

Khan smiled. "Oh, a little of this, a little of that," he said, putting out his cigarette in Madeline's palm. "Things got to be boring on Earth, so I took a little vacation. And here I am two hundred years in the future. Gosh!"

"There was the reconstruction of Earth after the Great Video Burnout to be considered. Many thought that a worthy venture," said Shmuck.

"Hey," whispered Jerk, nudging his first officer. "You gonna eat your braunschweiger?"

Shmuck wordlessly slid his plate over and started in on Khan once again. ''Why did you flee Earth at such a critical period?''

Khan's nostrils danced again. ''Very good, captain. Let your underling go for the throat, while you sit back stuffing your face and pretending you don't know what's going on.''

''Huh?'' said Jerk, his eyes still focused on his plate. ''What ya say?''

''Pardon me,'' interjected Shmuck smoothly and whispered in Jerk's ear.

Jerk wiped his mouth and glared at Khan. ''This is a social occasion, not a battlefield.''

''Many prefer open warfare to the metaphor of the cocktail party,'' snarled Khan.

Shmuck whispered, ''Sic 'em!''

Jerk laid down his fork and glared at Khan.

''Okey-doke,'' he said, swallowing the last of the sausage. ''You ran away, turned tail, went belly up, played the chicken at a time when Earth needed courage. What gives?''

Khan stood, enraged. A moustache sprouted on his upper lip and in a bad German accent, he shouted, ''Ve offered ze world *Order*!'' He slammed his fist on the table. 'Und zey *vould not take it*!''

''Aha,'' said Jerk. ''Gotcha!''

''I have a headache,'' said Khan, moustache vanishing along with the accent. ''I'd like to go down into the engine room and take over . . . I mean, I'd like to take a brief nap.''

''Humph!'' said Madeline as she flounced out in Khan's wake. ''You people are so *rude*!''

She crawled to his cabin.

''I wanted to grovel,'' she said. ''And the fact that they were snarky to you gave me a good excuse.'' She knelt at his feet.

Khan puffed up a bit. ''I yam a mystery to them, it's true.''

Madeline shook her head. ''But you're no mystery to me. I know *exactly* who you are.'' She nibbled at his boots.

Khan jumped. ''Oh, no, the jig's up . . . er, I mean, you do?''

She licked the back of his hand. ''You're Conan the Barbarian . . . the Incredible Hulk . . . Tarzan . . . Woody Allen. All those brave men come to life. . . .''

''Whew, what a relief,'' said Khan. ''I mean, how flattering. Now, will you help me take over the ship?''

''But my oath, my duties as an officer . . . I don't think . . .''

He planted a boot in her face.

''Okay,'' she said. ''You talked me into it.''

"No," said Khan. "You have not groveled enough. You must debase yourself further or leave my magnificent presence."

"Ooooh, please, let me help you take over the ship, pretty please?" She nipped at his sleeve and rolled over.

"'Well, all right, you may remain."

"What a guy," she sighed. "These modern quiche-eaters just don't measure up."

"Enough," said Khan. "Here's a Liv-A-Snap. Now help me take over the *Enteritis*, so that I may conquer the galaxy."

"Anything. Just keep ordering me around and feeding me those doggie treats."

Meanwhile, in the Conversation Pit, things were beginning to heat up some. Mr. Shmuck had found some old mug shots of a big television executive of the 1980s, and had matched them with the face of their visitor from the past.

"Khan Loonian Silverman," he pronounced. "Absolute dictator of over a hundred network affiliates. Wanted in almost every civilized nation for Extreme Bad Taste. He personally financed and developed the *Sing Along with E.T.* series."

Snot grimaced. "He's a baddun, all reet, but Aye must admit tae allus havin' a sneaking admiration for this one."

"He was the best of tyrants, and the worst of tyrants," added Jerk. "He saw the best minds of his generation, starving, hysterical . . ."

"All right," said Shmuck, cutting off their histrionics.

"But still," said Snot, "ye hae tae admit he was a darin' programmer."

Shmuck groaned softly. "You actually admire vermin like that? A man who was responsible for *Raiders of the Lost Mork*? Who enslaved millons of people through mindless swill?"

The humans burst out laughing. "We can hate him and admire him at the same time, Mr. Shmuck," said Jerk.

"Well, that's one for the philosophers," muttered the Vulgarian.

"Ah, me," chuckled Jerk. "That Khan. What a guy. Security, wake up La Rue. . . . Oh, you can't? Then send in someone like Coffey or Bates. . . . Right, put a guard on Khan. What the heck, eh?"

Sashaying over to Khan's quarters, Jerk made sure a guard was posted, then went inside. "We know who you are," he said, waggling a finger in Khan's face. "So 'fess up now."

"You could not understand my purpose," answered Khan.

"Why?" smirked the captain. "Because I'm not as highly inbred as you and your cronies?"

Khan smirked right back. "You are just plain inferior."

Jerk's eyes narrowed. "We'll see about that," he said, and left with a nod to Coffey, who lay napping with his back to Khan's door.

After a few minutes, Khan stuck a wad of plastic explosive (made from McAirhead's sculpting materials) into the door and blasted it open. He ran out, pausing only to give the still-sleeping Coffey an insurance tap on the skull. By the time Coffey had awakened and reported the escape, Khan had revived his people, beamed them over to the *Enteritis* instructed them to run the ship, and taken over most key positions.

"Good fast work, Coffey," said Jerk, a bit faintly, for Khan had already cut off life support to the bridge.

Khan called up from the engine room. "I have taken over the ship. You will surrender or die."

"I don't suppose even the microwave oven works at this point," said Jerk glumly.

"Might I remind you," complained Shmuck, "who it was that gave Khan the run of the ship, not to mention free access to all computer banks, ship's blueprints, and other vital information?"

"That's right, Shmuck," said Jerk. "Rub it in good, willya?"

"It is merely that you never seem to learn from similar experiences," sighed Shmuck shortly before they all passed out.

They awoke (most of them, anyway) in one of the minor party rooms. Khan stood over them, nostrils flaring away like rampaging tubas. "I yam superior. I yam also very handsome and dashing." He paused to smooth his hair in a mirror and continued, "Join with me in conquering the galaxy or I will subject you to unspeakable torture. I will force you to sit through every hour of television programming at my disposal."

Shmuck lifted a disdainful eyebrow.

"Very well," said Khan, "I see you need persuasion. Activate the viewscreen."

The screen lit to reveal Jerk, strapped to a chair in the Conversation Pit, his eyes propped open with toothpicks. The tinny theme to *The Dukes of E.T.* was already splitting the air.

"If you join me," said Khan, "I will save your captain's life . . . *plus* you will get what's behind this curtain!"

"Gwan," said McCrotch. "Y'all is jess foolin'."

"Each of you will be strapped into that seat to die!" ranted Khan. "I really mean it!"

"Khan," said Madeline, groveling over to him, "I don't have to sit here and watch this, do I?"

He sneered down at her. "What's the matter? Can't take a little rough stuff?" He booted her toward the door. "Go and fix my dinner."

Outside of the room, she picked up a convenient monkey wrench and sneaked toward the Conversation Pit.

"Now," resumed Khan, "if any of you join me, I'll give you what's in this box, *plus* what's behind the curtain."

"Hey," one of Khan's people protested, "we lost the picture. And it was getting to the good part."

"Never mind," said Khan. "Captain Jerk will be dead by now. Take Mr. Shmuck next."

"Maybe if you threw in what is behind the door . . ." suggested Shmuck as he was hustled out of the room.

In the Conversation Pit, Madeline crept up behind the strapping fellow who guarded Jerk. "Look!" she yelled. "What's that behind you?"

"Huh?"

She hit him with the wrench, then flipped the toothpicks out of the captain's eyes.

"Good timing," said Jerk. "*E.T.'s Company* was just about to start." He began throwing submachine guns and bazookas into a sack.

"Captain," begged Madeline, "I saved your life. Don't kill Khan."

He was about to answer when Shmuck popped in, dragging his guards behind him. He and Jerk exchanged glances.

"Aren't you dead?" asked Shmuck.

"Nah," said Jerk. "Never am. But we'd better gas all decks."

Shmuck operated the controls to do so. "Trouble," he said as he checked the results on a viewscreen. "Khan has escaped into the engine room."

"What a guy," said Jerk. "I'll go get 'im."

Dashing into the engine room, Jerk discovered that the ex-programmer was trying to overload the ion flux and get them all killed.

Jerk drew his Fizzer. "Hey, you, whatya trying to do?" he yelled. "Get us all killed?"

Khan turned slowly and began circling the captain menacingly. He casually reached out and grabbed the Fizzer. He crushed it against his skull. Then he ate it.

"Oh-oh," said Jerk.

Khan moved for him. Jerk took off running.

"You can never overcome me," growled Khan as he chased the captain around the engine room. "I yam far superior to you in every way—strength, endurance, intelligence—"

Jerk hit him over the head with a shovel.

"Whew," he panted into an intercom. "Somebody come and get this clown, huh?"

Once ship's operations had been returned to normal, a formal hearing was convened. A board of review consisting of Jerk, Shmuck, and McCoy sat to hear the charges against Khan and McAirhead, and also to act as the Victory Dance Committee.

"This lynching is now in session," said Jerk, chuckling. He faced Khan and McAirhead.

"What a guy. Sure would be a shame to send him off to be rehabilitated, where Bunky and Spunky would just try to make a good citizen out of him." He pondered. "Tell you what. We'll give you and all your dangerous pals a whole planet to play around with. We'll drop you off on Alpha Ceti something-or-other."

Shmuck's jaw dropped open.

"Oh, yeah," continued Jerk. "You, McWhat's-your-face. You wanna go with him or you wanna be court-martialed and hung out to dry?"

"I want to be Khan's doormat, wherever he is," she sighed.

"Well, then," said Jerk, "we're all set."

"Yes," said Khan with an evil grimace. "And you will recall what the great Scottish poet Doug McKenzie said." He exited, trailing followers and twirling the cape he had somehow obtained from somewhere.

"Captain," said Snot, "as loath as Aye am to admit it, Aye *hate* Scottish poets. What *did* the Great Poet say?"

Jerk quoted from the saga of the Great White North: " 'I'll come looking for you someday, you hoser.' "

Snot was silent for a long time. Then he said, "Aye don't know, captain. Aye think ye made a mistake. Aye think ye'll be sorry one day."

Jerk shrugged.

Shmuck slumped onto the table, face in hands. "Not as sorry as I'll be," he sighed.

ABOUT THE EDITORS

Although largely unknown to readers not involved in Star Trek fandom before the publication of *The Best of Trek #1*, WALTER IRWIN and G. B. LOVE have been actively editing and publishing magazines for many years. Before they teamed up to create TREK® in 1975, Irwin worked in newspapers, advertising, and free-lance writing, while Love published *The Rocket's Blast—Comiccollector* from 1960 to 1974, as well as hundreds of other magazines, books, and collectables. Both together and separately, they are currently planning several new books and magazines, as well as continuing to publish TREK.